The Claresby Collection Twelve Mysteries

The full collection of Claresby mystery stories with Rupert and Laura Latimer.

By Daphne Coleridge

For Alan, with thanks for all his ideas

Contents

The Treasure of Claresby Manor

Laura took a bottle of wine out of the fridge and made her way to the study. It was a longish walk, down the chilly corridors past dusty suits of armour, through the Great Hall with its high beams and carved musicians' gallery disappearing in the darks shadows above, and into the panelled room beyond. Had not every inch of the house been familiar to her, it might have felt eerie so empty and gloomy it was as the last beams of evening sun made their reluctant way through the mullioned windows, barely reaching the furthest corner. Her study, however, was warm and welcoming with a fire burning to ward off the chilly late summer nightfall and her favourite pieces of furniture in comfortable abundance about the place. She set the wine down and took a couple of glasses from an ornate oriental cabinet. As she did so, a bell rang from the front door. Again a longish walk until she could swing open one of the creaking double doors at the entrance. A tall, slightly gangly man with light hair and strong features stood waiting. He too held a bottle of wine.

"Ooh, more wine," commented Laura happily. "I just unearthed something from the cellar, but half the stuff is undrinkable, so it is just as well to have a backup."

The man bent to peck her fondly on the cheek and followed her in. Once back in the study, Laura sat down in a red, plush chair of great antiquity which oozed a greyish stuffing from one corner. She would not have considered the fact, but the dim light enhanced the attractions of her pale, oval face, delicate features and lustrous auburn hair. The man, turning to pass her some wine, cast a glance at her which suggested that he, at least, was not oblivious. Laura sipped the wine with some trepidation.

"Well, it's not corked." She observed the golden liquid in

the cut glass with a critical eye. "It's not cloudy either. I think it is a dessert wine; I hope it's not too sweet for you? I can't tell you what it is as the label had dissolved."

"It's lovely," replied the man, sitting down opposite her. "Now, tell me how you are today?"

Laura crinkled her nose, "Well, happier for seeing you Rupert, but I'm really having to face up to things now, and I can't say that I like it. I preferred being an ostrich, but I have bills I can't pay and they sit there ugly and insistent and I'm going to have to deal with them."

"Do you have a plan B?"

Laura shook her head. "Everything saleable had been sold to cover debts; starting with grandfather's death duties and ending up with the inheritance tax when father died. I have inherited this wonderful house, but it has swallowed itself up. The only thing I could sell is the title."

"You mentioned that before: I still don't quite understand," replied Rupert, sipping his wine with appreciation.

"Well, there is a title that goes with the Manor – Lord of Claresby Manor or Lady of Claresby Manor in my case. It is a property and can be conveyed in the same way as any other property: in other words I could sell the title," she explained, seeing Rupert looking vague.

"I thought I read somewhere that titles could not be sold – despite the number of websites promising you a certificate that makes you Lord or Lady Something-or-Another at inflated prices."

"Well, that is pretty much true," conceded Laura. "You cannot buy or sell the right to any title in the peerage, nor pay to become a Lord or Lady. There are only two titles which can be legitimately sold: that of a Scottish Feudal Baron or Lordship of the Manor. Lordship of the Manor does not make you Lord anything. Father was James

Mortimer, Lord of the Manor of Claresby – not that he would have ever styled himself as such. He wasn't Lord Mortimer. Anyway, the point is that I can sell that title – and there are people who buy such things. With the title goes certain historical rights such as a monopoly on holding markets and fairs in the Manor – oh, and fishing rights in the river; for all the good that may do anyone."

"Doesn't the title go with ownership of Claresby Manor?" inquired Rupert.

Laura shook her head, taking another sip of the wine. "No; the two are separate properties and I can sell either one without the other. As a matter of fact I think that they should stay together, but only for sentimental reasons. In any case, I don't think I can afford to retain either. I will have to sell the house even if it breaks my heart. Did you know that it has been in my family, give or take a few changes down the female line, since before 1066? I feel like I am letting down a whole host of ancestors, most of whom glare down at me from unsaleable, second-rate portraits whenever I make my way down the Gallery to bed at night!"

Rupert laughed, even though her wit was of the dour, resigned type. They both sat drinking the venerable golden liquor from their glasses in the firelight for a few moments until Laura spoke again.

"Of course, there is one hope – but it is a very forlorn and worn out hope."

"What is that?" asked Rupert.

"Well, I've not mentioned this before, because it has been tried by my ancestors down the centuries whenever they have hit hard times and never amounted to anything. It's just a story that has been passed down verbally, so it is probably apocryphal."

"Well?" prompted Rupert, when she became silent again.

"Oh, it's just so silly it's probably not worth mentioning."

Laura shook her halo of auburn hair before rushing off the tale in an almost embarrassed, off-hand tone. "Well, it is back to the sixteen hundreds and Oliver Cromwell and the Civil War and all that and of course my family were romantic and loyal and all the things it wasn't clever to be – in other words, they were royalists and supported King Charles, even though they didn't think much of him personally as far as I can tell. The practical upshot of all this was that, at some point, a group of roundheads were deployed in this direction to loot the place and generally teach the Mortimers a lesson. The Lord of the Manor at the time was one Gerald Mortimer who, rumour has it, took all the silver and gold and prudently stashed it away in a safe place. Luckily for him his cousin, Henry Mortimer, was on good terms with Cromwell - my family has been historically very good at hedging its political and religious bets - so nobody was killed at Claresby Manor. I think the soldiers tore some tapestries and roughed up a few of the servants, but all in all we got off lightly. As for Gerald, who was elderly at the time – he died of perfectly natural causes a few months later leaving the house to his daughter, Elizabeth, who had the good sense to marry her cousin, thus retaining the family name. Anyway, amongst the upset, furore, illness, marriage and dynastic changes, old Gerald entirely failed to tell anyone where he had actually put the treasure. On his deathbed, Elizabeth's diary tells us, he told them that "the treasure is in the pictures", but no one has ever made the slightest sense of this enigmatic comment. Hence the rumour of hidden treasure – and if ever the Mortimer family was in need of it to rescue their fortune, now is that time."

"The treasure is in the pictures..." mused Rupert. "I like a conundrum. Did he mean that some of the paintings were valuable?"

"Well, we only have two paintings of that era left. Gerald

was painted with his wife, Margaret, by Peter Lely, the fashionable portrait artist of the day. He was, by the way, the artist who famously painted Cromwell "warts and all". He must have been a shrewd man as well as a great artist as he served Charles the First, painted Cromwell and was still around to serve the restored monarchy. Anyway, that painting was sold ages ago and the profits swallowed up by this greedy estate. There were some exquisite miniatures as well, painted by Samuel Cooper, but they too have gone. There are only two paintings left from Gerald's time, both very inferior works by person or persons unknown."

"Well we had better start with those," replied Rupert enthusiastically, "if we are going to find that treasure."

Laura sighed and put down her glass. "Well, by all means take a look, but I can promise you that every effort has been made to decipher them and various demolitions and diggings have taken place and yielded nothing."

"Yes, precisely because I was not there to decipher the pictures: show a little faith in me, Laura!" Rupert's face was lit with enthusiasm. He was not a handsome man, his nose being too large, his mouth having a suggestion of the lopsided about it, but it was a pleasant face and Laura had been fond of him since they had shared an unhappy, dispossessed, first term at Cambridge. She rose reluctantly to her feet.

"Very well; they are pushed to one side in a junk room upstairs, not being deemed worthy of display."

The two of them walked through the chilly, dimly lit but nonetheless beautiful rooms of the medieval Clarebsy Manor, up the grand oak staircase and down a narrow corridor to one of the undistinguished back rooms. There were discarded objects old and new: brass bedsteads, boxes of books, folds of heavy curtains.

"All of it junk," commented Laura despondently. "My

9

family have long since ravaged the place for anything of value." She picked up two paintings and set them up against a wall and sat on the threadbare carpet to look at them, shivering a little in the cold of the evening. Rupert hunkered down beside her to study the paintings.

One painting was a heavy work in oils set in a cumbersome gilded frame. It depicted Gerald Mortimer looking rather smug in the foppish clothes of a royalist; long hair, lacy cuffs and large feather in his hat. Behind him was Claresby Manor.

"It really is a very bad painting," commented Rupert, examining it carefully. "It must have been painted by a student or an amateur."

"Family history suggests that he might have painted it himself. Anyway, it has been studied for clues and codes and suchlike. There is one obvious anomaly and perhaps a statement of intention; I'll be kind and let you have the satisfaction of spotting those for yourself."

Rupert duly studied the details of the picture. The first thing that inevitably drew his eye was the scroll of paper that Gerald held. "Sollicitae tu causa, pecunia, vitae," he read aloud. "Hmm, I wish I hadn't dozed through Miss Taylor's Latin classes." Rupert screwed up his light blue eyes, making his nose look even more pronounced on his pleasantly ugly face. "I make it something like – You, money, are the cause of an anxious life; am I close?"

"Pretty much," Laura nodded. "Sextus Propertius, a poet."

"Okay; so we deduce that Gerald had money on his mind when he, or someone else, composed the painting. And there is an anomaly, you say?"

Laura nodded. Rupert studied the picture further and then said, "I'm guessing that there is something odd about the house, but I can't work out what. Bear with me whilst I take it outside and compare art with reality."

Laure trailed behind Rupert as he bounded down the stairs, out through the front door and across the overgrown lawn to the place where Gerald was shown in relation to the house. He looked from painting to house a few times with rapt interest.

"Fascinating to see how little it has changed over the centuries. The chimneys are different, which could be accounted for by decay or strong winds. Those stables have gone and the entrance has been rebuilt, but other than that, remarkably unaltered."

"And the deliberate error?" pushed Laura.

"Well, the extra window on the front of the house, of course."

Laura nodded. "Yes, to the left of the entrance – the first area of wall at the far end before the angle where the library is set forward. There are only three windows there. That has traditionally been a music room."

"So, where the fourth window is shown – is there a secret blocked up room?"

Laura shook her head. "No, the extra window is set in an area of wall that is simply windowless. Exactly behind it is that nice chintz settee. Come back inside and I'll show you."

The two of them made their way down the moonlit lawn and inside to the music room. Laura turned on the light. It was a pretty, cosy room with a large piano, bookshelves and a number of tall backed chairs and a selection of settees with floral covers. There were indeed three large windows to the front – two at one end, then a gap, then another window. Inevitably Rupert started tapping at the wall and floor around the area where the window had been shown in the painting, pushing the settee away from the wall to do so. Laura watched him indulgently for a few minutes before saying, mildly;

"I can promise you that there is nothing there. The wall is

of normal thickness, there are no hidden spaces either inside or out. This part of the house has been taken apart to look for the treasure because of that painting. The only result is that, the walls having been rebuilt, this is the one part of the house that does not leak. Other than that..." she shrugged her shoulders dismissively.

"Okay," conceded Rupert. "But the position of the window must have some relevance, otherwise why bother drawing our attention to the spot. Let's go and take a look at the other painting."

The second painting showed a view looking away from the house to two low hills a few miles away. The view had changed very little in substance, although areas of trees had been cleared, a road constructed and a few more houses had appeared in the distance. In the foreground of the picture, very conspicuous and spoiling both the composition and the pleasant impression of a landscape at sunrise, was a gravestone in the shape of a cross.

"Before you ask," Laura intervened, "There is not and, to my knowledge, never has been a stone or monument in that particular place. Although the view of the sunrise over the hills is painted from Claresby Manor the gravestone, had it been there, would only have been about a hundred yards from the house itself. Nobody would have buried treasure there in full view. And, as before, generations of my family have dug holes there just in case: nothing!"

Rupert was squinting at the picture. "Something was written on the grave though, but is has darkened so much over the years that I can't make out what it says."

"Turn the picture over," advised Laura. "My great grandfather transcribed a version there when it could still be made out."

Rupert turned the picture over. A scrawling dark pen had written the words –*To the furthest reach where the sun does not reach.* "What are we supposed to make of that?" he mused.

"We have generally interpreted it as meaning death – or the state of death. You are welcome to form another opinion, but I doubt if you will get any sense out of it. Like I say, we have gone down this path before and only found a dead end." Laura yawned. "Anyway, I hope you don't mind an early night. You can help yourself to the blue bedroom – you know where everything is."

"Okay." Rupert placed the picture down and gave Laura a brotherly hug and kiss. Only his wistful glance after her as she left the room suggested feelings other than the purely platonic.

It was still dark when Rupert crept into Laura's room. Although purposeful, he paused a moment to relish the sight of her sweet face, peaceful on the pillow, her hair glowing in the soft moonlight. However softened he was by this vision, it did not stop him from gently shaking her shoulder and softly calling her name.

"What? What is it?" Suddenly awake, Laura sat up with a jump and stared at Rupert. "What's happened?" she asked.

"It's all right, don't worry," he said soothingly. "It's just that I have worked out the clues. I'm pretty sure that we can find the treasure – it's just that it might help if we watch the dawn."

"Dawn? It's still pitch black," grumbled Laura, nevertheless getting out of bed and slipping a dressing gown over her white cotton nightdress. "It must be about four in the morning!"

The two of them, still in night clothes, stumbled downstairs and out into the damp of a chilly pre-dawn. Fortunately the sky was clear, so there was the prospect of actually seeing a sunrise.

13

"You see," explained Rupert as he dragged a wooden bench over to a spot on the lawn just in front of the house where the music room was, "I realised that we just weren't thinking far enough – literally. Old Gerald made it clear that the spot where the window wasn't had significance. He also showed the dawn over the hills. Put those together and we have to follow the trajectory to the furthest reach where the sun does not reach. I think he means the most distant point of the grounds of Claresby Manor on the west side of the house. Wait, see the sun come up and it should make sense."

The situation of the hills in the East with just a small space between them meant that any dawn light would first penetrate that gap. As it did so, they both saw the sun first strike the house at an angle, where the window had been put in the painting. In response, Rupert leapt up and marked the angle at which the sun hit the house.

"Now it is a case of geometry," he said, happily. "We need a map to Claresby Manor and its grounds. I hope the boundaries haven't changed over the centuries. I'm going to follow the angle and continue the line through the house, out the back and to the furthest reach on the shadow side of the house!"

Laura obligingly provided map, ruler and pencil and even went to the cellar to find a couple of spades. She was not the smallest bit excited by Rupert's discovery; indeed she had long since given up any hope of rescuing Claresby Manor. Despite her reluctance, she was soon to be seen walking through the dewy damp of the grass, into the woods and to the mixture of broken down wall and wire fence that made up the boundary of Claresby. It was a pleasant, soft light now and the sun even bestowed a modicum of warmth to the air. Rupert had located the spot he wanted, but looked about him as if for some kind of confirmation. The mature beauty of the house could be seen through the trees and up a rise, and they were indeed where the sun did not currently reach. The ground was uneven and pieces of wall and fallen stone gathered in rough hollows. At last Rupert found a place that pleased him.

"It has all pretty much returned to nature and Gerald must have meant any hiding place to blend in with the landscape, but I still think that you can imagine that there is a slight rise in the ground and a dip where an entrance might be – a bit like where the ice house is over the other side."

"Well, I'm inclined to be sceptical," replied Laura, "but, yes, I guess there could be. Do we have to dig?"

"Of course."

Laura sighed but picked up her shovel. If she was reluctant to begin with, her reluctance soon faded. In all the time she thought about buried treasure being in or around Claresby she had imagined a chest buried in the ground. It was soon clear that they were uncovering something quite different. Rupert was correct; there was an underground structure, rather like an ice house. By the time they had uncovered the few steps down and the rotted wooden door the two of them might have been exhausted, but they were driven by adrenalin. Laura had gone back to the house for a flask of coffee and sandwiches to sustain them and had also brought out a couple of powerful torches. Once the earth was cleared from the entrance, Rupert was able to pull the damp wood of the door away with his bare hands and force it open on its rusty hinges, the lock itself having virtually fallen away. What met their eyes in the torch light was a beautifully constructed set of steps leading to a room below. Roots had broken through the stonework in places and hung eerily down, but other than that the space was remarkable dry and undisturbed with only a few earth falls.

"It looks sound," ventured Rupert cautiously. "I think it is safe for us to go down."

"Well, I'm not going to go away and leave it unexplored now!" exclaimed Laura, her cheeks flushed with excitement and anticipation.

"Let me go first – and step carefully."

The space below was just enough for two adults to stand up in. There was certainly treasure – two big chests and a shelf carefully stocked with gold and silver plate. But there was something else. Slumped in one corner was a skeleton, readily identified by the round helmet still on the skull as one of Cromwell's roundhead soldiers.

"Well," sighed Laura. "It looks like we've solved one mystery and found another!"

Pickled Toad with Diamonds

Rupert Latimer stared at the object with disgust barely concealed on his large, rather ugly face.

"What is it?" he ventured finally.

"What does it look like?" countered Laura Mortimer, rather irritably, as if she had expected a more enthusiastic response.

"Well," proceeded Rupert cautiously, "it *looks* like a pickled toad with diamond eyes."

"There!" said Laura, in a rather patronising tone, "you retain your reputation as a solver of puzzles. It is a work by Sebastian Fullmarks entitled "*Pickled Toad with Diamonds*". Apparently a toad traditionally represents evil or a demon and diamonds the opposite; purity and light. Hence the whole work is deemed to express the fundamental spiritual dichotomy of life itself: the choice between light and dark, good and evil – or a dangerous symbiosis of them both!"

"Oh," replied Rupert, clearly underwhelmed. "It's rather ugly: did it cost much?"

"I refuse to answer," replied Laura with dignity. "It is a work of art and therefore price is not important." A statement such as this is always euphemistic for a price tag that would pay the national debt of a small third world country and, indeed, there had been seven figures on the label when Laura had first laid eyes upon it.

"Is it an investment?" questioned Rupert, trying to extract some logic from Laura's actions in purchasing the obnoxious item.

"Yes; exactly. Since we found the Claresby treasure I have all this money sloshing about and I didn't want to put all my eggs in one basket. There is no point in putting all the money in the bank in these days of credit crunch and fiscal meltdown. I thought I'd put some into object d'art so that if the world's banks collapse, I still have something."

"You might just as well have left the treasure where Gerald put it," commented Rupert.

Laura quelled him with a look and, as a semi-permanent guest in her house, Rupert was in no position to level any criticism at her life-choices. The two had met in their first term at Cambridge when both were struggling with homesickness and the shock of actually being expected to work for their grades. Rupert was in Gonvilles and Caius (which Laura dismissed, rather crudely, as sounding like a venereal disease) whilst Laura was very nearly of Newnham College studying History of Art. In fact she had dropped out after her first term and returned to her beloved Claresby Manor, whilst Rupert had gamely stuck out his three years of Archaeology and Anthropology. The friendship had endured and when, as a first class honours graduate in Arch and Anth, Rupert had inevitably found himself making an inadequate living selling crosswords over the internet, Laura had invited him to share her very large and rather lonely house. Everybody naturally assumed that they were lovers and, as Laura was vivacious and pretty with a halo of auburn hair, Rupert rather hoped that they would eventually be proved right. In the meantime he was left pointing out to those inclined to disparage his occupation given his excellent qualifications, that it takes a genius to format crosswords for Kindle.

"At least it will give us something to talk about over the weekend," mused Laura. "I'm beginning to doubt my wisdom in inviting Delilah Hawkes alongside Samantha Pearson; Samantha is an art critic – I think I showed you her blog "Sublime Art". She is an outspoken adversary of everything modern, particularly installation art and anything she considers a gimmick. Delilah, on the other hand, loves anything controversial and hates what she calls "fusty" art or anything representational."

"At least," intervened Rupert, "they should agree in disliking your toad; it may be a gimmick, but it undoubtedly represents, well, a toad."

"Of course," continued Laura, pushing her hair behind her ears and ignoring him, "Floyd Bailey will argue with anyone after he's had a few drinks – and he has always had a few drinks, even at eleven o' clock in the morning. I do respect his constitution."

"He is a brilliant portraitist," conceded Rupert. "If you ever consider adding a portrait of yourself to your remaining ancestors in the gallery, he's the man for the job: I don't know anyone else who stands a chance of capturing the beauty of your colouring and the delicacy of your features."

Rupert's comment was made in a matter-of-fact tone, but it still brought a pink tinge to the porcelain skin of Laura's pretty, oval face.

"Anyway," she persevered, despite her mild embarrassment, "it shouldn't be dull. I've asked Simon Forrest along as a make-weight and because he always rather gets on with Delilah's husband, Conran. They were at school together and neither of them has ever grown up in any meaningful sense. Also, I feel a bit sorry for Simon as he has just lost his job."

"I didn't think that lawyers could lose their jobs," said Rupert, with an uncharacteristically bitter undertone. As one of those men unlikely ever to land a conventional job, he was inclined to be slighting of those who looked like they had successfully manoeuvred themselves into a job for life.

"Well, he was a conveyancing lawyer and a downturn in the property market has hit the firm he worked for quite badly."

"Poor chap." Rupert shrugged his large, angular shoulders

dismissively. "I feel so sorry for estate agents too."

"Well, be nice to him, anyway."

Rupert turned his mild, light blue eyes on Laura. "I'm always nice to everybody."

"I suppose you are," she smiled at him fondly. "Don't mind me; I'm just out of the habit of houseguests. It is only because I've got all this money now that I have no excuse to not return a few favours. I thought I might as well ask everyone I owe an invitation to at once and get it over and done with. At least Claresby Manor is big enough to swallow them all up. I'll give them rooms in all four corners of the house so that they can avoid each other if need be."

In fact it was the first time in years that Claresby Manor had been heated throughout come November. The boiler had been installed in Laura's grandfather's time but still worked very well owing, she speculated, to the fact that they had never been able to afford to run it. Admittedly the long picture gallery and grand oak staircase would always be hopelessly draughty, but she could manage to make the Great Hall quite tolerable if there was a good fire going in the fireplace as well. She hadn't had a chance to really spruce up any of the rooms, but the faded grandeur of Claresby was sufficient to impress now that it didn't require the guest to dress in three layers of clothing at all times just to survive. The fact that hot water came out of the taps now, albeit chokingly, she regarded as some sort of miracle.

Laura had delighted in ordering the food over the internet and she and Rupert collected it on the Friday afternoon and companionably stowed it away into the fridges in the rambling kitchen. There were sandwiches, canapés and sushi; also mini jellies, cheesecakes and cupcakes as well as lobsters, shellfish platters and a rather delicious looking salmon and lemon mascarpone terrine. Rupert was alternately popping strawberry and chocolate cupcakes into his mouth as he helped. His long, rangy and rather lopsided physique could accommodate any amounts of food without him ever showing the smallest sign of any real flesh on his body.

"How can you?" Laura wrinkled her delicate nose. "Doesn't that make you feel sicky and gooey after a while?"

"Yes, but not yet," came the muffled reply.

"Well, I've got two of the girls from the village to come in and cook a full scale roast lunch tomorrow; you should enjoy that. Apart from that, there's plenty of bacon and eggs, so I can manage the breakfasts myself. Hopefully, after breakfast on Sunday everyone will pull themselves together and push off again. Then it will be just you and me again, thank goodness."

Even through the cake, Rupert picked up the unintentional compliment of the fact that he was accepted as part of her home and life, despite her oft-mentioned dislike of any outsider. He knew better than to remark about this out loud, even if he had been capable of doing so with a full mouth.

After that, they arranged the Great Hall in a welcoming fashion: baskets of logs ready by the fireplace, the long oak table polished and set with crockery and fairy lights strung around the gargoyles and gryphons of the musicians' gallery above. Personally, Rupert thought the gargoyles that cropped up both inside and outside the house rather ugly and best left in darkened recesses; but Laura had named them individually as a child and was fond of them. Indeed, one of her favourites bore an uncanny resemblance to Rupert.

The assorted guests started to arrive at about seven. Dishevelled and damp from the stormy weather outside, they stamped their feet and flattened their hair as they entered, lifting their eyes to examining the splendour of the oak panelling and plasterwork ceiling.

"Darling; it's the devil out there!" exclaimed Delilah Hawkes, shaking her wet coat as she took it off, so that everyone else was rendered wetter than she was. Her husband, Conran, a head smaller and looking dark and grumpy followed in her wake. In fact Laura knew him to be a good-hearted, amiable fellow whose only fault was his inexplicable adoration of his demanding and selfish wife. The Hawkes' were quickly followed by Samantha Pearson, tall, elegant and confidently un-fashionable in her favourite Burberry: a grey chambray trouser suit with a regency blue check cashmere scarf. She cast a disparaging glance in Delilah's wake and kissed Laura politely on the cheek. Floyd Bailey and Simon Forrest followed concomitantly, Simon blond and dapper and Floyd in a loose linen suit and cashmere scarf not dissimilar to Samantha's. Suddenly the Great Hall was filled with chatter to the high plastered ceiling with its geometrical patterns and arcaded frieze. True to character, Floyd had made a beeline to the drinks table and poured his spirits neat whilst Simon and Conran fell into easy conversation. Samantha and Delilah, finding themselves thrust together, conversed in slightly frosty tones. The very educated, old-money Samantha rather despised the parvenu Delilah, and Delilah, in her turn, thought the elegant but plain faced Samantha not worth her time – mainly because she had an unfortunate tendency to rate people in accordance with how much they could do for her, and she knew that Samantha would go out of her way to avoid doing her a favour. Laura, with the training if not the instincts of a good hostess, slowly made her way around to all her guests and inquired after their well-being and current traumas, whilst Rupert took care to see that everyone's glass was kept filled whilst Floyd was kept as far away from the open bottle of Aberfeldy 21 as was humanly possible.

It wasn't long before conversation became general. Laura

knew her guests well enough to anticipate that tempers would at some point become frayed as strong personalities mixed with alcohol and clashed. It was for this reason she was keeping the toad up her sleeve, figuratively speaking. She thought that, at the opportune moment, it would serve as a distraction. As it was, Simon's mind was fixed on his own redundancy, so employment and un-employment – always an issue to touch raw nerves – became the subject of discourse.

"It's all right for you," said Simon, rather resentfully, addressing Laura. "You inherited this place and enough money for several lifetimes."

"Yes, in the end I did – but if you remember, it wasn't long ago that I was surviving on vegetables from the garden and expecting to have to sell the place to pay my family's debts. I agree I was incredibly lucky in the end, but I don't see why I should apologise for the fact. Anyway, when you are finally destitute, you know you can come and stay in one of the rooms for as long as you need."

"Can I join you in your bedroom?" asked Simon with a wink.

Rupert bristled visibly but Laura just replied, amiably, "No; I bet you snore and grumble. You can have the blue room – or the stable if you prove to be a nuisance."

Simon chuckled. "That's a deal – but I think I've got something else lined up. I'm going to specialize in family law – well, divorces. There's going to be plenty of business in that arena, recession or no recession."

"So you are willing to batten off the misery of others?" queried Floyd, giving up on the bottle of Aberfeldy 21 which Rupert had placed just out of reach and settling for the Bowmore Darkest.

"I'm a lawyer," replied Simon succinctly.

"We all struggle from time to time," Conran commented

comfortingly to Simon. They all had reason to know that this was the case. Delilah was a high maintenance wife, not least because her love of the modern art world had led to radical changes in the style of her husband's formerly quietly prosperous gallery. He was too much of a gentleman to complain about his troubles, but Delilah intervened.

"Conran hasn't been able to make the Hawkes Gallery pay recently," she said bluntly. "But, as you will have heard, we are offering the inaugural "Hawkes Prize" for the most challenging work of modern art in 2011! And," she said with some pride, "we will be out-classing both the Man Booker Prize and the Turner Prize in terms of the value of the award. The winner of the Hawkes Prize will receive one hundred thousand pounds! That is more than twice what the Turner Prize gives their winner."

"How will you fund that?" queried Samantha, disingenuously. "Also, the value of winning the Man Booker or the Turner Prize comes mainly from the prestige and subsequent publicity. Can you offer those things?"

Conran was seen to wince slightly but Delilah could not be so easily put down. "Oh everyone knows that you hate anything modern, Samantha.   I read your blog once and you advocated the destruction of modern art "like the dross and rubbish it is!" – I think those were your very words."

"I'm not against everything modern," replied Samantha coolly. "There are innovations I admire, if they demonstrate actual technical skill and artistic merit in the work. I've seen some brilliant ipad art, where the artist can change the images displayed daily. I have no problem with modern methods if the artistic content is still there. Now men like Sebastian Fullmarks..." in a tone that promised the deepest vitriol.

This seemed to Laura to be the moment to unveil her new acquisition.

"Funny you should mention him..." she began, tentatively leading them over to where the object was covered with something that looked like a red velvet tea cosy.

Of course discussion broke out amongst them as they compared the merits and demerits of the pickled toad with the diamond eyes. Samantha declared it an abomination that disgraced Claresby Manor. Delilah said it was "cute".

"Sebastian, eh?" was Floyd's contribution, as he struggled to focus on the toad. "He used to be able to draw. We were students together. He borrowed other people's paints and never gave them back!"

"Well I feel sorry for the toad!" declared Simon. "What say did it have in the matter? Cruel, I call it."

"Oh, I think it must have died peacefully of natural causes," said Laura, suddenly concerned.

"What's it in, anyway? Formaldehyde? It will start going off in a while, you know."

"Actually I believe it is pickled in wine vinegar. I think Sebastian Fullmarks was trying to express something important about the mutability of all life, so perhaps a little bit of natural decay is part of the art."

Samantha was heard to give an uncharacteristic snort of derision. It was at this point that Rupert decided to mention food and, the sight of the toad not having caused anyone to lose their appetite, they moved away to start on the buffet.

Somehow they got through the evening without any further disagreements. A little political chat did not seem to rouse the same controversy as matters artistic and soon only Simon and Conran were discussing economics as the others basked in the rosy glow of firelight. Floyd was heard muttering about the flavours of caramel and liquorice versus chocolate and toffee as he cuddled two bottles of whisky to himself. Eventually they all wandered up to bed, with the exception of Floyd, who looked immovable; so Laura settled for placing a quilt over him and left him to sleep it off in situ.

The following morning, Laura made her way down to the kitchen to start cooking some bacon. Floyd, still in the Great Hall, did not appear to have moved at all, and wasn't even disturbed by the sound of Laura rekindling the fire. Soon she had bread ready on the kitchen table along with fresh coffee and heaps of crispy bacon and sausages. Even in a house as large as Claresby Manor the aroma of bacon will reach male nostrils, and Simon and Conran soon appeared and helped themselves to quantities of food. Shortly after Rupert came down too, but he did not make his usual dash towards the breakfast.

"Um, I think it's gone..." he began tentatively as he entered the kitchen.

"What's gone?" asked Laura distractedly, turning more bacon in the pan.

"The pickled toad...with diamonds!" said Rupert.

Laura handed the spatula she was holding over to Simon and followed Rupert through to the Great Hall. Sure enough, whilst the red tea cosy was still there, the jar containing the toad had gone.

"Has someone moved it?" asked Laura, agitated – after all, the artefact had cost her around a million pounds.

"Why would they?" asked Rupert reasonably.

Laura spent a few moments looking about the place.

"Perhaps it has been stolen!" she exclaimed.

"I looked around when I first came down and saw it was gone. I can't immediately see any signs of a break-in, but I haven't checked all the rooms."

"You don't need to," muttered Laura under her breath. "If you think about it, we have five people in this house all with a possible motive!"

"You can't really think that. Why would any of your

friends take it?"

"Well, Simon and the Hawkes' are pretty desperate for money – we saw that last night. And Samantha – well, she might consider destroying it as a matter of principle."

"What about Floyd, there's nothing suspicious about him."

"Rupert, everything about Floyd is suspicious; although, I agree, I can't immediately see a motive for him to steal it."

"Well, what about me? Do you suspect me? After all, I've got less money than either Simon or Conran and Delilah."

"Don't be silly," snapped Laura. "I'd trust you with my life."

Before Rupert could respond to this touching expression of faith, the two other ladies came into the Hall.

"What's the matter?" asked Samantha.

"The toad has gone," replied Laura, slightly sulkily.

"Oh, good; it was vile," retorted Samantha, and went to have her breakfast.

Laura and Rupert exchanged glances.

Delilah expressed more concern. "Oh, my God: gone! It was worth a fortune. I hope you are insured. Have you called the police?"

The look on Laura's face instantly told Rupert that she had not got around to arranging any form of appropriate insurance.

"What about calling the police?" he urged.

"Not yet," she said. "Let's ask everyone if they saw or heard anything. After all, Floyd was in the room the entire time. He must have seen something."

"I wouldn't bank on it," commented Rupert, looking at the still comatose figure of the artist.

By then, Simon, Conran and Samantha had joined them, all clutching bacon sandwiches and, in the case of the men, expressing surprise and dismay. At some point Floyd was stirred into a bleary consciousness and plied with coffee. His immediate response on hearing the news was to assure them that he had witnessed no intruders in the night, whilst admitting that someone could have probably stolen the building from about him and the clothes from his body and he would not have been aware of the fact.

"To be absolutely honest, I'm not feeling at all well this morning," groaned Floyd, prising himself out of the chair and wincing. "I don't wish to complain, Laura, but I'm wondering if there wasn't something a little bit amiss with that whisky."

"There was nothing wrong with the quality of the whisky," Laura responded with mild indignation. "It was the quantity in which you imbibed it that was the problem."

"You may well be right; but my insides are feeling awfully queer." Indeed, Floyd looked both pale and sweaty with a greyish skin colour.

"Well, leaving Floyd's insides out of it, perhaps we should all make a search of the house, just in case the toad was simply misplaced or to see if there are any signs of a break in. Whatever one's artistic attitude to the object, it was valuable and we are going to have to call the police if we can't sort this out ourselves," insisted Rupert.

Everyone acquiesced to this plan and they all wandered off in different directions to search. Laura herself was rather dispirited; something told her that the "Pickled Toad with Diamonds" had disappeared for good and she was equally sure that, when the matter got out, it would be received with as much hilarity as sympathy. The fact that she had failed to insure the beastly thing didn't help.

Sometime later the group reconvened, shrugging their shoulders and muttering about the skills of professional burglars. It was at this point that Floyd re-emerged, looking a slightly better colour but somewhat sheepish.

"I think I may be able to help you solve your mystery," he began, delicately.

"Do you remember seeing or hearing anything last night?" asked Laura eagerly.

"Well, several memories are beginning to emerge, and none of them very pleasant. You have to understand, I wasn't in a good way last night."

"We do understand," said Laura, with gentle encouragement. "Just tell us what you remember."

"Well," began Floyd, cautiously, "I think I must have been tired and fallen asleep. When I woke up, you had all gone and the fire had died down. The whisky had left me feeling slightly odd inside, but surprisingly hungry. I thought I'd look out a snack – something savoury to offset the over-sweet liquor."

"You *ate* the toad!" exclaimed Laura with horrible realisation.

"I'm rather afraid I did, my dear," said Floyd apologetically.

"But you were very drunk and your memory might be betraying you. Can you be sure you ate it?" asked Rupert.

"Regrettably, yes," replied Floyd. "You see, feeling rather unsettled, I paid a visit to the bathroom. It was as I sat there that the memory seemed to float inexorably to the surface of my mind. Distressed at the loss to Laura I felt obliged to see if I could at least...retrieve the diamonds!" He opened his clasped right hand to reveal the two stones.

There was a stunned silence before Delilah said, "I really hope you washed your hands well."

"I did. I am mortified at what has occurred. Of course the work of art cannot be returned to you, Laura. All I can do is to humbly offer to paint my own portrait of you in recompense."

With the return of the diamonds and this generous offer

from the great Floyd Bailey, Laura was feeling much happier. Perhaps she would even be able to see the funny side of events in due course. As for Rupert, he thought the replacement of the Pickled Toad with Diamonds by a portrait of Laura a definite improvement.

An Uninvited Guest

Of all the unwelcome guests you hope will *not* turn up at your wedding: ex-spouses, drunken relations and voluble friends in possession of all the facts about your misspent life, a corpse is amongst the most undesirable. However, on the day of the marriage of Rupert Latimer, the dazed and fortunate groom, and his very lovely and wealthy wife, Laura, they not only returned from Claresby parish church to find a corpse already in attendance in the Great Hall, set out as it was in full splendour for the reception, but that very corpse was seated at the top of the snowy clothed, flower bedecked table in the large oak chair predestined to receive the groom, its limbs spread-eagled in careless, slightly tipsy abandon. Worse still, after the screams and shrieks of one or two of the first ladies to arrive had been silenced, a helpful medical friend took a brief look at the unwanted guest and indicated that, far from being recently deceased, it was probably a day or so since it had breathed its last.

It was characteristic of Laura that, on entering to find this scene, rather than dissolving into hysterics or clutching herself to the manly, if rather bony, chest of her newly acquired husband, she lifted the skirts of her elegant satin dress, bent towards the offending figure, sniffed her delicate nose and said, "Typical!"

Once a semblance of order had returned and a number of guests, in need of reassurance, had made their way to the table set out with sherry and glasses, a few of the more sensible souls had emerged to take responsibility for the situation.

"Where were the caterers?" was the first question asked by Paul Mayfield, the doctor who had already made his assessment of the uninvited guest. "I tell you, that fellow did not make his own way over to the chair. Someone must have carried him in, and someone should have seen that happen."

There werc half a dozen caterers about the place for the occasion: two based in the kitchen preparing food, two girls to serve the food and drink, one to wash-up, and one in charge of the wine. They were not a large party for the wedding; only twenty guests, twenty-two to include the happy couple and twenty-three if you wanted to be particular and include the corpse. Certainly the two girls should have been on hand to start pouring the sherry when the guests returned from the church pretty much on time. As it was, the guests were proving themselves perfectly well able to pour their own drinks and the girls were only just emerging into the Great Hall from the kitchen, flush faced and flustered. There was a pause whilst they noticed the dead body, noticed that everyone was looking at them and became very nervous. Eventually one, a mousy, hesitant sixteen year old with a propensity to blush managed to answer the queries.

"Well, we'd set everything up, and Maureen told us to come into the kitchen. Then Ken suggested we all took a sip of the champagne, just to drink Miss Mortimer's health, like... I mean Mrs Latimer..."

"I presume that the fellow in the chair wasn't there when you finished setting up?" queried Rupert.

"No, he weren't. I'd have noticed him for sure 'coz he's a funny colour."

"How long were you out of the Great Hall for?" asked Paul Mayfield.

"Well, just a minute of two...well, maybe ten. We was all ready early. We meant to be back in by twelve-thirty when you was all due back." The girl glanced awkwardly at the clock which showed twenty-five to one.

Rupert shrugged. "The DJ was here first thing to set up some of his equipment, but he won't be back until this evening, so I doubt that he saw anything. Ten minutes is all it would take to lug a body in here, and if no one was about at that particular moment to witness the event then it's anyone's guess who it was that did the deed. The question is: why? And who is the fellow anyway?" He gazed quizzically at the corpse as if hoping it would deliver up an answer, his amiable, intelligent but rather ugly face expressing bemused interest.

The corpse itself, sprawled in ungainly but casual attitude upright in the chair suggested a tall, bony man of perhaps sixty. The face was discoloured and hideous in death and it was difficult to deduce whether or not the man had been more attractive in life. The clothes were of rather good quality tweed, the shirt fine linen, perhaps suggesting their owner had been a well-to-do man of decent taste.

The group of people-who-are-interested had been joined by sometimes lawyer, Simon Forrest, and a dishevelled looking man with a ruddy face.

"Have you solved the crime?" asked the dishevelled man, prematurely.

"Well, we don't know a crime has been committed," said Rupert, reasonably. "For all we know, he sat down feeling a little unwell and passed away."

"Yes, but as I have pointed out," said Paul Mayfield, "he may well have died of natural causes, but he didn't do so in the last twenty minutes – that corpse is post rigour mortis, of that I am certain."

"Perhaps someone put him here as a joke?" suggested the man with the ruddy face. "A rather black joke," he added seeing the expressions on the other's faces.

"Assuming he did die of natural causes," Rupert said, turning to Simon Forrest, "what are the laws concerning the disposal of a dead body? Has a law been broken here?"

"Well," said Simon, thoughtfully, "not really my area of expertise, but whilst it is generally recognised that a corpse has no rights, the failure to dispose of a dead body properly is an offense; there are questions both of what is decent and respectful as well as public health issues to be considered. Also, unless someone has already ascertained how he died, a post-mortem would be required. And," with a spark of legal remembrance in his eyes, "it is a crime to hold a body as security for an unpaid debt!"

"The latter not an issue," commented Rupert, "but we will need to call the police."

"Is there any urgency? Can't we stick it in the corner and worry about it after we've eaten?" suggested one heartless and hungry guest who had just joined the throng.

"Well," said Rupert, "we could call the police but put him quietly in the study until they arrive..."

"You shouldn't move..." began Simon; but no one was willing to attend to him. Two none-too-fastidious men were summoned to lift the chair bodily and remove it to the study whilst celebrations were resumed with the added relish of unexpected drama.

It was only when they had sat down to eat the hors d'oeuvre of smoked salmon with dill cream that the man with the ruddy face – coincidently the best-man on this occasion – commented to Rupert, "You know, the funny thing is that I was talking to that very man in the churchyard just before the wedding, and whatever your doctor friend says, he was very much alive then!"

A traditional English wedding follows a certain course, so notwithstanding the interruption, food was eaten, speeches were made (with humorous reference to "our friend in the study"), toasts were drunk in champagne and the triumph of white icing and marzipan flowers that was the wedding cake was cut with a Cromwellian sword, removed from its station over the fireplace by an enterprising guest and wiped thoroughly but covertly on a napkin by the bride. A couple of policemen moved discretely about the place, and as guests relaxed and mingled, formalities having been completed, they apologetically cornered Mr and Mrs Latimer.

"Well," said a young, pink-faced policeman, "there is no sign of violence on the corpse, although we will have to wait for the coroner to tell us how he died; but we've not been able to establish his identity. We'll have to question your caterers and the guests of course and I understand that you had someone setting up some musical equipment, so we'll be talking to him. In the meantime, is there anything you can tell us about the man?"

Laura shook her head. "He was here in a chair when we returned from the church; nobody saw anything and nobody seems to recognise him. It's a bit of a mystery." She had removed her veil, but still wore a crown of tiny, white fabric flowers in her glossy auburn hair and this, coupled with her wide eyes and gentle expression gave her a look of almost conspicuous innocence. It made the young constable feel rather brutal as he revealed his next piece of news.

"Well, we do need to find out more about him, because while you were eating a discovery was made in the churchyard. I'm sorry to say that another dead body has been discovered there – and I don't mean the usual kind, buried and all. This chap was slumped in the chair in the garden of remembrance."

Rupert's eyes started in surprise, "Do you know anything about that man? And are the two deaths connected?"

"Well, I couldn't comment on any of that, sir. But, I've been down to the churchyard myself, and it would appear to be the same man as that one in your study, only fresher, so to speak!" He looked somewhat shocked, confused and out of sorts himself, so Rupert patted him reassuringly on the arm.

"If it is all right with you, I will come and look at the man in the churchyard; I'm beginning to have a worm of suspicion about the identity of these two men. Let me just have a word with my best man."

The uninvited guest having been properly removed, the invited guests continued to enjoy the abundance of free flowing wine into the evening when the DJ arrived and the Great Hall was transformed into a disco. Rupert eventually returned from his foray to the graveyard and, whilst he said nothing to Laura at that time, she could tell from the set of his broad, ugly, but to her completely lovable face that he had found out some conclusive yet disturbing truth about the identity of the two dead men. As it was, they continued the evening as planned and only fell into the newly refurbished Elizabethan four-poster in the scarlet bedroom in the wee hours of the next morning. There were a handful of other guests spending the night there by arrangement and a few uninvited (but live) guests who crashed in corners, too drunk or tired to make their way home. It was only after they had explored one of the comforts of married life appropriate to their wedding night that Rupert and Laura lay in each other's arms and Rupert told her what he had discovered.

"I think I had the inkling of the beginning of a niggle in my brain from the moment I saw the man in my chair, but I was too confused by events – the excitement of the wedding and then everything else – to really think straight."

"Not the great detective today," commented Laura, kissing his shoulder affectionately as she rested her head against his chest.

"Not my top priority today," admitted Rupert, stroking his wife's silky hair. "Anyway it was that twit, Martin, who suddenly said something that made the penny drop: he told me that he had spoken to the corpse we found in the chair and that he had been alive that morning in the churchyard. Of course he was wrong; he actually spoke to another man who looked just like the corpse – and who later died anyway."

Laura lifted her head to look at Rupert, her interest now aroused. "Were they twins?"

Rupert nodded. "Yes, and as soon as I realised that I knew who the men were and could guess something of what had happened. Martin, if he had the wits to think about it, had been told the truth. When I went back and asked him what had happened when he spoke to the man in the graveyard, he was quite dismissive. He said the man was slurred and possibly drunk and didn't make sense. In fact what he said was that he had promised his brother that he would see that he got to his son's wedding, whatever it took!"

"His son's wedding! That man was your father? You never met your father!"

"No," continued Rupert gently and pensively. "As you know, my mother married after I was born and George brought me up as his own son and my two half-sisters were really sisters to me. My mother spoke a little about my real father, and quite fondly. He used to send her sporadic and generous amounts of money to help with my upbringing, and apparently he turned up to one or two of my sports days and school plays, although I was never aware of his presence at the time. Anyway, I don't think I ever mentioned the fact to you, but I did know that he was one of identical twins: Peter and Michael Gordon. The man in the graveyard did have a wallet on him and was Michael Gordon. Of course I knew the name, and in fact I could see from his face that he was related to me – same ugly visage! It wasn't really possible to tell from the man in the chair." He paused for a moment.

"How awful for you, Rupert! What must you be

feeling...?"

"Honestly; at the moment nothing but happiness that I am in your arms. The rest is just too much for me to process straight away. If anything, I'm touched that my father wanted to be here – although perhaps not in the way things turned out! I suspect that both my father and uncle were ill – I know there was a history of heart problems in their family – my mother told me useful stuff like that for my sake. I think my father may have been unwell and Michael was determined to fulfil his last wish. He must have lost his senses a bit to have continued after his brother died – but there you have it! Perhaps the exertion killed him too; we'll have to wait for the coroner's report."

"Was a crime committed?"

"Possibly, by Michael, if he didn't report the death or dispose of a body appropriately, but perhaps he was in a state of diminished responsibility. Anyway, he's dead too, so it becomes irrelevant."

"Perhaps if your mother had been alive she would have recognised your father, but I don't suppose anyone else would. Well, Rupert, I hope the rest of our married life is more conventional than our wedding day." Laura wriggled into a comfortable position preparatory to going to sleep.

"Who knows," commented Rupert in the voice of one who expected anything but the conventional from life with Laura, as he snuggled against her and closed his eyes at last.

The Claresby Mystery

It was a matter of record, as witnessed by the Domesday Book in 1086, that the Lord of the Manor of Claresby enjoyed exclusive rights to hold both a market and a fair on his lands. It was a matter of fact that, although there were various faded sepia photographs to bear witness to the reality of Claresby Fair as a happy tradition, no such fair had been held in living memory. It was Laura Latimer (née Mortimer) who was now the rightful custodian of these tattered photographs, which had been long retained by her family on the basis that they were of negligible value on the open market, everything that was of value having been sold at prestigious London auction houses or, more recently, on eBay. Laura had, however, perused these pictures as a child and nurtured a dream of one day reviving the custom. The recent restoration of her fortunes, which had resulted from the discovery of treasure concealed by her family in the time of Oliver Cromwell, meant that she now had the wherewithal to host such an event without any anxiety about whether or not it would be profitable. As a student of Fine Art – albeit one who had dropped out after her first term at Cambridge – it was inevitable that she should choose to have an Arts Fair, despite the invasion of artists that this invited.

Thus it was that Laura awoke in bed on a sunny June morning, the tousled hair and benign, ugly face of her husband, Rupert, on the pillow beside her and the prospect of a chaotic day of stalls being erected, ice-cream vans claiming their pitches and the smell of hog roast from dawn until dusk ahead. The inevitable consequences of a beer tent being available in her grounds had not escaped Laura's practical mind, but there was a row of portable toilets on site and she planned to keep the door to the manor itself locked and out of bounds, the fair being set at the far end of the grounds. Nonetheless, despite a tendency to reclusiveness and inhospitality, she did have an assortment of artistic minded friends who were taking part at the fair sleeping in her house; a side-effect she rather resented.

"Remind me, Rupert," she asked, rubbing her sleepy eyes and smoothing her glossy, auburn hair, "who is in the house?"

Rupert hauled his long, angular frame upright in their four-poster bed – which creaked protestingly – and put his arm around his pretty wife, screwing up his eyes in thought.

"Floyd is in the green room and Sebastian across the corridor – malice aforethought; I love watching those two bicker! Delilah and Conran are in the King's Room, because we spent so much money restoring it and Delilah loves something a bit flashy. Samantha is in your old bedroom, because all the best paintings are in there and she will appreciate them."

Laura nodded approvingly at the logic of her husband's dispersal of their guests. She was glad to hear that the King's Room was in use. It was the grandest bedroom in Claresby Manor, with the best view across the gardens, an ornate bed with newly restored rich purple hangings and seventeenth century Flemish tapestries on the walls. Its name derived from the fact that   Henry VIII was reputed to have spent a couple of nights sleeping there, arriving with his retinue on a royal progress and almost bankrupting William Mortimer, the incumbent at that time. Still, it was never prudent to fail to please the great monarch, although rumour had it that William had taken care that his young and famously beautiful niece was not about the place when the King had arrived.

With a view to the fact that the day was to be a very hectic one, Laura placed a perfunctory kiss on her husband's large nose and rolled out of bed and headed for their bathroom.

Rupert watched her slim, graceful silk-clad body with the enthusiasm of a man still in the honeymoon years of early marriage.

"You had better rout out Sebastian and Floyd; Floyd was putting away my vintage Armagnac with gusto last night, and Sebastian is notoriously idle." Laura emerged from the bathroom rubbing her face dry with a towel. "Floyd won't have much to do as Jinny is arriving with his paintings today and will no doubt set up stall for him – he does take shameless advantage of his wives – and Sebastian is much too much the "great artist" to do anything other than set up an easel and impress people. At least Floyd will muck in and take part; I appreciate the favour, even at the price of having him as a houseguest again."

Rupert nodded obligingly. It was the nature of their relationship that Laura took the lead and he made things work. The fact that the house and money were hers and that the nearest Rupert came to a paid occupation was writing crosswords could have made for an awkward dynamic between them, but for the fact that it suited their personalities. Even without the house and the money, Laura was one of those people who went their own way whilst others followed, or not, at their own inclination. Rupert, in turn, was the type to be utterly devoted, as he was to his lovely wife. The reason the financial reality and balance of power was not emasculating to him was the underlying reality that Laura could not possibly manage, let alone be happy, without Rupert by her side. She would never have dreamed of acknowledging the fact, even to herself, but the tall, awkward, ugly man in her bed was the light of her life.

Whilst Laura proceeded to wash her hair, Rupert pulled on jeans and a tee shirt without feeling the need to wash or do more than smooth his light hair into abeyance. As he opened the heavy door to their bedroom onto the slightly musty, cool corridor with shafts of sunlight playing on the dusty air, he could hear no sound of movement within the house itself, although the muffled noise of cars arriving and other "setting-up" sounds came from the grounds as others prepared for the resurrected Claresby Fair. The volley of creaks that the oak floor boards reported as he made his way towards the corner of the house where Sebastian and Floyd were separately ensconced, was enough to waken any but the most robust sleeper, even without the gentle taps he made on the doors belonging to the Hawkes' and Samantha Pearson. When he reached the room allocated to the well known installation artist and occasional inventor, Sebastian Fullmarks, Rupert turned the knob and stuck his head around the door.

"Nice, sunny morning; are you thinking of getting up? There are bacon and eggs and everything else in the kitchen in a help-yourself kind of way."

Sebastian, a white haired ruddy cheeked man with a perpetually disgruntled expression was already sitting up in bed.

"You needn't have bothered waking me," he grumbled. "There was no prospect of my sleeping with Floyd's stentorian and vulgar snores bellowing across the corridor all night! I believe you put me next door to him deliberately. I had the misfortune to share a room with him for a couple of nights forty years ago, when we were students together, and have made a study of avoiding such proximity ever since!"

Rupert gave his lopsided grin. "Sorry, Sebastian; we can always give you a different room tonight."

"Very well," came the slightly mollified reply." I will get into the bathroom before Floyd and make sure I have had my breakfast before he emerges. Did you say there were sausages? Will you be cooking?"

"Yes, I'm just going down to get things going. I'll just stick my head around Floyd's door."

Rupert crossed the corridor and peered into the room inhabited by Floyd Bailey. The green bedroom was on the west side of the house, so it was necessary for Rupert to readjust his eyes to the gloom after the sunlight of Sebastian's bedroom.

"Good morning, Floyd," began Rupert brightly. There was no reply. This was not too surprising; Floyd did not so much "go to sleep" at night as "fall unconscious into his bed": rousing him the following morning was a challenging and sometime unsuccessful operation. As it was Rupert knew that Laura's vision of the day included the presence of this unreliable but likeable and talented artist. He entered the room and repeated his greeting in a louder voice. Still no reply. As Rupert's eyes became slowly accustomed to the dim morning light that filtered through the curtains a few anomalies began to register on his brain. The room was a pleasant sage green and plainly rather than grandly furnished. The bed was a fine brass bedstead with a cream coloured bedspread and Floyd was reposed on his back, the covers up to his chin. On the wall were a number of scrawlings which caught Rupert's eye. For a moment he thought that Floyd, with drunken artistic enthusiasm, had been undertaking some sort of impromptu mural. Rupert examined the walls with greater attention and finally turned to the recumbent figure in the bed.

Breakfast had been initiated by Samantha Pearson. Already immaculately dressed in her uniform of a smart grey trouser suit softened by a lush purple scarf and modern, silver jewellery she was turning the bacon rather stiffly at arm's length with the air of a headmistress who had been forced to substitute for the school dinner-lady. Sebastian, pale knees protruding from beneath a dark blue dressing gown, was seated at the long, oak table and watching her, his bright blue eyes focused on the progress of the sausages. The kitchen was a lofty, medieval affair with lots of brass cookware hanging along the walls.

"Thought I'd get in before Floyd arrives," Sebastian was saying. "Since he is usually drunk from midday onwards, breakfast is the only meal he makes a proper job of. I don't want to see the sausages go to feed the production of his tedious, out-moded paintings."

Samantha turned and delivered him a plate and forked several sausages onto it, sliding a fried egg out of a second frying pan. She didn't say anything but, at her disapproving look, Sebastian put his legs together, pulled his dressing gown straight, and turned to the table to more properly address his food. In fact Samantha was perfectly indifferent to the man's state of dress or undress, and her disapproving look was a professional one that related to Sebastian Fullmarks' modern style of art which she regarded as nothing short of an abomination and an insult to the beholder. Leaving the food to keep warm at the back of the stove, Samantha helped herself to a good English breakfast and sat at the table a reasonable distance away from Sebastian.

"Why are you here, anyway?" asked Sebastian through a mouthful of egg. "This is an arts and crafts fair; your speciality is eviscerating decent artists in that blog of yours, "Supine Arts" – that is destructive, not creative." His tone was not as aggressive as his words suggested, and he and Samantha were old friends and adversaries. Certainly she was unruffled by his address. Sitting straight backed and prim, she finished the food she was eating before she spoke,

"I am here to support Laura; and I will be judging the best flower arrangement competition."

Sebastian snorted.

"And it is "sublime" not "supine" although I understand that you would find it hard to differentiate between the two. Anyway, I wonder that you are participating – since when was a display of dried meat either art or craft – unless Laura has included a farmers produce section at the fair?"

"Simply because my presence ensures the attendance of the press and a little publicity for her venture," responded Sebastian complacently.

Unfortunately this was quite true and Samantha was, for once, silenced. She maintained a dignified interest in her bacon.

"As a matter of fact, I have brought an easel and oils and will be painting a record of the day. I have a four foot square canvas," continued Sebastian. "I was hoping to twist Floyd's arm to follow suit, if he can deal with a little friendly rivalry." He looked towards the door as if hoping that Floyd would enter. As it was, Delilah and Conran Hawkes came into the kitchen.

"I hope you left some for me?" Conran, a short, dark man with a round, pleasant face headed for the stove and helped himself to a plate and started piling food on it.

His wife, a slim and immaculately dressed woman who topped her husband by at least six inches wrinkled a delicate nose and headed toward the large refrigerator. When she joined the others at the table, it was with a small pot of Greek yogurt in front of her.

"So, what have you been drafted in to do?" Samantha pointedly addressed her question to Conran, for whom she had some respect. His art gallery, The Hawkes Gallery, had held exhibitions of exquisite traditional works which she had reviewed favourably and with real interest – right up until the point when Delilah had arrived and started to impose her taste onto the formerly quiet, reserved little gallery.

"There will be an open air exhibition of works by the Claresby Art Society. I will be choosing the winner and presenting the inaugural trophy: I'm rather looking forward to it. Will you be painting al fresco, Sebastian?"

"Indeed – I had hoped that Floyd would join me, but I think he is setting up stall with some of his works. I imagine that will be the job of Jane or Jinny, or whatever the dear little thing he recently married is called. One wonders that women continue to marry Floyd, given his track record."

"He could have sketched portraits, like they do at Montmartre," commented Samantha.

Sebastian grunted.

"Where is Floyd this morning anyway?" asked Delilah, who had scraped out the remains of her yogurt and licked it delicately off her spoon with the tip of a pink tongue. "And why aren't Rupert and Laura up yet?"

Laura, fully dressed in a summer frock of a cream material sprigged with roses and a little white shrug to protect the fair skin of her shoulders, was staring at her husband with incredulity.

"Dead! Are you sure?"

"Pretty sure," nodded Rupert with a furrowed brow. "I didn't touch or move him, but there was something so very dead about his whole demeanour, I didn't need to."

"Couldn't he just be unconscious? I mean, no one can drink themselves comatose like Floyd."

"Not with his eyes wide open and fixed on the ceiling. No, Laura, Floyd is dead."

Laura moved about the room and opened a wardrobe almost absent-mindedly and picked out a straw hat with a red ribbon about it.

"That is peculiarly awkward," she said slowly. "So many

46

people have so much going on today, and a death in the house is rather distracting. Any idea how he died – I mean, it was natural wasn't it?"

"I didn't examine him; there were no signs of violence, if that is what you mean. He was just dead – untouched and staring up, as if it was sudden and unexpected."

There was something about Rupert's slightly dazed and detached demeanour that irritated Laura.

"You are not suggesting that someone crept in and performed the Avada Kedavra curse, are you! I imagine it was a heart attack or something. One way or another Floyd was always going to drink himself to death."

"I was not suggesting anything," replied Rupert, mildly, "except that there was something odd, if not about the body, about the room. Someone – and it may have been Floyd – had put inscriptions on the wall."

"What sort of inscriptions?"

"Well, it was gloomy in there, and I was rather taken aback, but my impression was that they were hieroglyphs."

"Hieroglyphs! Why would Floyd be scrawling hieroglyphs on my bedroom wall?" This time Laura really was astonished.

"I don't know," mused Rupert, "but it does make me want to check up on a couple of things. I'll put in an appearance downstairs – I think they have sorted out their own breakfasts – and then try and make sense of this. We don't need to call anyone in straight away, do we? – after all, I might not have noticed that Floyd was dead."

"To be honest, no one would question Floyd Bailey's non-appearance, even if it was his own exhibition; not even his current wife. No, you do what you like and sort it out," said Laura briskly. "I must see to things outside. And, anyway, if anyone can make sense of hieroglyphs, it would be you." Suddenly Laura paused and then added, with some show of real feeling, "I actually rather liked Floyd."

After Laura had left Rupert started to act with some purpose. First he went down the stairs and quietly into his study. He could hear the rumble of voices from the kitchen, but was intent on finding something in his desk, indifferent to the summer's morning sun which filled the room, winking off two silver andirons in the fireplace and illuminating an elegant room furnished in an eighteenth century style. Soon he had found the notebook and pencil which he had wanted and made his way back up the stairs and into the cool gloom of Floyd's room. There was an uncomfortable feel to the bedroom, not least because the light through the green curtains created an eerie glow, but also because the inscriptions on the wall had been written in gold and seemed to gleam ominously. The presence of the corpse with its staring eyes fixed on the ceiling didn't help. Although it would have been both helpful and reassuring to open the curtains and let in some daylight, Rupert was determined to disturb nothing. Instead, squinting a little, he started to copy down the hieroglyphs from the wall.

As a Cambridge graduate in Archaeology and Anthropology, Rupert was not a complete stranger to the forms in front of him, and it helped that they were often illustrative of their meaning. A circle with a dot in the middle was clearly a sun disc. The profile of a bed with a shape on it was a mummy on a bier – or was it Floyd on his bed? A set of legs walking backwards – someone running away? Sometimes the symbols could represent sounds, but what he was looking at seemed quite rudimentary – pictures to tell the tale. He took them down quickly into his little book and left the room, closing the door softly behind him.

When Rupert reached the kitchen he found the Hawkes'

still there.

"Not much left for you," apologised Conran. "One sausage I think. Your good wife just popped in for coffee and a croissant. Any sign of Floyd?"

"I did call in to him, but he wasn't very responsive," said Rupert with complete honesty as he popped a sausage between two slices of bread.

"He'll probably emerge mid-afternoon; we'll go and help Jinny set up his stall. I think he has some prints to display." He stood up and Delilah followed him out of the room.

Rupert dispatched the sausage in no more than two bites and headed through the Great Hall and out of the double doors at the front of Claresby Manor. The sun was full on the eastern side of the medieval building and the lawns stretched away to where the fair was taking shape. Stalls, awnings, tents, canopies and gazebos were being erected and he could already see woven baskets, dried flower arrangements and other craft works being unloaded from the boots of cars and backs of vans. He saw Bill Smith of Claresby Art Club setting up boards on which to mount the display of paintings under a striped gazebo. Bill, a diminutive, rotund, rosy cheeked man in his late sixties who reminded Rupert of a robin redbreast gave a cheery wave which Rupert returned. He could see Laura's pretty flowery dress and despite preoccupations a smile rose to Rupert's face at the sight of her. She seemed to be holding a heated discussion with two men, both of whom towered over her. Nonetheless, he could tell from the body language of the players that it was his wife who was exerting her authority. In one corner of the grounds, he could see Jinny Bailey setting out Floyd's stall and his stomach seemed to twist within him. Laura had caught sight of him and came over.

"You would think that two grown men could agree to share the sale of ice creams between them without my having to threaten to bring in the UN," she sighed. "How are you doing?"

"All right. Did you want an update on the Floyd thing?"

"Yes. Is it bad news?"

"Not really. I took down a note of the hieroglyphs; let me show you." Rupert displayed the little drawings.

"Not any the wiser," commented Laura as she glanced at them "What are these things, and who drew them on the wall?"

"Well," began Rupert, with something of a scholar's enthusiasm, "this one is the best." He pointed to a cluster of hieroglyphs which looked to Laura like a feather, saw, wave, circle, line and crouched figure. "This is Amun-Ra, kind of top Egyptian god. The circle and dot represent the sun. This one I don't get," he pointed to a horizontal shape. "It is a mummified crocodile."

"Rupert, *what*, are you talking about! A mummified crocodile! Why would Floyd be drawing these things on the wall? And what do they have to do with his death?"

"Well," hesitated Rupert. "I wonder if he did draw them. You see Floyd, Sebastian and I ended up in the junk room last night – Floyd wanted to borrow an easel as Sebastian was trying to get him to paint today and..." Before he could say more, one of the ice cream men advanced on Laura and she was obliged to turn away. Rupert gave her a sign to mean that he would try and talk to her later and then headed back to the house.

In fact Rupert's memories of the previous night were coloured by the fact that he and Sebastian had been helping Floyd in the matter of the bottle of Armagnac. They had been in the Great Hall when the banter between the two rival artists had resulted in Floyd agreeing that he too would make an alla prima painting of Claresby Manor in full view of the fair-going public. All he required was an easel and Sebastian would allow him to use the paints and brushes that he had brought along for the purpose. This led to the three men repairing to the junk room of Claresby Manor. The contents of that room did fit the category of "junk", virtually everything worthwhile having been sold to pay death duties in the past. Somehow the Armagnac had made its way up with them, and Floyd and Sebastian had rifled through the artefacts, crockery, old prams and discarded paintings that filled the room.

"Some abominations here," commented Floyd of the paintings. "Now Laura has some money she should stock up on some real artworks for Claresby,"

"Well, she tried," responded Sebastian acerbically, "with my *Pickled Toad with Diamonds*; but some drunken fool consumed it!"

"Oh, you heard about that," said Floyd, sheepishly. "Well I did replace it with my lovely portrait of the fair lady, so all's well."

"You robbed posterity!" exclaimed Sebastian, but without any real rancour.

At this point Floyd had yanked an old suitcase out of a corner. It had a brown leather strap around it and the initials T.M. embossed on it. Floyd proceeded to pull out some clothes and papers. Amongst the papers was a leather bound sketch book which Floyd flicked through.

"These aren't half bad," he commented showing the other two men a series of sketches of Egypt. "Nice watercolour of the Sphinx at Giza; oh, and someone went to the Valley of the Kings too – typical nineteenth century English tourist: I'm surprised he didn't bring a mummy home with him, bandages and all."

"Who was the owner of the case?" asked Rupert, with some interest in Laura's ancestors.

Floyd flicked through the papers and said, "Tom Mortimer

– he signed his pictures and dated them. 1882, I think. There are a few notes on the back of the pictures." He poked through the suitcase a bit more and picked out a dirty looking ring and tried to rub it down with the cuff of an old shirt which was still in the case. "Valuable artefact, perhaps?"

"No," replied Rupert firmly. "No family disposed of everything of value more effectively than the Mortimers. Just a trinket from the market, probably."

"Let me see?" Sebastian put down the broken umbrella he had been trying to open and reached out a hand for the ring. Just at that moment a voice called in to them.

"If you lot can leave the brandy alone and come down, somebody ordered enough Chinese takeaway to feed an army – the Great Hall will smell for days," added Laura with distaste.

"Oh, that was me," smiled Sebastian, happily. "Special set dinner for four, twice: my treat!" They all stuffed the things they were holding back where they came from and followed Laura down the carved oak staircase towards the tempting aroma of Chinese food.

Returning to the junk room in the morning light, Rupert saw that the suitcase had been left open, the clothes and sketch books stuffed in any old how. He couldn't now remember if it was Floyd who had been still holding the ring or if Sebastian had taken it and whether or not it had been returned to the suitcase. Unbidden, stories of ancient Egyptian curses and scenes from *The Mummy* films rose to the forefront of his mind. Carefully he took the sketch book from the case and read all the notes that Tom Mortimer had written as a record of his trip to Egypt. Then Rupert searched through the mess of clothes and other personal effects until he saw the ring. It was tarnished and grubby, but appeared to be a turquoise stone set in gold. The stone may have been just a stone, but Rupert had a nasty feeling that there was just the suggestion of the scarab about it. He took a fresh linen handkerchief from his pocket and carefully lifted the ring within it and folded it up, returning it to his pocket.

Claresby Fair was scheduled to start at noon. The weather was sunny with just the hint of a cooling breeze and a scattering of light, white, fluffy clouds. As Rupert returned to the grounds he saw that everything was taking shape and there was a tendency for people to gravitate to the refreshments tent, which was already serving coffee to the participants. He could see that Conran was helping Jinny and, knowing what he knew, felt a reluctance to go over there. Unfortunately for him, Conran caught his eye and beckoned.

"Is Floyd up and about?" asked Conran.

"'No," replied Rupert. "You look like you are managing well enough."

"On this sort of occasion, Floyd is an optional extra," smiled Jinny, a slight and pretty woman in her thirties. "We just have prints of some of his most famous paintings. Sebastian said that Floyd might be setting up an easel and painting the house. I'll wander around and look for him later. I can see Sebastian over there; I think he has started before the crowds arrive. Is there an official opening?"

"Not really; just gates open at twelve. The highlight of the day is the award of prizes in various categories at four this afternoon. Would you like me to fetch you a coffee?"

"Oh, yes please!" Jinny smiled at him.

Once Rupert had done this, he went over to see Sebastian. He wasn't sure what he was looking for, but somehow he thought that the artist might give him a clue to what had happened to Floyd – after all, he too had looked at the ring, and he had been sleeping right next to Floyd's room and might have heard something. He found Sebastian at the point of having set up his easel and placed a small folding table beside him with his paints lined up, his palette already sporting bright worms of colour squeezed from the tubes and a scent of turpentine in the air. Sebastian himself was striking in cream chinos and a white linen shirt, his shock of white hair and pale skin emphasised by a bright red neck cloth which protected the back of his neck from the sun, and a light straw hat with a red band around it. His face also showed a red tinge about the cheeks. His large canvas already looked imposing and the artist had taken a thick brush and was boldly marking out the area of sky in what looked like purple lake and the foreground in patches of raw sienna and burnt sienna. If Rupert hadn't had more important things on his mind he might have been tempted to watch Sebastian Fullmarks at work. Famous mostly for his controversial modern work, there might have been cynics who questioned whether he was actually capable of good, solid, conventional painting. Still, he seemed confident enough with easel and brush, so perhaps he was about to prove his detractors wrong.

Still vigorously applying purple paint to the sky, Sebastian indicated another table. "See – I have set out some limited edition replicas of my latest work: *Plate of Meat*! The original is in the Tate Modern, of course, but any money I raise from these today will be donated to repairing Claresby parish church."

Rupert glanced at what he had originally taken to be Sebastian's lunch, but at the same time acknowledged the generosity of the gesture. If the Claresby villagers bought these from Sebastian today at whatever they paid for them, they would be able to resell them for a great deal more; Sebastian was, after all, very famous. And Laura would be happy for the donation to the church.

"No sign of Floyd then?" Sebastian asked casually.

"No; perhaps he had a bad night."

"Well he certainly slept – he was snoring continuously from midnight until four in the morning."

"Any sounds from him after that?" asked Rupert.

"Well someone went for a pee in the bathroom at our end of the house at about six. Why, are you worried about him?"

"Not really; Floyd was never the most reliable man around. Still, it would have been nice to watch him paint." Rupert's eyes travelled to the new colour that Sebastian was squeezing onto his palette. "Goodness! Is that actually gold? I didn't know you could get a gold oil paint."

"Oh yes," smiled Sebastian happily. "This is actually a renaissance gold – I find the Winsor and Newton gold a little too buttercup coloured for my taste. I have a tube of silver too: nice in clouds." He proceeded to dab some of the gold into the foreground as highlights. Somehow the picture that was beginning to take shape seemed to bear no resemblance to the view of Claresby Manor as it stood in front of them, but Rupert supposed that this was all part of the great artist's modern interpretation, or perhaps he was just building up an under-painting. Rupert didn't really know much about paintings and was inclined to go for photorealistic scenes of the English countryside left to his own taste.

Rupert could see Laura a little way off, standing with a cup of coffee in her hand and surveying the scene before her with some satisfaction. He left Sebastian and went over to join her.

"I'll go and help sell programmes at the gate come twelve," she commented, glancing at her watch. "How is Sebastian getting on? I want the painting for in the Great Hall if it is any good; we need a modern interpretation of Claresby Hall."

"Hard to tell," said Rupert, absent-mindedly. "He is using

55

gold paint – the writing on the walls in Floyd's room was in gold."

"Is that relevant?" asked Laura, squinting her eyes against the sun as she looked questioningly at him.

"Probably not; I just happened to notice."

"Did you find out anything new? You were saying something about the junk room earlier."

"Well, it linked to that fact that there were Egyptian hieroglyphs on the wall. Just before you called us down for that Chinese takeaway, when we were looking for an easel, Floyd somehow managed to unearth an old suitcase belonging to Tom Mortimer."

"There has been more than one Thomas Mortimer over the centuries."

"This one was a nineteenth century Tom. There was a sketch book in there covering a trip to Egypt. It would have been in the eighteen-nineties."

"I think there was a Thomas Mortimer who used to be a bit of an artist. There are a couple of his watercolours in the library – of Cornwall, not Egypt. I think he was the one who had a perfect fetish for knick-knacks; he used to collect Dresden shepherdesses, that sort of thing."

"Well, he had collected an Egyptian artefact; a ring. When I looked through his writings he seemed to think that it had belonged to Nesperennub."

"Nesperennub? I know that name. Is it from one of the *Mummy* films?"

Rupert smiled. "No, you remember the name from the time I dragged you around the British Museum. Nesperennub is the mummy who is famous for having been subjected to a CT scan so that his body could be examined in a non-intrusive way. He is thought to have been a priest of Amun-Ra in the temple at Karnak."

"You said that one of the hieroglyphs on the wall in

Floyd's wall represented Amun-Ra: is someone playing games, or should I expect some of those squealing resurrected mummy things to start popping out of the windows?"

"I would be interested to know if the ring is genuine. As far as I remember, Nesperennub was discovered at Luxor at about the same time Tom was in Egypt. The fact that the mummy was sold to a curator of the British Museum suggests that someone was happy to flog the bits and pieces; at a price, no doubt."

"But," mused Laura, "even if this ring is genuine, you are not seriously suggesting that the discovery of it has anything to do with Floyd's death? I know that mummy curses make for good television, but does anyone really take them seriously?"

"Lord Carnarvon may have done. He died a year after the celebrated excavation of Tutankhamun's tomb – as a result of a mosquito bite. But you have to hand it to the ancient Egyptians, they just knew how to write a curse: "They that shall break the seal of this tomb shall meet death by a disease that no doctor can cure!" and "Death shall come on swift wings to him who disturbs the peace of the King!" – these are quality curses. There are a host of rational explanations given, such as a deadly fungus growing in enclosed tombs and infecting those who enter. It is a case of sceptics and believers – take your pick – and perhaps belief in a curse is enough to bring a man down; that is the basis on which any good ancient gypsy curse could work."

"Yes, but we didn't open the tomb; so no curse and no nasty bacteria. We don't even know what killed Floyd."

Rupert sighed. "You are right, and I am going to have to inform Dr Lowe that he is dead. Sooner or later someone will go and find him, so it is better I sort things out quietly and tell Jinny. Like you I am a sceptic about curses – and yet

I did pick up that ring pretty gingerly. Mike from Cambridge works at the British Museum; I'll get him to look at it and see if it is genuine."

"Who did touch the ring then: just Floyd?"

"Well, Sebastian wanted to look at it, but I'm not sure if he did, because we all came downstairs. Anyway, he is still happy, healthy and painting. I won't panic unless he dies mysteriously too!" And with that Rupert gave his wife a fond kiss and made his way back to the house.

Laura watched Rupert go with a mixture of fondness and concern and then promptly forgot about him as she returned her interest to her pet project: Claresby Fair. It was beginning to get hot and the colourful stalls stood out on the lawns like flower blooms. Even before the arrival of villagers and other visitors, there seemed to be a lot of people about the place. She let her eyes sweep over the displays of dried flowers, embroidered purses, exotic silk screen prints, woven baskets and polished carved wooden bowls. She could see Samantha chatting to members of the Claresby Art Club and wondered what they would make of the ferocious and blunt spoken art critic. She had deliberately chosen Conran Hawkes to judge the art because he was less likely than Samantha to say anything downright offensive in his critique. It had seemed fairly safe to put Samantha in charge of judging the flower arranging – after all, flowers were nice, what could she find to be scathing about? Nonetheless, Laura decided it was prudent to move Samantha away from the mild-mannered but sensitive amateur artists.

"It is so lovely to see some plain, honest good painting," Samantha was saying in strong tones to Bill Smith, the top of whose head barely reached her shoulders. "One wonders who the real artists are – the likes of Sebastian Fullmarks and Floyd Bailey or the worthy members of your club. It is just a case of showmanship and cheap celebrity that makes them their money if you ask me. I'm not saying that Floyd can't paint, but I would happily say that Sebastian can't – or if he can, he never does."

"And yet," intervened Laura with a light smile, "he is currently working away at a painting of Claresby Manor. I have not seen it yet, but I'm sure it will be a work I can display with pride."

"Let's hope so," replied Samantha, scepticism in every syllable.

"I was just going to ask you if you would help me at the entrance? We are due to open in five minutes."

"Of course," replied Samantha, and the two women made their way towards the sweep of the drive and the recently erected wrought iron gates at the main entrance of the manor. The next hour was a swirl of greetings and payments and despite growing heat and a pain starting to blossom behind her eyes, Laura experienced a swell of satisfaction at seeing how popular Claresby Fair was turning out to be. She also spared a grateful thought for Samantha, who worked hard beside her without complaint. Fortunately, come one o'clock two of the villagers Laura knew well came and took over and she and Samantha were able to repair to the beer tent for a glass of Pimms with a whole fruit salad floating in it. Then they made their way over to the hog roast and were gifted rolls with a mere smidgen of salad and a hunk of crispy meat. Laura felt herself perk up and even the immaculately groomed Samantha was tucking into the ungainly fare with enthusiasm. Then the two ladies drifted around the stalls and Laura made some courtesy purchases of handmade cards and a paperweight with an arrangement of rosebuds in it.

"Well," said Laura as they thanked the woman who had

made the cards, "perhaps we should venture up and see if Sebastian is making headway with his painting. I must confess to being curious as to how he will pull off a conventional landscape with building. I sometimes think he is more of an inventor at heart than an artist."

"A charlatan, more like," sniffed Samantha. "But I must confess that I was impressed that he was prepared to expose his talent to public view by painting alla prima in such a populous venue."

They could both see his easel now, top heavy with its enormous canvas. A small group of people were looking and Frank Bowler, organist at Claresby church, moved away and caught sight of them.

"Nice painting," he said with a wink. "I wonder where he spent his holiday!"

Bemused, Laura hastened up the slope and turned to look at the canvas. The painting that met her eyes depicted a turbulent sky of moody blues and purple. Below, emitting a sense of heat and menace, was the Sphinx.

"Well!" exclaimed Samantha. "I'm astounded. With art I cannot lie, and this is a wonderful work: strength, energy, brooding, ominous – brilliant! And I'm going to have to admit as much to Sebastian. How galling."

"Yes, but aren't you missing the obvious," returned Laura. "What on earth was he thinking about? He is meant to be painting Claresby Hall."

"What does it matter?" replied Samantha dismissively. "The painting is good."

"I suppose it doesn't matter, but I am just wondering what was in Sebastian's mind. And where is he? The painting doesn't look quite finished and he has left his little stall of...meat."

"Perhaps he went to the beer tent; we'll soon find him."

But they didn't. Exhaustive search of the fair, grounds,

beer tent and kitchens did not reveal Sebastian and no one had seen him, nor had he spoken to anyone.

Laura sighed. "I'd better go and tell Rupert. Samantha, one more favour; could you just look after Sebastian's stall. He is selling those replicas of *Plate of Meat* for the benefit of Claresby church. And his work is, after all, quite valuable."

"What me? – Sell that?" Samantha was incredulous.

Laura, however, did not seem to register this reaction. "Yes, if you would be kind enough." And with that Laura set off in the direction of the house with her mind full of concern. She was not so consumed by this concern, however, that she didn't take just one look over her shoulder to enjoy the ironic spectacle of Samantha Pearson having to tout just those goods which she despised most on behalf of her adversary, Sebastian.

Laura was not sorry to be returning to the house. Not only did she want to appraise Rupert of Sebastian's disappearance, but she also felt in need of a freshen up. As she made her way through the Great Hall, she encountered Keith Lowe, the local doctor. Keith was a very good looking and pleasant bachelor in his forties, one of the few locals whom Laura actually welcomed to the occasional dinner party which she felt obliged to arrange.

"Oh, hallo Laura, is everything going well out there? When I'm finished I hope to take a look around. I've arranged for the body to be taken away. There will have to be a post-mortem of course, but I imagine with Floyd's lifestyle we can assume heart attack – that's off the record, by the way!"

"Thank you. We will have to tell his wife, Jinny – she is down there looking after his stall."

"Not easy; she is much younger isn't she? Rupert said she wasn't staying here last night, which perhaps explains why nobody found his body for so long."

"Yes; we just assumed a hangover and left him undisturbed," Laura lied fluently.

"That's pretty much what Rupert said. The press will make a story out of it, I imagine."

Laura winced. "I suppose so. There is a photographer coming to take pictures of Sebastian and his painting later – that's if we can find Sebastian."

"Well, if you will mix with artists: unreliable lot." Keith winked and made his way out in a brisk, businesslike manner.

Laura carried on up the stairs and met her husband on his way between the green bedroom and their own room He followed Laura in and flopped down on the bed. Laura went to quickly slosh a bit of water on her face and then came and sat beside him.

"Keith seemed satisfied," she said. "He thinks heart attack."

"Hopefully he is right. Anyway, I spoke to Mike Herbert. As luck would have it he was staying with his parents who are only about ten miles away. He became very excited when I told him about the ring and mentioned a possible link with Nesperennub and got straight in his car – it's just his field of expertise. He's on his way over here now. Any objections if we offer to donate it to the British Museum if it is genuine? I just have this feeling that things might be better if the ring and the owner were reunited so to speak."

Laura looked mildly surprised by this indication of continued superstition on Rupert's part, but agreed readily enough. "If you like," she said. "Will you wait in here for him?"

"I've got to wait for one of those private ambulances to collect Floyd. Hopefully its arrival will go relatively unnoticed if everyone is otherwise occupied. How is the fair going? I'm sorry I've been so out of it."

"Not your fault," Laura gave him an affectionate peck on the cheek and smoothed his light hair off his forehead. "Anyway, I better go and talk to Jinny – she might want to see Floyd before they come for him. Oh, and I thought I should tell you – Sebastian seems to have disappeared. And he was painting a strange Egyptian scene on his canvas."

Rupert, who had been propped up on one elbow in a weary stance, suddenly sat upright at this sudden revelation. "That's what I didn't want to hear. Are you sure he is gone? Couldn't he just have wandered off for a drink?"

"Maybe, but Samantha and I had a pretty good search for him. Don't worry too much now. See your friend and when you are free come and find me and we'll have a good Sebastian-hunt. Oh, and remember that we are presenting prizes at four. I'd really like you to be there if you can."

After his wife had left to find Jinny, Rupert took himself down to the kitchen for a cold drink. He wasn't sure what to think. It had been reassuring to have Keith walk into the green bedroom, pull the curtains and dispel the eerie green light, and examine the body with a practical, professional manner. When Rupert had glanced at the hieroglyphs even they seemed to fade to nothing in the bright daylight. Keith did not seem to see anything to arouse his suspicion above sniffing the air and commenting that artists always seemed to carry about with them the smell of turpentine. And then there was the apparent disappearance of Sebastian. Still lost in thought, Rupert sliced himself some bread and cheese and took a jar of pickles out of the large, walk-in larder. He had just cut a piece of Victoria sponge when he heard voices which he recognised to be those of Delilah and Jinny. Bracing himself, he went out to meet Floyd's now fully informed widow. He found her dry-eyed but obviously upset, Delilah flustered but comforting.

"He had been warned by the doctor last week about his drinking," Jinny was saying, "but you could no more ask him to stop drinking that to stop painting: it's what he lived for!" She gave a sad little laugh at this irony.

"He lived his life the way he wanted to," said Delilah.

"Yes, and he didn't suffer. I just wish I had been with him last night. I was going to come, but my mother had been in hospital after a minor operation on her knee. I wanted to visit her and spend the evening with my dad. It seemed to make sense to come down here this morning – and I just expected Floyd to turn up; late, disorganised, unapologetic and adorable as ever."

Delilah patted her arm.

"I'd like to see him and say goodbye," sniffed Jinny. She looked imploringly up at Rupert. "Would you come with me and show me his room?"

Rupert nodded and rapidly swallowed the rather dry cake crumbs in his mouth. He took Jinny up the stairs, leaving Delilah behind in the kitchen, obviously reluctant either to confront a corpse or to intrude on a private moment.

It was four o' clock and prize giving time. There were a greater number of clouds in the sky and a little breeze had picked up, but it was still a beautiful afternoon. The photographer had pictured Sebastian's lonely, abandoned easel and looked eagerly for those two great artists: Sebastian Fullmarks and Floyd Bailey. So far disappointed, he and an associate had stayed only after hearing rumours that Floyd was dead and Sebastian had fled. The rivalry between the two was well known.

Laura had been explaining procedures to her friend, Wendy, from Claresby village. "I'm going to hand out the raffle prizes, then Samantha Pearson will announce the prize for a flower arrangement and Conran Hawkes will choose a winning painting from Claresby Art Club. The Bishop is choosing "Best Stall" – I thought I ought to slip him in somewhere."

Wendy nodded. She knew that Laura was actually talking about the churchwarden, Monty Howard. During the interregnum following the retirement of Reverend Pierce, Monty had been the big power in church affairs and would have been offended not to be given a significant role in Claresby Fair. Laura was now looking around for Rupert, reluctant to proceed without him. Luckily at that moment she saw his head bobbing through the crowd, head and shoulders above most of those around him. Laura sighed with relief and mounted a small podium to a gentle ripple of applause. The awards went well, with general good humoured appreciation, a few clever words from Conran, and a surprisingly gracious announcement from Samantha admiring the lovely flowers. They had just reached Monty Howard, a bulky, bullish man with an oddly high pitched voice which was at odds with his stature, when a bellow from the back of the crowd made them all turn around. Sebastian had reappeared; very flushed in the face and gloriously drunk. The cameraman nudged his companion; things had become exciting at last.

Laura was sitting beside a gently weeping Sebastian in her study. It was a comfortable, chintzy room with a warm feel to it despite the stone doorway with fifteenth century mouldings and the high ceiling with its ornate plasterwork. Sebastian was drinking the black coffee which Rupert had brought him and was hiccupping gently.

"Floyd came to me last night – he was very superstitious and started asking me whether I thought the Egyptian ring was cursed - he'd picked up one of your old university books, Rupert, something on Egyptology, and was filling his head with nonsense. He was mumbling on about Lord Caernarvon and Tutankhamun and I told him he was a silly fool and that it was all balderdash. Then he got a bit argumentative and told me that just because I was insensitive and prosaic, it didn't mean that there weren't strange things at work in the world. You know: "There are more things in heaven and earth, Horatio, than are dreamt of in your philosophy." After he had finished quoting Shakespeare at me he started casting aspersions on *Plate of Meat.* We ended up having a bit of a bicker – the usual thing. As a matter of fact we are old friends; but you know that."

"Of course we do," Laura reassured him with all sincerity. The two artists may have squabbled their way through forty years, but the friendship had been a steady one.

"Well," continued Sebastian, "he can't have been too troubled in his mind, because once his head touched his pillow all I could hear from his room were colossal snores. It was driving me crazy and I hardly slept a wink. Then, at about six-ish, I heard him make his way to the bathroom. I suppose I was filled with mischief and a desire to get my revenge on him, because I had a sudden urge to give him a bit of a scare. I meant it as a joke. Well, I know very well that Floyd takes an age in the bathroom – I don't even want to contemplate why – but even so I took a bit of a chance. I took a brush and a dab of gold paint on my palette and went to scrawl a spooky message on the wall. Then I had a bit of a scare myself as I heard his footsteps returning. As luck would have it, he actually carried on past his room and went downstairs, perhaps to have a quick drink in the kitchen – the water from the upstairs cold tap comes out an interesting yellow shade that even Floyd could not miss. Then I had an idea. Seeing the Egyptology book beside his bed I picked it up and copied out a few hieroglyphs at random. In the dim light the paint seem to glow: it was very effective. Anyway,

I hot-footed it back to my own room and waited for his response. As it was I heard nothing and I must have dozed off for half an hour after that."

"So what you mean," said Laura with dawning understanding, "is that when you found out that Floyd was dead, you thought that you had frightened him to death?"

"I was painting Claresby Hall," explained Sebastian. "At least, I meant to, but all I could see in my mind's eye was that painting of The Sphinx that Floyd showed us from the suitcase, so I painted that. I don't know why I did that; it was almost as if Floyd's superstition had rubbed off on me. And then Rupert came up and mentioned that Floyd hadn't showed up and I became worried about the old reprobate. I carried on with the picture until I had got the main thing in place, and then I went to look for Floyd. Of course I found him stone dead, staring at the ceiling. My writing was still on the wall glowing with such an eerie light that it half frightened me. I went to my room and put some turpentine on a cloth and tried to rub it off the wall. Sorry, Laura, it stuck in the flock of the wallpaper, but I got most of it out. And then I went to The Claresby Arms and drank a toast to Floyd."

"Ah," said Rupert, "that explains why Keith could smell turps when he went to examine Floyd – and I thought that the hieroglyphs had faded. But really, Sebastian, you can't blame yourself. Floyd has been drinking himself to death for years. Even Jinny was unsurprised."

"I do feel some responsibility for Floyd's death," said the remorseful Sebastian. "I shall have to make a tribute to him. What about my commissioning and designing some new stained glass for Claresby church? I was going to donate the money from the sale of the *Plate of Meat* replicas anyway. That would be a fitting tribute to Floyd."

Laura wondered what Floyd would have had to say about

this; but as for the generous gift for Claresby church, she was ready to accept.

Later that night Rupert and Laura lay side by side in the four-poster in the scarlet bedroom. There seemed to be a lot in the day that they had needed to talk over and digest, but now they were silent, Laura absent-mindedly stroking her husband's arm as it embraced her.

"Did you really believe that there could be a mummy curse at Claresby?"Laura asked eventually, just at the point when Rupert was dozing off.

"Well," replied Rupert sleepily, "Let's just say that I am glad the ring has gone back to join its owner. I interpreted the little hieroglyph of walking legs which Sebastian had put on the wall as meaning "return" – and assumed that Nesperennub wanted his ring back. Frankly I'm glad it's gone: perhaps we are all a little superstitious at heart, or perhaps there was more going on in Claresby today than we like to admit."

The Black Widow of Claresby

It was a rather dismal Sunday in February, the rain having lifted at dawn to reveal a cold, misty landscape and iron grey skies. Fortunately the interior of Claresby Manor provided a cheerful haven with log fires burning in the Great Hall and the red drawing room and the aroma of roast lamb wafting out from the kitchen. Laura Latimer, the Lady of Claresby Manor, was in the process of cooking the Sunday lunch herself. There were to be only six for lunch, including the new vicar whom she barely knew. Nonetheless, Laura had decided to keep things informal and to serve dinner in the kitchen rather than the Great Hall, which was always inclined to be draughty and gloomy, even with the fire alight. Eating in the Claresby kitchen was no hardship; it was a fine, stone medieval structure with a large scrubbed oak table at the centre and tall-backed, carved walnut chairs with green silk damask upholstery. The dinner had reached a stage where it could look after itself for a short while, so Laura made her way to the drawing room where Rupert was already entertaining two of their guests with sherry and gossip. In fact when Laura entered it was Wendy Lloyd, an old friend, who was providing the gossip whilst her husband and Rupert stretched out long limbs from the comfort of a fat, red leather settee which was amongst the new acquisitions at the manor.

"I've actually quite taken to Veronica, although she is a pragmatic rather than a warm personality. She is organized and looks like doing her job thoroughly – which is more than Henry did, bless him!"

Laura, who understood Wendy to be referring to both the new Vicar of Claresby and the old, took the glass of sherry which Rupert was proffering her and said, "Yes, I thought she seemed practical and capable when I met her. I don't think we want touchy-feely in our vicar, do we?"

"Not really. On the down side, it is a pity that she is quite so attractive and that she is a widow; not that the poor woman can be blamed for either of these facts. But the practical upshot is that half the men in the congregation have a crush on her and the rest disapprove of her, as if beauty is somehow inappropriate in a member of the clergy."

"Yes, well physical beauty wasn't an issue with Henry," observed Laura, "although I'm sure that problems with young, handsome curates must have been an issue for centuries before the coming of women vicars. I don't see why the fact that the vicar is an attractive woman should cause controversy."

"Well, she doesn't do herself any favours," said Wendy. "There are rumours. Allowing Strider to come into the vicarage for food and the occasional shower doesn't help."

"I think that reflects well on her," commented Rupert. "It is part of the vicar's job to help the needy."

"Strider was certainly in need of a shower," guffawed Wendy's husband, Phil. "He came into The Claresby Arms and stood next to me at the bar, so I was left in no doubt!"

"There isn't any water or electricity in that caravan of his, and they won't have him in the farmhouse with the children. Not that I think there is any harm in him, but he is odd," Wendy replied.

"Yes," mused Laura, "and he turned up about a week after the Reverend Dahl, which made it look like there was some connection."

"Also, the Bishop is set against her, which isn't going to make for a peaceful parish."

They all nodded in agreement with Wendy, understanding that by the Bishop, she meant the churchwarden, Monty Howard, so called because he acted with such highhanded authority.

"To be honest, though, Monty did need bringing down a peg or two," said Phil. "He is only the churchwarden. I'm not saying it isn't a vital job and he does work very hard, but as Henry got older Monty was taking one in three of the morning services and nearly all those in the evening. During the interregnum he was virtually omniscient – and would have been if he could have presided at Holy Communion."

"He was pretty impossible to work with on the PCC," agreed Wendy, who was both a longstanding member of the church choir and currently a member of the parochial church council. "What I don't understand is why he finally agreed to recommend the appointment of a woman vicar to Bishop John. He seemed implacably opposed to the idea, but when we interviewed candidates, Veronica was by far the most impressive."

"It struck me," said Phil, "that he agreed to it with the air of someone who foresaw that the appointment would be a disaster and relished the future opportunity of saying "I told you so!" when everything went wrong."

"Oh, don't say that," sighed Wendy. "Veronica has had a bad enough time over the last year or so, let's hope that that she settles in and is happy."

Laura had left the little group whilst she basted potatoes and put the vegetables on to steam and by the time she returned to the red room the Reverend Dahl had joined them as had Dr Keith Lowe, the village GP and a handsome man in his early forties. As a bachelor he was always happy to dine at the manor house and, to Laura's knowledge, he had not had a girlfriend in the six years he had lived in Claresby. The story told was that his fiancée had run off with his best friend weeks before their wedding and he was broken-hearted. He certainly never gave the impression of romantic melancholy, being a cheerful, humorous man with twinkling blue eyes. Laura could not imagine what the best friend could have had to offer that this man did not. Discussions had turned to the painting, The Sphinx by Sebastian Fullmarks, which looked very striking over the fireplace.

"I thought he was more modern than traditional," the Reverend Dahl commented, looking closely and with admiration at the painting. "I've been reading up about him because he is helping with the design of our new stained glass – a tribute to the late Floyd Bailey."

"Yes, well he does do a few traditional paintings as well as his more exotic and challenging works," said Laura. "This was meant to be a view of Claresby Hall – but that's another story. In fact Sebastian did go on to do a splendid painting of Claresby which is in the Great Hall; I'll show you after dinner."

"I'd like that." The vicar turned and smiled at Laura.

"There used to be a handful of watercolours of old Claresby village on the walls in the vicarage," began Keith Lowe. "Are they still there?"

Whilst he engaged Veronica in conversation Laura took the opportunity to look more closely at the woman. She was wearing black tailored trousers and a clerical style shirt with her dog collar. Rather than taking the edge off her femininity and beauty, these rather dour, masculine clothes had the effect of enhancing these attributes. Voluptuous was the word to describe Veronica Dahl. Of mid-height, she had an hourglass figure, her trim hips and slender waist enhanced by the cut of the trousers, whilst the sombre shirt failed to conceal the swell of her breasts. She had a wide, sensual mouth, green almond-shaped eyes, a nose a little sharp for absolute perfection and a heart-shaped face with well defined cheek-bones. Her hair was thick and lustrous and so dark a shade of brown as to look almost black. She did not appear to be wearing make-up other than the burgundy coloured lipstick that traced the full curve of her lips. Laura noticed, with the merest twinge of annoyance, that even Rupert seemed unable to take his eyes off her. She was speaking in a pleasant, low, slightly musical voice.

"The pictures and a few cumbersome pieces of old furniture were resident when I moved in. In fact the vicarage here at Claresby is so much bigger than my previous one that I am rattling around a bit. I moved just after Christmas, so everything was a bit chaotic and even after nearly two months I've still got things in boxes. I suspect a few of the inessentials will never see the light of day. I have a wall mounted bookshelf to reconstruct. The removal men took it apart for me, but I see no immediate likelihood of my developing the DIY knowhow to put it back together."

"Oh, I could pop around to the vicarage and help you with that," volunteered Keith Lowe.

"Thank you, I'd appreciate that." The hint of a glow passed between them, but Laura interrupted the moment by suggesting that they went in to the kitchen as dinner would be ready to serve.

During the course of the meal the chat was casual and encompassed subjects such as the merits of nineteenth century literature and the popularity of the local allotments. After dessert had been eaten, Wendy asked Veronica how the services had gone that morning in church.

"Well enough," replied Veronica, her cheeks becomingly flushed by wine and the warmth of the kitchen. "I was cheating a bit because I virtually recycled an old favourite sermon of mine. Just as well because of course I was a bit flustered and wasn't up to the challenge of new territory."

"Why flustered?" inquired Wendy, draining the last of her wine.

"Oh, I suppose none of you were there. I forgot - you've

been out of the choir this week, Wendy, because you've only just got over that nasty bout of laryngitis. Well, some kind soul had daubed "HARLOT" across the wall in nice, red capitals. I suppose Monty will have to find a way of getting it removed. Anyway, by the time we noticed there was nothing we could do before everyone started to arrive for the family service. Goodness knows what they all made of it. Nobody said anything to me, but I could see them all looking. I had hoped that I had left that kind of thing behind."

"That sounds rather unpleasant," Laura commented. "But you make it sound as if this isn't the first time that something of this nature has happened?"

Veronica sighed rather wearily. "Unfortunately this isn't the first time. There was a certain amount of unpleasantness after Rory died, although I was too wrapped up in my own grief to really be bothered by it then. I'm surprised the whole story hasn't preceded me here, but you may as well hear it from me. Rory, my husband, was quite a bit younger than me: twenty-six to my thirty-five. We had been married for just over a year and I think that people had just got over commenting about our age difference when Rory died. Well, when a young and apparently healthy man like Rory dies it is an outrage against nature and reason and I think people look for something or someone to blame," Veronica rationalized. "Since I was the person closest to him they picked on me. It wasn't a matter of common knowledge that he had a congenital heart defect, so they speculated on their own explanations for his death – very creative they were. And then there were his parents. Of course they did know about his heart, but they still blamed me. The fact that they refused to come to the funeral if I was there caused no end of gossip, as did the fact that I eventually stayed away – simply because I didn't want to cause them any more distress."

"Why on earth did his parents blame you?" exclaimed Wendy

"They had disapproved of our relationship from the start. Rory and I first met when he was only sixteen and I was briefly dating his older brother who had been at university with me. Rory and I had a bond from the start and stayed in touch. It wasn't until he was in his twenties that we became romantically involved, but his parents still disapproved. Added to that, I encouraged Rory to live life to the full – which is what he wanted. His parents convinced themselves that his heart would have held out longer if he hadn't had such an active life. The irony is that he died whilst quietly reading a book."

"Perhaps just gently let it be known that your husband died of a heart attack and then any rumours will just fall flat here," suggested Rupert.

"That's pretty much what I intend to do," said Veronica. "My hope is that as I settle in and people get to know me, all the gossip will just fizzle out. With any luck this incident is a one-off."

But in these hopes Veronica Dahl was to be severely disappointed.

A cold February was blown into March by a series of blustery gales. Claresby Manor was left looking windswept and littered with small branches and large boughs along the margins of the woods. Having overseen the refurbishment of the house itself, Laura was beginning to turn her mind to the grounds, fluctuating between grandiose schemes to have the whole estate landscaped, to merely going out herself with wheelbarrow and gardening gloves to help Bob, the gardener, in trying to just keep the place in some semblance of order. Within the parish of Claresby the appointment of the Reverend Dahl continued to cause controversy.

Opposition to her took two forms. There was the persistent grumbling of the old-guard of parishioners, headed by Monty Howard, who objected to the fact that their new vicar was a woman on principle and resisted every little attempt she made to bring the parish into the twenty-first century. A crèche for children was met with horror, the use of different forms of prayer were treated as sacrilege. Her sermons were considered to be too informal, her humour treated as an outrage. The suggestion of a service dedicated to parishioners' pets resulted in the boycott of the church for two weeks by objecting parishioners, although Veronica observed wryly to Rupert, when he and Laura had lunch with her one day, that this was an absolute blessing, and she was considering substituting half the congregation with hamsters and rabbits on a permanent basis if it kept the complainers out for good.

There was, however, a second way in which objections to the Reverend Dahl were expressed and whilst the constant griping of elderly parishioners opposed to change was unpleasant, these attacks were both more sinister and more personal. They mostly took the form of notes being left in the hymn books accusing her of being a whore or a witch and even a murderess. Sometimes notices on this theme appeared on the board where hymn numbers were meant to be displayed and sometimes they were sent to the vicarage. Monty, as churchwarden, was suddenly and infuriatingly slow to remove any of the writing that occasionally appeared scrawled on the walls of the church and the word "HARLOT" was eventually removed by Dr Lowe on his afternoon off. Perversely the result of all this was a sudden increase in the congregation at Claresby Church, the newcomers made up of those curious to see the controversial new vicar and those hoping for a bit of scandal and possibly even an outbreak of abuse during the Sunday service itself.

Wendy, making one her regular visits for morning coffee with Laura, gave the folks at the manor their twice weekly update.

"Monty and his minions actually refused to follow her in prayers this week," Wendy said, helping herself to an all-butter shortbread. "They talked amongst themselves. It was very awkward."

"They sound like badly behaved school children; why didn't Veronica chuck them out? In fact, why do they still attend every service if they are only going to try and undermine everything Veronica does?"

"Simply because it is undermining her. If they stopped coming, the problem would be solved. In their eyes it is their church and she has no right to be there. They want to drive her out. And Veronica is trying her best to ignore them – that's what you do with bullies."

"What percentage of the congregation is against her?"

"Well, that's just the thing, only a very small percentage. I swear that Monty Howard is at the root of it all. Without him, there would have been one or two who grumbled a bit, but he is orchestrating a sustained campaign of hate. I never liked the man, but now I loathe him."

"Is Veronica getting the support she needs?"

"The choir are squarely behind her. Anne Jones left in protest, but she was always a semitone flat, so we won't miss her. Frank, our organist, is picking up the slack by doing a lot of the churchwarden's duties about the place and checking up that Monty hasn't failed to do something that will make problems for the vicar."

"Perhaps, if this carries on, I ought to make more effort to come along to church: but I don't want to look like I'm interfering, just give a bit of moral support."

"Why not come and sing with the choir? We are one alto down, and I know how nicely you sing. Martin Gordon from

The Claresby Arms is just starting, so you could learn the ropes with him."

"Martin! I never thought of him as a church goer. More beer and birds, if you know what I mean."

"Word is that he has set his sights on Veronica," replied Wendy with a wink. "Being a bit of a Romeo he finds the village girls too easy a conquest."

"Surely not Veronica's type? Anyway, she would have to be daft to go anywhere near him if people are already questioning whether or not she is a femme fatale. Which reminds me, what is behind the rumours about her and Strider? I've met him once or twice in the village and he would be a fine looking fellow if he wasn't so unkempt. I take it he has drink problems?"

"Well, I can promise you that they are not romantically involved," said Wendy with the ghost of a smile.

"Why?" asked Laura suspiciously.

"Because he is her brother! It isn't even a secret. Everyone knew in her last parish; it's just that the facts haven't followed Veronica as fast as the rumours."

"Why doesn't she tell everyone and stop the tittle-tattle?"

"Like I say, it isn't a secret. I told Anne Jones and she said – "So she says!" – Even if the vicar put a notice about Strider being her brother in the parish magazine, people would still think whatever they wanted."

"I suppose you are right," said Laura, pouring more coffee into their cups. "Oh, well – I'll show my solidarity by joining the choir."

There was a hint of spring in the air on the Saturday morning when Laura made the walk of a mile or so to Claresby Church. There were carpets of crocuses in the woods and around the church and the daffodils were promising a good show to come. As the low Saxon tower of the church came into view, Laura pondered the fact that it must have weathered its share of controversy over the centuries. Like Claresby Manor, the church was mentioned in the Domesday Book. It had been built in the tenth century and there was a list of incumbents from 1254: she reckoned they could tell a tale or two between them. The church was entered through an arched doorway and the interior was cool and exuded a feeling of mellow contemplation, despite recent events. The dozen or so members of the choir were mostly present and Wendy gave Laura a welcoming smile and beckoned her over.

"I hope you are in good voice? We are just going to sing a couple of favourite hymns to see how your voice and Martin's blend in. We'll start with Blake's "Jerusalem". It will have to be a quick practice because Veronica wants to fit in a wedding rehearsal before lunch. Ah, here's Frank; it's unusual for him to be late."

Frank Bowler, the organist, was a tired looking man in his fifties. He came in looking flustered, but smiled when he saw Wendy and Laura.

"Small catastrophe at home: the washing machine was leaking. Just a matter of tightening a few things up and a bit of mopping, but it threw me out."

"I had that a couple of months ago," said Wendy. "But it was only a small leak and the first thing I noticed was a damp smell. It's hard keeping on top of everything about the house."

"Especially now I'm on my own," commented Frank. His wife had died a couple of years previously. "Ah well, we better make a start. To be honest, I have my doubts about Martin. I do wonder if he will be reliable. Having said that, has anyone seen him this morning?"

As if on cue, Martin Gordon came through the door at that moment, dazzling them with a white smile. He was just short of six foot tall with a lean, fit physique. He habitually wore jeans and white shirt with a tweedy sports jacket which had a couple Rolling Stones badges on the lapel as a permanent fixture. Laura knew him well enough from the pub and, whilst having nothing specific against him, had never particularly taken to him.

"Morning all," he said. "Where's Veronica?"

"The vicar doesn't attend choir practice," said Frank, coldly. "But if you are ready, we don't have much time this morning."

Martin winked at Laura and Wendy behind Frank's back and they all made their way to the choir stalls. After leading them through some warming up scales, Frank sat at a small piano whilst they began on "Jerusalem". After a bit he stopped them.

"Too powerful, Martin," he said. "You are drowning out the others. Control your voice, there's no need to belt it out."

They tried again. In the second verse Frank stopped them for a second time.

"Still too loud, Martin. Your voice isn't quite good enough for a solo! Lovely, Laura; you are blending in nicely."

They had moved on to "All Things Bright and Beautiful", with Frank making only a couple more snippy comments at Martin, when Veronica came in. She waited until the singing stopped and then said,

"Sorry to interrupt, but I've got to ask if any of you have seen Monty? His wife called me this morning. He didn't return home last night." She looked tired and took in the shakes of their heads and general mutterings of "no" rather despondently.

"Did Molly say where he had gone last night?" asked Wendy.

"She said he was slipping down the pub for a nightcap at about half past nine."

"Well, he didn't come in for a drink last night," said Martin, the landlord of the local pub which was Monty's regular watering place.

"I was going to ask you that," said Veronica. "Well, Molly has called the police, Monty's disappearance being so entirely out of character. Let's hope he turns up fit and well."

"Would he have been over at the church yesterday?" asked Laura.

"There wasn't much going on," said Veronica. "We had our coffee morning in the James Mortimer Rooms, but as far as I know everything was locked up after that and I don't think Monty had any reason to come back."

The James Mortimer Rooms were a small extension on the northern corner of the church which provided a space for Sunday school and other church related events and incorporated kitchen facilities and toilets. It had been built about ten years before with a bequest from Laura's own father. She now regretted that she had rather resented the money at the time, Claresby having been left in such a parlous state, and still thought the room spoiled the external harmony of the church, although it had been sorely needed. They trooped down and searched the room and toilets, but found nothing untoward.

Choir practice having been effectively abandoned, the search for Monty was extended from his familiar haunts around the church to the short walk between his house and The Claresby Arms. The police arrived, at first gently inquiring, but gradually more insistent in their searches and questions; but there was no sign of Monty Howard. It was as if he had disappeared off the face of the earth. In the course of the next few weeks there was some speculation that he had "done a Reggie Perrin" and gone off to start a new life somewhere else, but this was largely dismissed. Then the story made the national news and press speculation included reference to the death of Veronica Dahl's first husband and the fact that she had been referred to within the parish by the sobriquet, "The Black Widow of Claresby". Then there was an interesting interlude when Strider was arrested on suspicion of murder.

Wendy, sharing a glass of sherry before a Sunday lunch at Claresby filled in details of this incident.

"The trouble started because Ian and his wife were suspicious of Strider. They can see his caravan from the farmhouse and thought he had been acting oddly the day of the disappearance, although they didn't say how. Anyway, there were no lights on in the caravan that night and they were left with the impression that Strider didn't come home on the Friday evening in question. Strider's real name, by the way, is Arthur Dahl. Like everyone else, they suspected him of having a drink or drugs problem and just being an all-round dodgy character."

"I assumed he had a drink problem," admitted Laura.

"As a matter of fact, Phil has seen him a couple of times at the pub and he has only ever ordered lemonade. No, Veronica hasn't been very confiding, but I gather that her brother has learning difficulties and is not really able to hold down a job. She has supported him since their parents died, but he refuses to move in with her – for some reason he is happier in the caravan. Veronica cooks him food and lets him use her bathroom; he's there most days. I've bumped into him and he is really rather sweet; only a bit lacking, if you know what I mean. He also has a mild form of epilepsy and was not well the evening of the disappearance."

"He has an alibi, then?" queried Rupert. "So why did the police arrest him?"

"Well, Ian was wondering whether he should tell the police about his suspicions when he saw Strider setting off with a rucksack late in the afternoon the day before yesterday. Then he jumped to the conclusion that Strider was making a run for it, so he called the police and said goodness knows what. The police turned up and tracked Strider down making his way out of Claresby. He was confused and panicked and tried to run away from them. They assumed the worst and arrested him."

"Poor chap," said Laura.

"Unfortunately they couldn't get hold of Veronica that evening – there wasn't any sign of anyone at the vicarage, so he spent the night in the cells. Once they got hold of her, sometime after ten in the morning yesterday, she explained that he had been unwell the day Monty disappeared and she thought he might have had a fit. She had taken him in to casualty and they kept him in overnight for observations. He was at the hospital from seven and Monty was last seen at about nine. To my mind it is just as well that it wasn't Veronica alone providing the alibi – she said the police seemed a bit mistrustful of her until the hospital corroborated the story."

"So where had he been going with the rucksack?" asked Laura.

"To visit his parents."

"I thought you said they were dead?"

"They are, but from time to time he forgets that."

"I see. So does that mean that Veronica has an alibi for that Friday too?"

"Well, no. She took her brother to the hospital, waited with him, but had left by nine."

"And why couldn't they get hold of her the evening that her brother was arrested," pursued Laura.

"Ah, well that I don't know," replied Wendy. "I have a sneaking suspicion, but wild horses won't drag that out of me in case I'm wrong."

"Nothing the police should know?"

"Like I say, it is my suspicion; I don't actually know anything."

"Oh well, let's hope the police find out something concrete soon. We could all do without any kind of suspicion hanging over us."

But the police made no headway at all and the disappearance of Monty Howard remained a mystery. Without a body there wasn't even any evidence that it was a case of murder. A new churchwarden was appointed in the shape of Bill Smith, a mild mannered man of gentle artistic temperament who nonetheless had the organisational abilities to make him an efficient if lower profile successor to Monty. It was hard to tell if the Reverend Dahl benefited or not from the disappearance of her chief antagonist. There was no doubt that the vocal opposition of the old-guard was reduced to the faintest murmur and a handful simply defected to the church in the neighbouring parish. Certainly all the writing on the walls and other obvious manifestations of hate ceased. Whether this was because Monty had been solely responsible, objections had lessened, or Monty's disappearance had frightened others into silence was anybody's guess. On the downside, Veronica was now routinely described as "The Black Widow of Claresby" – in local press articles and even at the pub. Laura was actually impressed by her fortitude throughout and her apparent ability to carry on working for the good of the parish despite many awkward moments. When she gently complimented Veronica of this, she merely replied,

"Worse things have happened to me: I can cope with this." But she was beginning to look her age, even if her natural beauty was untouched.

Easter came in the latter half of April and Laura took it into her head to take some flowers to the church to help Veronica decorate for the Easter Sunday Service, particularly since she would be singing in the choir that year. She and Rupert had put a dozen flat boxes full of blooms in the back of the car and she was carrying the first of these up the path to the church when she was surprised to meet a sour-faced Anne Jones marching in the opposite direction.

"Are you helping with the flowers too?" asked Laura.

"No I am not!" came the swift response. "I was here to tell the vicar that if she had any decency she would not conduct the services tomorrow and telling everyone else that it was their Christian duty to refuse to attend."

"Oh," said Laura, slightly taken aback by the vitriol evident in this declaration.

"And you of all people should set an example. It is a positive disgrace, with parishioners disappearing and the police at their wits end, for people to continue to show support for that evil woman."

"Parishioner," corrected Laura rather coldly.

"Oh, so you haven't heard? We've had another disappearance. Martin Gordon hasn't been seen since yesterday afternoon and that woman who lives with him over the pub says the last she knew he was heading for the church. It is common knowledge that he was having an affair with the vicar. How many more deaths do we need before she is made to leave? Everyone knew what she was when her first husband was killed."

"You should be careful not to make accusations like that," warned Laura. "Her husband died of natural causes."

"Oh, you're just like the rest of them; you won't see the truth!" And with that the woman stormed off.

Laura carried on to into the porch and through the low arched doorway. It was news to her that Martin had gone missing and news too that he was thought to be romantically involved with Veronica. She would have thought it very improbable had not she recalled what Wendy had said about Veronica being missing from the vicarage one night and the fact that she had "suspicions". But it didn't make sense that she had spent the night with Martin, who already had a partner – unless she had been away that night for some reason.

"What was that about?" asked Rupert, coming up behind with a couple more boxes.

"Martin has disappeared," hissed Laura, as they joined the others in the church.

There were flowers all over the place, but nobody seemed bothered about arranging them. Veronica was sitting in a pew looking anguished, Frank was hovering around looking anxious, and Wendy and Bill Smith, the new churchwarden, were looking bemused.

Veronica looked up with an almost panicked expression on her face, but relaxed just a little when she saw Laura and Rupert.

"I suppose you've heard? We'll have police all over the place again soon. Unfortunately word is that Martin was heading for the church last night before he disappeared, so one way or another I will be implicated."

"Oh, I don't think anyone will blame you," Frank put a reassuring hand on her shoulder. "Martin was a bad lot; he must have had plenty of enemies."

Veronica gave a wan smile but said, "Of course people will blame me – I know that there were rumours about us having an affair, but there was no truth in it. He did try to flirt with me once or twice, but he was experienced enough to know a gentle but firm rebuff when he met one."

Frank was shaking his head. "Martin was not one to give up; he was too sure of his own charms."

"Why would he be at the church yesterday?" asked Laura.

Veronica shook her head. "I don't know. It was Good Friday, so we held a vigil between twelve and three, but there was nothing happening after that."

"Was that what Gordon came for?"

"No; it wasn't well attended to be honest, and Gordon definitely wasn't there."

"Gordon had a bit of a reputation with the ladies – isn't it possible he just spent the night with one of them and mentioned the visit to the church as an excuse," suggested Rupert.

Wendy shook her head. "I spoke to Kim myself; she knows what Martin's like, but he never spends the whole night away even if he has been known to turn up in the early hours of the morning from time to time. Anyway, he might be an unreliable partner, but he is a very reliable landlord and he missed a Friday evening – that is unheard of. Kim had to get a couple of the girls in from the village at short notice to help her out."

"Did she say why he might be visiting the church?" asked Laura.

"She said he had talked a lot about his singing recently and she thought it might have been something to do with the choir."

"We don't have a practice in Easter week," Frank said quickly. "We have a very full Sunday tomorrow, so we miss our Saturday practice out. Anyway, Tuesday evening is our weekday evening practice – Gordon knew that."

"Has anyone checked the church and grounds yet?" Rupert asked sensibly.

They hadn't, so everyone apart from Veronica, who seemed too upset to function, searched up and down the church, in the churchyard, in the bell tower and around the James Mortimer Rooms. It seemed as if there was nothing to be found until Bill Smith, who was searching near the chancel, let out a little cry. They all flocked to him to see what he had discovered.

"It was on the floor just under the edge of the piano," he explained, holding up a small, red, shiny object between finger and thumb.

"That's one of the badges that Martin wore on his jacket," exclaimed Wendy.

"What exactly is it?" asked Laura. "It looks like a red mouth and tongue."

"It is the Rolling Stones' logo," said Bill knowledgeably.

"Well, it was certainly Martin's," mused Rupert. "Anyone who spent any time in The Claresby Arms would recognise it. So... Martin was here...but where is he now?"

"Yes, another church-based disappearance," considered Laura. "We all expected Monty to be here – he spent half his life here – but we couldn't find him. Martin was definitely here and we can't find him. I've never heard of any hiding places in Claresby Church, despite its age and history, but we might be missing the obvious."

For a while Laura poked around the walls of the church paying special attention to the plaques and memorials on the walls. Rupert sat with his head in his hands, apparently thinking, and Veronica and the others started to decorate the church with flowers. After a while Laura gave up and came and sat next to her husband. He raised his big, plain face with its strong features and large nose and looked at her thoughtfully.

"The only real building work in centuries has been the James Mortimer Rooms?"

"Yes," confirmed Laura.

"What do you remember about it?"

"Just that a feasibility study was done, the PCC was in favour and father had left the money for funds, so it went ahead. There were some archaeological investigations in the area where the extension was going to be built, just because of the age and history of the church, but nothing was found. The building work was undertaken by local builders: George Bowler – Frank's brother. He's dead now."

"Hmm," said Rupert. I wonder if a little look around the extension might pay."

The James Mortimer Rooms had been built at the northern corner of the church and the flints of the north side of the nave had been left as an exposed internal wall. The rooms were accessed from the eastern end of the church where the font stood. On entering, the first door was to a storeroom, the second to the toilets. Once in the main meeting room, which was on the other side of the wall to the nave, the kitchen could be accessed. The unit of the toilets, store and kitchen were at the eastern end of the extension. All this Rupert examined, pacing up and down and tapping walls. The storeroom, which he examined carefully, was clean and tidy and contained shelves of hymn and prayer books as well as such items as an old tea urn and a box of decorations for Christmas and props for the annual nativity play. As well as the internal door from the church a passage extended to make an entrance to the rooms by the east doors of the church itself – this enabled the place to be used even if the rest of the church and internal door were locked.

After a while Rupert came and gently touched Laura on the shoulder. She had been arranging a large vase of flowers to go on the entrance table. He led her outside through the porch on the south of the church. Turning right, he walked her around to the eastern end of the church, past the oak double doors to the little entrance of the extension. All the time he was guiding her insistently by the elbow. Straight in at the entrance, the first door on the left was the storeroom door and they went single file through the entrance and into the storeroom.

"What do you notice?" asked Rupert, a hint of pride in his voice.

"Ah, nothing," said Laura, looking around the clean, tidy little room.

"Yes, that is what is so clever about it. Because no one is looking for anything, no one sees it – and yet it is blindingly obvious. Walk in and out again."

Laura obliged, wondering what on earth it was that Rupert was expecting her to see. Rupert was grinning at her as if almost pleased by her obtuseness.

"If you can see something I can't, you'd better tell me," said Laura with a hint of irritation.

"Well, when you enter the storeroom you see a couple of feet of wall on your left before you reach the room. Why? The external wall of the storeroom is in line with the rest of the eastern wall of the church, with just the external door in it."

"So I should walk through the door straight into the room. This wall on the left isn't the external wall."

"Exactly! Between the external wall and the doorway is an unexplained space – and nobody has noticed."

"And Frank's brother built this. Why would he want a concealed space?"

Rupert shrugged. "Who knows; maybe he had a sideline in stolen goods, maybe it just amused him. But what's the betting that Frank knew about it?"

"Frank! – Organist Frank?

"Yes. And I reckon if I take a close look at the wall in the storeroom that encloses this interesting space I'll find..."

"Monty and Martin? Oh, Rupert, for once I really hope you are wrong!"

Rupert moved the couple of boxes of Christmas things that

were against the wall. The wall exhibited a panel painted the same magnolia shade as the rest of the room and about four foot square. It was fastened at each corner by a flat topped brass screw which sat flush to the surface. A casual observer might well have assumed that this was an access panel to electrics or some other area that only needed to be reached for maintenance. Laura waited whilst Rupert went to fetch a screw driver from the car. When he returned she moved back and waited with wary anticipation as he removed the panel. Some part of her had been expecting two bodies to come tumbling out, so it was with some sense of anticlimax that she saw another tidy space, about three feet deep and four feet wide with carpet tiles at the base. Two boxes of wine were stacked there: one stated that it contained twelve bottles of Fair Trade white altar wine, the other a pale red, fortified sweet Communion wine. Undeterred, Rupert lifted these boxes out and removed the carpet tiles. Underneath was a well sealed, large steel manhole cover. Standing to one side in the cramped space, the large limbed Rupert was just about able to lift the cover and rest it against one wall. Below was a concrete lined chamber about ten feet deep containing two large bags such as might have been used in the delivery of mattresses. The bags contained bodies.

The final post-mortem, if not of the bodies at least of the whole affair of the missing parishioners, took place at the home of Dr Lowe. Those in attendance were Rupert and Laura Latimer, the Reverend Dahl and Dr Lowe himself. The table was littered with the remains of a magnificent Indian takeaway and three bottles of wine, two of which were already empty. It was one of the joys of Claresby village that you could dine with a friend and home was within walking distance, so wine could be provided liberally and conscience free.

"So has Frank actually confessed to anything?" Laura asked, nibbling at a remaining poppadom.

"Apparently not," said Keith Lowe, absentmindedly caressing the back of Veronica's neck as he spoke. "But once they found all the pictures of Veronica on his computer, they knew there was something odd going on: he was obviously obsessed. He had been taking pictures on his mobile phone at every opportunity. Unfortunately some were taken through the vicarage window."

"They think that he killed Monty in a deranged attempt to help me," said Veronica. "There was paint on Monty's hands, so the police think that he had gone in to write some other abomination on the church walls – he knew I had a wedding rehearsal the following day. It seems likely that Frank was on the lookout and attacked Monty. He was strangled, as was Martin."

"Yes, that's what I was told," said Laura. "What a pity the police didn't make a better job of searching the church at the time; it might have saved Martin's life."

"Well, these are the same police who arrested poor Arthur because he looks odd," said Veronica, bitterly.

"And I suppose he killed Martin out of jealousy?" said Rupert, "There were some people who were saying that you were having a relationship with him?"

"Well, there I am guilty," said Veronica. "I actually felt a bit insulted that people thought I would fall for someone like Martin, but of course it suited me for them to be following this red herring, because it meant no one thought to suspect Keith – not that there is any reason why we shouldn't have fallen in love – it's just that with so many rumours already flying around, I didn't want to provide any more fodder. And I didn't want Keith to have to suffer. The only person who seemed to have guessed the truth was Wendy and she was kind enough to keep it to herself."

"It doesn't worry me," said Keith. "I think we should be quite open about our relationship."

Veronica gave him a loving smile and continued, "It is also possible that Frank thought he was protecting me from Martin. My guess is – and it is only a guess – that Frank told Martin that he wanted to test him out for a solo and got him up to the church on some such pretext."

"But Martin was a fit man," said Rupert. "You would have thought that he could fight Frank off."

Keith shrugged. "Frank had the advantage of surprise, attacking from behind. And Frank was a well built man too, if older."

"I feel quite sorry for Martin," said Laura. "Monty was playing dangerous games, but the thought of Martin coming to the church with hopes of a nice singing part makes me sad."

Rupert put his arm around his wife. "Well, it is all over now. Hopefully we can settle down to a quiet year in Claresby. Everyone is glad you have decided to stay, Veronica."

"It was Keith who convinced me. As well as the obvious advantage of being near him, I will have to get over the shock of all the things that have happened wherever I go. And if I start in a new parish, all the gossip will still follow me and I will be back to square one. I might as well stay here and deal with those who still insist on seeing me as the root of the trouble."

"There can't be many," said Laura.

"A few, but I'll cope."

Keith, looking at Veronica, glowed with admiration.

Making the walk back to Claresby Manor arm in arm an hour later, Rupert and Laura had moved on from the repercussions of recent events. Laura was gently suggesting plans to landscape the Claresby estate and Rupert was wondering if his wife was so tired that she would want to go straight to sleep. With his arm slipped comfortably around the gentle curve of her waist, he had other ideas.

The Claresby Ghost

In the twenty-first century people tend not to talk in terms of "heirs"; unless they happen to be referring to Prince William on the eve of his wedding to Kate Middleton and contemplating the future of the British monarchy. Laura Latimer (née Mortimer) was an exception to this rule. Her family had held the title of Lord of the Manor of Claresby in a succession far more direct than that of the royal family and without any member of the line ever having had their head cut off. Admittedly the fortunes of the family had fluctuated from the time Claresby Manor was mentioned in the Domesday Book in 1086, but the recent discovery of family treasure lost since the time of Oliver Cromwell saw the house refurbished and the family flourishing in the year 2011. The term flourishing related mostly to the fact that Laura was eight months pregnant with the child she and her husband, Rupert, tentatively referred to as Humphrey, without any firm evidence as to whether the expected child was actually a girl or boy. Gently feeling the lusty kick of the unborn baby one morning as he sat beside his wife Rupert commented,

"The trouble is, I am used to the name now, and if the baby is a girl I'm sure I will continue to call her "Humphrey". We should have picked a name with masculine and feminine alternatives such as George and Georgina."

"Yes, you can't really do much with Humphrina, although there is, strictly speaking, nothing to prevent us from using the name."

"Except perhaps the cost of future counselling for the poor child! I rather like the name Jane, for a girl."

Laura rose cautiously from her chair at the breakfast table. Her slender figure made the advanced pregnancy very obvious, but she retained her delicate beauty, even if her

95

oval face was slightly fuller and her porcelain complexion carried the hint of a rosy bloom. To Rupert she was still the image of perfect beauty, and it was his fervent hope that if they did have a daughter she would inherit her mother's pretty face rather than the large and slightly lopsided features of her father.

"I hope I didn't keep you awake last night?" inquired Laura. "There didn't seem to be any position in which I was comfortable and Humphrey will fidget and keep me awake."

"No, I was fine," lied Rupert, who had been kept awake for much of the night by his wife.

"Hmm," said Laura, returning the milk to the fridge. "Well, if I can't settle tonight, I may go into one of the spare rooms: there isn't much sense in allowing our offspring to prevent both of us from sleeping – although I suppose there will be plenty of sleepless nights later on. Anyway, as it is raining today, I was hoping that you would drive me in to buy a few more items of baby clothes – you don't mind, do you?"

"Of course not. I'll just check my emails and then take you into town."

"You are kind." Laura gave him an affectionate kiss on the cheek.

Sure enough Rupert allowed his wife to spend the morning musing over unbelievably cute outfits which seemed to him improbably tiny – he couldn't believe than any child of his could be squeezed into such garments. However, after a few moments of sharing his wife's raptures, Rupert proved himself to be human, and wandered off to look at laptops whilst Laura completed her shopping. Lunch at a restaurant was followed by a damp walk and an afternoon of reading and an early night. Laura, however, was still restless and after a while she sat up in the big four-poster they shared in the scarlet bedroom and said,

"I'm sorry, Rupert, but I just can't settle. I think I'll take myself off into one of the other rooms; at least that way you can sleep."

"Where will you go?" inquired Rupert drowsily.

"Not the green room; I still don't fancy sleeping in there after poor Floyd died in that bed. I think I'll go into the dowager's room."

This suggestion made Rupert lift himself on one elbow and look curiously at his wife. In a large house like Claresby Manor you were spoilt for choice in the matter of bedrooms and of all the options this seemed the least appealing. The room was situated in the north corner of the house and was gloomy and damp. Amidst all the refurbishment of the last couple of years, this particular room had remained untouched: there was just something about it that had made them feel that it should not be subject to changes. The result was that it still held a centuries old tall bed surrounded by shabby, dusty hangings in elaborate brocade. Other than the bed, the room was sparsely furnished with heavy, dark Jacobean items which added to the rather sinister atmosphere. There was scarcely a more neglected corner of Claresby.

"Will the bedding be clean and dry?" was what Rupert finally asked.

"Probably," said Laura, who was pulling on a light dressing gown. "I was just thinking about the room as I lay here, so I'll go and take a look. If I'm not comfortable, I'll come back."

"I'll come and check on you in a little while," said Rupert solicitously. In fact, once Laura had left Rupert descended into the first restful sleep he had enjoyed for a week and did not stir until the morning.

Laura, meanwhile, made her way down the creaking

corridor to the room which had unexpectedly filled her imagination. Opening the heavy door, the first thing that greeted her was a musty smell and a stirring of ancient dust. It so happened that the curtains were open and the moon full, so she could move about the darks shapes and shadows without turning on the light. The covers felt coarse but pleasing against her bare legs as she slid into the bed and snuggled down, trying to produce some warmth in the chill of the unused room. For a while she tossed and turned, until eventually falling into an uneasy slumber.

Sometimes dreams and reality seem to merge together and it is only when a person is fully awake that they can sensibly disentangle them again. It was this state into which Laura had sunk that night in the dowager's room. One minute she was looking open-eyed at the unfamiliar outline of the furniture lit as it was by the white moonlight, the next with her eyes closed but seeing with equal clarity the figure of a woman standing in the room. As can be the case with dreams, the details of what Laura witnessed were remarkable: she could see the woman's elaborate dress with its tight bodice, her curled hair, the pearl necklace, her pale blue eyes and the hard line of her mouth. There was something remorseless about the progress the woman made towards Laura, sitting down on the bed beside her, the dress rustling, the bed dipping with her weight as she leaned forwards, cold breath on Laura's cheek, icy fingers on her neck. Awaking with a frightened jump, Laura could still feel the chill on her skin where the fingers had touched and squeezed. Gently she touched her neck to feel the tender skin, and then fell back into a now dreamless sleep.

When Laura awoke the next morning, a pale hint of daylight penetrating the curtains about the bed, the first thing that she noticed was the tingling sensation about her neck. Rising swiftly from bed she went to a small mirror, speckled with the effects of age, and examined herself in it. Sure enough, there was what appeared to be a red rash about her throat. She hastened back to her own bedroom to show Rupert. Her husband had obviously woken early and refreshed and was pulling on some clothes.

"Oh, I was just coming to find you," he said. "Did you sleep well?"

"Yes and no," said Laura. "I did sleep all night, but I was having vivid, rather unpleasant dreams. The odd thing is that I dreamed about a pale, cruel looking woman trying to strangle me – and when I woke up I found red marks on my neck. Is it a rash? Should I see the doctor?" Unspoken worries about any how any ailment might affect her unborn child were foremost in her mind. Rupert led her gently to the light of the window and studied her neck.

"It is curious," he said, "the marks do almost have the pattern of fingers, with what looks like thumb marks in the middle of your throat. It seems a bit symmetrical for a rash, but that bed can't be clean – there may have been some bugs in it or just an irritating dust. Or, of course, you may have just become entangled with a cover in your sleep if you were restless. I'm sure it's nothing important, but I can ask Keith to drop in if you like?"

Laura nodded. Keith Lowe was both the Claresby village doctor and a close friend and could be relied upon to drop in at short notice whenever his duties allowed. Sure enough, he found time to pop in at lunch time to share a sandwich and reassure Laura by checking her over.

"They are curious marks," he conceded, "but they do seem to be fading. Anyway, I am certain that they are of no significance and will not cause any harm. You are in perfect health, Laura, and the baby is moving well – definitely nothing to worry about. They do look faintly like finger marks – not been driving Rupert to the end of this tether?" he joked.

"No; but I have been keeping him awake at nights because I am so restless. Thanks, Keith, I just wanted to check with you, I get a bit anxious at the moment; it's not like me at all. And I have had some vivid dreams."

"All quite normal for an expectant mother," said Keith, helping himself to another sandwich. "Take a rest in the afternoons if need be."

"I might even do that," said Laura with a grateful smile.

When Laura went to take her nap she told herself that the dowager's room was a more sensible choice than her bedroom, because her own room got the full sun in the afternoon, whereas the north facing room was dim and restful. In the daylight it looked even more dismal and gloomy than the night before, the hangings and seat covers more threadbare and faded. Entering through the door was like stepping back in time to the seventeenth century when the room had originally been furnished. Undeterred, Laura pulled the curtains half shut and settled down on the bed and was very quickly asleep. Her dream began almost immediately. She was in the same room but as an invisible presence, looking at the bed which had the very brocade hangings they still possessed, the oak furniture, and the mirror she had looked in herself – but without the pockmarks of age which had disfigured it over the centuries. There were differences however. It was night time and the room was lit by candles and a small fire which was burning in the fireplace. The woman of her earlier dream was also present: she sat by the small black walnut desk and was concentrating on what looked to Laura like a diary. After a while she finished her writing, shut the book and placed it in a narrow drawer. On this occasion Laura was able to look at the woman's face more closely. She was aged perhaps in her late thirties with a face which might had been beautiful had it not been hardened by an expression both haughty and bitter, with tight lips and narrowed eyes under high curved brows. For a moment it seemed to Laura that the cold blue eyes of the lady looked unseeingly into her own, and she experienced a shudder of horror at their bleak depths. It was at that precise moment that she awoke with a little start. A glance at her watch told her that she had slept for just less than an hour, although the dream had seemed to last only moments.

When Rupert found his wife she was staring distractedly at a painting which hung in the upper corridor of Claresby Manor. It was not a very distinguished painting – if it had been, it would have been sold by the Mortimer family in hard times. It was a rather dark picture which depicted a man standing with his hand on the shoulder of a younger man who was seated.

"Did you have a nice rest?" asked Rupert, putting an arm around his wife and stooping to kiss her.

"I think so," said Laura. "I was dreaming again: the same woman that tried to strangle me!" She instinctively put her hand to her throat.

Rupert increased the pressure of his arm about her. "Perhaps you shouldn't sleep in that bedroom again."

"Perhaps not," said Laura. "I'm beginning to feel that the pale lady haunts that room. In my dream she was writing in a diary. I woke up and looked where I had seen her place the diary and it was still there! I'll show you in a minute. The diary was written in the late seventeenth century – the woman was a contemporary of Samuel Pepys – I think diaries must have been in fashion."

Rupert looked down at his wife's white face with some

alarm. "Come down into the kitchen and I'll make you a cup of tea," he coaxed.

"All right," agreed Laura, "but I'll go and get the diary first."

Down in the lofty but comfortable kitchen of Claresby Manor, Laura sat at the large scrubbed table as Rupert handed her a mug of hot tea. The diary she had found was clasped in her hand and for a few moments she flicked through the pages whilst Rupert made some toast and buttered it thickly. He came and sat opposite Laura.

"That looks old," he observed.

"It was written in the time of James II," said Laura. "Judging by the opening page it was intended to be an account of God's divine providence in the life of Eleanor Mortimer. Quite a bit of it tells me about the food they were eating at Claresby – goose pie, pigeons stuffed with gooseberries, that sort of thing." She riffled through the ancient pages with little respect for their historical value.

"Who was Eleanor Mortimer?"

"The wife of Geoffrey Mortimer, according to this," said Laura. "Which is interesting, because I didn't know that Geoffrey Mortimer had a wife. That's why I was looking at the portrait upstairs. I know from my father that Geoffrey Mortimer – the man in the picture – adopted his nephew as his heir. The young man seated in the picture is Bevis Mortimer, one of the few really successful and respected Mortimers: he was something of a thinker and a friend of Sir Robert Walpole's. To my knowledge there is no record of Geoffrey having a wife – and I'm pretty familiar with our family history. So that leaves me wondering who Eleanor was, what else she wrote in her diary, and why she has suddenly decided to make a spectral appearance at Claresby after all this time."

"Well, don't wonder about it too much for now," said

Rupert. "We have been asked to take part in a quiz evening down at The Claresby Arms tonight. Two people have dropped out of the pub team with flu and Veronica phoned up to see if we would fill in. I said that I would check with you, but the answer was probably yes. The other team come from Sunley Church – Veronica has arranged it as Claresby Vicar with the Reverend Jones from Sunley, the proceeds going into the church funds. What do you think?"

Laura thought that she would prefer to sit at home in Claresby Manor and unravel the secrets of Eleanor Mortimer's diary, but it seemed churlish to refuse to help out Veronica, so she reluctantly agreed.

When Rupert and Laura Latimer returned home that night, it was after an evening of entertainment which suited Rupert down to the ground. He had the kind of mind that retained an encyclopaedic knowledge of everything from films to physics and a wit that was readily sharpened by any challenge. Consequently the Claresby team had swept the board and Rupert had been well supplied with pints of beer from fellow team members and Claresby residents alike. The net result was that by the time they reached the imposing doors of the manor, he was a little the worse for wear. Laura steered him up to their bedroom and decanted him into the marital bed, removing only the shoes from his prone body. After eying him with a mixture of disapproval and concern, she decided that he would probably sleep off the ill effects of drink quite satisfactorily, but that she would rather not be in the same bed as him if he was unwell in the night. Picking up her nightdress from her pillow, she gently closed the door behind her and made her way back down to the dowager's room.

Before she and Rupert had gone out for the evening, Laura had placed the seventeenth century diary on the walnut desk, and it was from there that she picked it up after turning on a small bedside lamp which shed a dim light into the room. Laura changed into her night clothes, clambered into the big bed and opened up the book again. Despite her interest she found that she was tired and her eyelids already drooping. She flicked through a few pages and a couple of entries caught her eye. The first told her only that the family at Claresby Manor had been drinking syllabub – a sweet wine with cream. The second, more interestingly, detailed Eleanor's bitter regrets about the fact that she had not been able to provide a child for her husband: "Why has God, in his wisdom, not so blessed us?" Eleanor questioned. More regretfully still, she spoke of how she felt that her barrenness had caused her husband's affection for her to fade. Thus it was that Laura fell asleep again, the diary slipping from her hand, a vision of Eleanor's sad face in her mind along with her sad regrets about the child she never had.

Laura's dream on her second night in the dowager's room differed from her previous dreams in that she was no longer victim or observer: in this dream she was Eleanor Mortimer. It was a summer's morning, a light mist still clinging to the ground on the north side of the house as Eleanor looked out of her bedroom window, but the clear blue of the sky and heat of the sun promising a beautiful day ahead. None of this touched Eleanor at all: her heart was bleak and cold and bitter. It was months now since her husband had come to her bedroom. Indeed, the removal of her to this room on the north of the house was an insult in itself. He had pleaded the need for the large room which had been hers for the use of his sister and her husband when they visited, but they had long since departed, and she was still banished here. They ate their meals together and he would pass a few instructions to her on the running of the house, but his eyes never lifted from his plate and cup to meet her own. When visitors came, she was no longer summoned from her room to meet them. She knew it was not uncommon for men to lose interest in their wives after a decade or more of marriage, but when she recalled how he had adored her in their first years together, and how the hope of sharing the joys of raising a family had filled their lives with a bright glow of expectation, she still felt tears start in her eyes. Eleanor dashed these tears away impatiently. She would cry no more. She would harden her heart.

Eleanor could hear sounds of the house beginning to stir. She was no longer central to the life of the house, but the day when her husband started to lock the door to her room had not yet come, so Eleanor crept down the corridor in softly shod feet. A moment standing by her husband's door brought to her ears the sound she both expected and feared – the sound of a woman's happy laughter and her husband's voice, inaudible, but with the low, caressing tone he had once used when speaking to her. There was silence for a while, and Eleanor placed herself behind the half closed door of the room opposite. One of the servants went past but did not see her. Eleanor waited, silent as a statute. It was another half an hour before the door to her husband's room opened. Eleanor, peering through the crack between door and door frame, saw a swish of blonde hair and the sweep of a grey dress. She knew, without seeing the face, that this was Flossie, one of the kitchen girls.

For weeks Eleanor withdrew into herself, fired only by an obsessive need to watch for the times that her husband, Geoffrey, spent with Flossie. She might have been able to accept the fact that he was satisfying his carnal appetite by the use of a servant – such things happened. What she could not bear was the growing evidence that her husband actually loved this girl! She saw the way his eyes followed her when they were in the presence of others, saw him slip into the woods to walk with her hand in hand, listened to the warm soft confidential tones of their conversation as they lay in bed at nights whilst she stood outside the door, banished from the place by her husband's side that was hers by God-given right as his lawfully wedded wife and social equal. From the ashes of Eleanor's broken dreams rose the phoenix of a burning hatred.

It was one of the last days that Eleanor was ever to leave the confines of Claresby Manor, but she did not know that at the time. The spring of another year had come and she was sitting on a bench beneath the large yew tree in the grounds of Claresby. On the ground beneath her feet were needles from the tree. She knew now that Flossie was with child. The servants whispered and she heard them. The love Geoffrey had for Flossie could not be consummated by marriage but was to be sealed by the birth of a child. Of course the illegitimate child could never be recognised, but its very existence would be an insult to Eleanor and a degradation to the family. Eleanor knew that she could not allow this to happen. It fell to her to save her husband from this disgrace – and she knew just how to accomplish this task.

Laura awoke, a cold sweat on her brow. She knew what Eleanor had planned – what she herself had planned! Looking down, she saw her hands were shaking from the strength of the borrowed emotion which she had felt. But was what she had experienced just her own imaginings based on the diary entries which she had read, or were they memories which had been somehow played out in her dreams? Laura could hear the sounds of Rupert playing the piano downstairs. He had not had the opportunity to learn to play as a child and had taken up the instrument as an adult just the previous year. His natural talent was obvious; his

106

playing improved in leaps and bounds and right from the start he played simple tunes with real musicality. Now he was exploring a prelude by Chopin with both caution and style. Feeling a little unsteady on her feet, Laura descended the grand staircase and entered the music room. On seeing her, Rupert stopped playing and came over to her. Laura almost collapsed into his arms.

"You look as pale as a ghost!" he exclaimed. "Come and sit down and tell me what has happened?"

Laura sat down and accepted the small brandy which Rupert poured from a decanter and handed to her. Hesitantly, Laura told him about her dream.

"Firstly," said Rupert, after listening carefully, "you are not under any circumstances to sleep in that room again! For whatever reason, the room seems to have a bad effect on you. Secondly, I will find out all about Geoffrey Mortimer: whether he really did have a wife called Eleanor and if there was a girl called Flossie at Claresby and all about the younger man in the portrait. Obviously we must get to the bottom of this story to put your mind at rest. I will do a little research; but in the meantime you must put the matter from your mind. I'm going in to the library and will pick you out some light reading and I will play you some of my favourite tunes – but no more sleeping in the dowager's room – is that understood?"

Laura nodded her head, feeling the weight lift from her shoulders. She did feel that Eleanor's story had to be told, but what better person to investigate it than Rupert? She tucked her feet comfortably under her as Rupert disappeared, returning with a small selection of light fiction and settling himself back at the piano with a music book open in front of him.

Laura spent the final week of her pregnancy padding

around the house, reading, and playing chess with Rupert in the evenings. She had successfully put her dreams out of her mind, although she was aware of Rupert spending time in the library, which held a wealth of untouched documentation relating to Claresby Manor and the Mortimer family. He also disappeared into the attic once or twice and even went down to visit the vicar, Veronica Dahl. It was impossible for Laura to tell if he was achieving anything, but he seemed to be happy and occupied, which was always a good sign. The baby's "due date" arrived – although Keith had warned them that no baby arrived on cue and it was quite possible that Laura and Rupert might have to wait a week or more longer to meet their offspring. Apart from the lethargy which had overtaken her, Laura was in good health and there was every indication that the baby was doing well too. Nonetheless, it was with a sense of anticlimax and irritation that Laura reached the end of the day with no sign that labour was about to begin. Rupert had set out the chess pieces after they had eaten, as had become their custom. The set depicted characters from the film version of Tolkien's "The Lord of the Rings", and Laura had given it to Rupert as a present on his birthday. Once the pieces were in place, however, Laura sat back with a dissatisfied sigh.

"I'm sorry, Rupert, but I just can't get my brain around a game of chess this evening."

"We could watch a film," suggested Rupert.

Laura shook her head, "There's nothing I fancy."

"Do you want to read?"

Again Laura shook her head. "No – I just don't think I can settle to anything."

Rupert seemed to think for a moment and then he said, "I could tell you all about Eleanor Mortimer if you like?"

Suddenly Laura perked up. "Have you found out everything; what happened to Flossie, and if there was a child?"

"Yes; but it took all my detective skills. Your ancestor, Geoffrey Mortimer, did everything he could to erase the memory of his wife from the face of the earth. Happily, there was a record of their marriage and her death at Claresby church, so I knew that he did have a wife called Eleanor and that she died the same year as he adopted his nephew, Bevis – being childless himself. And he never remarried. Flossie herself - Florence was her proper name, by the way – is buried at Claresby church with a very nice gravestone which just has her name and a word I make out as "Beloved" beneath it."

"Oh, I must go and look at that," said Laura.

"It's in the south-eastern corner, by the big yew tree," Rupert added. "But I can find no marked grave for Eleanor and she is not mentioned in the family vault."

"What did she do so wrong, apart from failing to provide Geoffrey with an heir?"

"She murdered Flossie," said Rupert, bluntly. "I don't know how – that's the one thing I couldn't discover; but I did finally unearth a mention of the facts in a letter that Geoffrey left for Bevis. Apparently Bevis had been told along with everyone else that he had been adopted – all official documents still say he was a nephew – but Geoffrey wanted him to know that he was really his natural son after his death. He even names Florence as being Bevis's mother and describes the grave: Geoffrey writes that Florence was killed by "That Witch"! I'll show you the letter if you like – it's in my desk now. He doesn't mention Eleanor by name, but he does try to explain to his son why the death of his mother was hushed up for the sake of family honour."

"I suppose Geoffrey just didn't want a scandal – but what did he do with Eleanor?"

"He locked her up in her room and she was never seen

again: she probably got off quite lightly. Geoffrey didn't know how she killed Flossie and suspected witchcraft. Gentlefolk would probably have been beheaded for a crime like murder – if it could be proved. But even if Eleanor had been merely suspected of witchcraft she would have very likely been put to death. Tens of thousands of people were executed for being witches in the seventeenth century. I think Geoffrey just dealt with things in his own way. He obviously didn't trust his wife even after locking her up, because it wasn't until after her death in 1694 that he brought Bevis to Claresby – he was eight by then."

"And Bevis knew that Flossie was his mother?"

"Geoffrey's letter told him so. He didn't say that Eleanor killed Flossie in so many words, but I think that we can deduce that it was her from Geoffrey's actions – I can't think who else the "Witch" would be."

Laura was quiet and thoughtful for a moment. Then she said, "I don't think it was witchcraft – at least we wouldn't see it that way. And I think I know how Flossie was killed. Do we know which year she died?"

"1686 – the year that Bevis was born; that is in the parish records, but not on her gravestone."

"Well," began Laura hesitantly, "when I dreamed about being Eleanor she was sitting under a yew tree and remembering what she had heard about how women could get rid of an unwanted child. Of course for her the unwanted child was the baby that Flossie was carrying. Anyway, yew is poisonous, and a tea made from yew was used to help women lose an unwanted baby. On the other hand, Flossie didn't lose the baby, but she did die, so there may have been something else at work."

"Interesting," mused Rupert. "Yew is certainly toxic, but I didn't know that it was used to induce an abortion. There is taxine in the needles from the tree and if you used them to

110

make up a tea or some other potion you could certainly kill. Maybe Eleanor somehow gave Flossie a drink in the hope of aborting the baby and it killed her?"

"But then surely the baby would have died too? Perhaps she arranged for a bottle with the poisoned substance in it to be left for Flossie and she didn't drink it until after the baby was born. Do we know anything about how Flossie died?"

Rupert shook his head. "I'm still looking, of course: there are missing pieces to the puzzle and we already seem to be relying on your dreams to supply some parts. If Flossie did drink something poisoned by yew she would probably have hallucinated and fallen into a coma – death would be fairly swift."

"I'd like to see the letter that Geoffrey wrote sometime," said Laura.

"I could fetch it for you now," offered Rupert.

"Maybe not this moment," said Laura, with a little smile. "I've been having a few contractions in the last hour: nothing very strong yet, but they are noticeable. I think maybe we should go to bed and get some sleep whilst we can."

Laura sat up in her hospital bed looking exhausted but happy. Rupert – who had driven her to the hospital at four in the morning – had spent the following hours pacing corridors and occasionally checking up on his wife, who seemed to prefer to manage the matter of childbirth without too much involvement from him. Now the task was complete, however, he had finally been summoned and entered the room feeling bulky and awkward and somehow unnecessary. Laura's smile, however, made him realise that he was not only necessary but an integral part of this miracle. The small bundle of shawls with the wrinkled face was central to the miracle of creation and Rupert stared at the tiny creature with wonderment.

"You have a daughter," said Laura, her face beatific.

"She is beautiful," whispered Rupert with awed sincerity, but for once ignoring the visual evidence in front of his nose – for although his daughter would indeed prove to be a beauty, the newborn face gave no indication of this fact to anyone other than the parents. "What shall we call her: she doesn't look like a Humphrey now I come to meet her face to face."

"She certainly isn't a Humphrey," acknowledged Laura. "I do have two names in mind, but only if you agree."

"Tell me?" said Rupert, stretching out a large index finger to cautiously touch the soft skin of his infant.

"I thought Florence Eleanor," said Laura.

"Florence Eleanor," repeated Rupert, perfectly aware of why these two names were uppermost in his wife's mind. "Yes, they are pretty names, and both in your family: perhaps a way to quieten our ghost too. Yes, I think the name is very nice: Florence Eleanor Latimer. Do you like the name, little one?"

But Florence Eleanor Latimer was sleeping peacefully and did not heed her father.

Death of a Clarinettist

"Ah, they are starting with the William Tell Overture," commented Laura approvingly as she flicked through the programme for the concert at the New Millennium Hall in Maidstone that she and Rupert were on their way to attend. "Then Dvorak – oh, and a little sample of Kirsten Norman before the interval. She's playing Debussy's Petite Piéce for clarinet and piano; then the Weber to begin the second half. It should be a good concert – if you don't doze off like you did in the Mozart last time!"

"I wonder if the chap in the aviator hat will be there?" mused Rupert, his benign but ugly face a mask of concentration as he manoeuvred the Range Rover through the busy evening traffic.

"He's always there," replied Laura. "I'm pretty sure that he lives in the underground car park; it is one of the cleanest I know – probably because the NMH is so new."

"I'm mildly surprised that they let him in," said Rupert.

"Presumably he pays like everyone else; and even if he doesn't, you can tell that he enjoys the music – he taps his toes and waves his arms about."

"Last time he almost elbowed the lady next to him on the nose," smiled Rupert reminiscently. He and Laura were regulars at the New Millennium Hall and recognised and looked out for the other regulars, including the vagrant with the aviator hat which he wore indoors and out whatever the weather.

"We'll try and meet Suzy behind the scenes during the interval and then have supper with her and Kirsten after the concert." Laura closed the programme and pushed it into her handbag.

"Are the two of them – um...an item?" asked Rupert, carefully.

Laura cocked her head on one side thoughtfully, so that her auburn hair fell across one shoulder. "Hard to say: Kirsten is a bit of a diva and Suzy is always in attendance. As far as I remember, Kirsten had a boyfriend a few years back, but found that the relationship was too intense and got in the way of her music just as she was becoming really successful. So he had to go and Suzy took over as chief companion and general factotum."

"They came to our wedding as a couple, as far as I recall."

"I suppose so. Of course I asked Suzy as my cousin, and I think the invitation said something about including a partner. That was the first time I met Kirsten Norman, although I had a couple of her recordings and had heard her playing on the radio."

"I've never been a big fan of the clarinet," commented Rupert. "In any case, I prefer a symphony."

"Well, you are getting the New World – even you can't sleep though that. Anyway, I think you will like the Carl Maria Von Weber, even if it is a showcase for Kirsten's clarinet playing."

Rupert swung the big car around and down into the underground car park of the New Millennium Hall, stopping at the barrier to take a ticket. Ten minutes later and the two of them were on their way up to the beautifully designed Art Nouveau bar and a glass of champagne apiece. As they sat exchanging the odd comment, they saw the vagrant whom they had spoken about make his way in and deposit a wheeled shopping basket – no doubt containing his worldly goods – in a discreet corner. The uniformed men who stood at the doors checking tickets and directing people aright, far from looking at the scruffy man with his bulging coat and hat pulled over his ears disapprovingly, seemed to smile in his direction indulgently. Laura watched him as he walked past her, fumbling in his pockets for goodness-knows-what.

114

Beneath the hat was a face that showed small, unusually dark intelligent eyes and a pleasant mouth. Despite the ravages of outside living it was quite a young face; probably that of a man in his twenties – albeit one who had suffered in ways she could not imagine. He seemed to find what he was searching for and glanced distractedly about him without actually focusing on anything and moved onwards. Laura's attention was withdrawn from him as Rupert nudged her gently in the ribs.

"Mr and Mrs Posh look nervous tonight." He indicated a well dressed couple at one of the glass tables, champagne glasses poised in front of them. Both were sitting bolt upright, staring straight ahead and only occasionally lifting their glasses to their lips as they sat in silence. This was another regular couple, named by Rupert for their expensive grooming and aloof bearing.

"They do look more than usually uptight," agreed Laura. "I wonder if they will sit in their usual places in the front row with us." She looked beyond the couple and suddenly exclaimed. "Oh, look! There are Suzy and Kirsten." She rose a little in her seat and waved at them. Suzy, a short plain girl with a snub nose and neat figure waved back and the two women made their way over. Kirsten, appropriately to the fact that she was performing a solo that night, was dressed in an emerald green satin evening dress with chiffon overlay. She wasn't exactly beautiful, but had a rather exotic look with slanted eyes, high cheek bones and a well sculpted mouth. Perhaps the reason she missed beauty was that her expression was rather tight and hard. She smiled, however, in a friendly way, and her face was momentarily softened.

"Suzy told me you were coming to see my performance tonight, so I thought we'd come out and look for you. I'm going to sign some of my CDs after the concert, but I've got a few moments now." The young musician cast her eyes around, quite aware of the stir that her presence was causing. For a moment she seemed to pause, looking at Mr and Mrs Posh; but they had just got up and turned to walk away.

"I thought..." she began; but then shook her head. "I'm sorry – I thought I recognised someone, but probably they have just been at one of my concerts before. Where will you two be sitting tonight?"

"Oh, right up at the front of the stalls," said Laura. "We have favourite seats here: being our local concert hall we have been regulars ever since it was built. There are quite a lot of people in the Kent area who make use of this fabulous hall – we are really rather lucky. I think the acoustics are meant to be the best of any concert hall in the country."

"I've not played here before," admitted Kirsten. "I'm quite excited – or is that nervous! That's why I came out here. Sometimes sitting in the dressing room before hand is the worst time."

"You must be used to the pressure by now," ventured Rupert. "Or is it one of those things you never get used to, however long you have been performing solos?"

Kirsten wrinkled her nose thoughtfully. "It becomes a familiar sense of anticipation, but I've never lost my pre-concert anxiety. I always feel nervous right up to the point when I start playing – and then I just forget everything and am lost in the music: that is why I love it so much. It's the most important thing in my life."

For some reason there was a silence after this final remark. It wasn't that Kirsten said it with particular emphasis; it was simply a statement of fact.

"Well," said Laura, smiling at her cousin. "We can meet up afterwards for supper, if that is all right?"

"Oh, I thought you were coming to my dressing room in the interval?" intervened Kirsten. "Then you can tell me if you enjoy the Debussy."

116

"I'm sure you'll be wonderful," Rupert smiled at her. Suzy moved off with a little wave at her cousin and Laura and her husband resumed their drinks.

"Like her?" asked Laura, bluntly.

"No opinion either way," replied Rupert.

"Something about her..." mused Laura. "She was friendly enough, but somehow one senses an intensity."

"I imagine that a degree of obsession is a prerequisite in a musician of her calibre," said Rupert.

"But obsession doesn't come in degrees; it is by its nature all-consuming."

"As long as it results in music inspiring enough to keep me awake, I'm happy," said Rupert. "Champagne always makes me drowsy."

Settled in her front row seat, the stage rising in front of her, Laura took a look around. Mr and Mrs Posh were in their usual place to the left of Rupert and the vagrant was two removed from Laura on the right. The lights went up and a muttering of applause broke out as members of the orchestra made their way onto the stage. Once the orchestra was settled, the conductor came out to more prolonged clapping and soon there was an anticipatory silence before the melancholy opening strains of the music commenced. The audience lapped up the enthralling subtlety of the music and its stirring climax. More applause broke like a wave as the piece finished. The audience settled and then sat back to enjoy the Dvorak. The man in the aviator hat had his eyes closed, but the smart couple were staring ahead as if transfixed. Applause again, and then the audience rustled with excitement as they waited for Kirsten Norman to come on stage. A sweep of green satin and rapturous applause. Just the piano and clarinet sounded, weaving around each other in the lyrical piece. Rupert's concentration was broken

117

by Mr and Mrs Posh getting up and leaving just as the first note of the clarinet sounded, and by the time he was back with it, the music was over.

"That was hardly worth bothering with," commented Rupert as the audience rose en masse and made for the exits and a drink in the interval.

"Just a warm up for Kirsten, I suppose," said Laura. "We had better find our way around backstage."

Suzy was waiting for her cousin. Kirsten had returned, flush faced, and deposited her clarinet before rushing off to have a quick word with the conductor. Just after she left, a man's head popped around the door.

"Can I bring you two ladies some coffee?"

"Oh, yes please," replied Suzy.

"Milk? Sugar?"

"Black no sugar for me. Milk no sugar for Kirsten – thank you." The man disappeared and Suzy went out to see if she could spot Laura and Rupert and show them which room they were in. Eventually she found them and led them in.

"Did you enjoy the first half? I didn't make it out there; I was sorting out things in here."

"Oh yes: Kirsten was wonderful – brief, but wonderful!" commented Laura.

Rupert, as was his custom, was walking around examining everything he saw with interest.

"Kirsten has a spare dress?" he commented, noticing a rose coloured confection on a hanger.

"Oh, yes. We are prepared for all eventualities."

Rupert was now studying something that looked like a laptop case. "Is this hers? – K.C.N." he read the initials aloud.

"Yes: the C is for Cleo. She should be back any moment." There was a gentle knock at the door and Suzy opened it.

118

"Oh, here is our coffee."

Rupert glanced up and briefly caught sight of a familiar face – that of Mr Posh – handing two cups to Suzy. The door closed.

"Does she have a spare clarinet?" Rupert asked, putting the initialled bag down.

"Yes," Suzy put Kirsten's coffee on the side and took a sip of her own. "That is the bag for the one she is using. In fact our spare is still in the boot of the car. Do you two want a drink? – I should have had some wine in here."

"Don't worry," said Laura. "We just wanted to see backstage. I have some water in my bag. You have your coffee whilst Rupert turns the place upside down. It's his way, you know: incurably nosy!"

Suzy laughed and drank some more of her coffee.

"What is this?" asked Rupert, holding up a little plastic case.

"That's to put the reed in from the mouthpiece of the clarinet. Kirsten won't leave it in the instrument as it needs to dry flat. You just slide the reed in under a ligature. When she puts it into the clarinet before the performance she has to wet it in her mouth – it won't play if it is dry."

"Interesting," mused Rupert.

Suzy watched him tolerantly as she finished her coffee. "I'm not a musician myself, but I find the whole musical world fascinating. I met Kirsten when she was studying at the Royal Academy of Music and got to know a lot of the other musicians she knew there. Now, of course, I see a lot of the orchestra backstage."

Rupert was glancing around, "Where is her clarinet? I won't touch, but I'd like to look."

Suzy looked around too. "That's odd," she said. "I thought Kirsten put it down in here. Why would she take it with her?" She started to look around the room lifting magazines

119

and other objects, slightly flustered. Rupert, meanwhile, was looking at the cup of coffee that had been left for Kirsten with more interest than it seemed to warrant.

"Does Kirsten take sugar in her coffee?" he asked.

"What? No." Suzy's reply was rather abrupt.

"Curious," commented Rupert, who had lifted the cup and was sniffing it cautiously. "There's quite a bit of sugar spilled in the saucer."

"Well I told the man no sugar. I do hope Kirsten has her clarinet...but I'm sure she left it here."

Just then Kirsten swept in and Suzy looked up flushed faced.

"Do you have your clarinet?" asked Suzy swiftly.

"No. I left it in here." Kirsten's smile faded.

"Well it's not here now," said Suzy.

The two women continued to look around in something of a panic. As they did so, Rupert quietly beckoned his wife over. "Take a sniff of this," he indicated the coffee. Laura sniffed. "Can you smell anything?"

"Just coffee!" said Laura. "Rupert, what are you playing at?"

"I'll tell you later."

"Suzy, go and get my spare. I must be ready. Where the hell can it have gone?" There was a note of real fear in Kirsten's voice.

"All right. You keep looking; I'll run down to the car." Suzy bustled out.

"Can we help?" Laura asked.

Kirsten gave a weak smile. "Oh, no, don't worry; it is a crisis, not a disaster. I just can't work out where it has gone. Was Suzy in the room all the time?"

"She did come and look for us and the room was empty when she brought us in," said Rupert. "Someone could have stolen it, I suppose."

"I'll go and ask around and find out if anyone saw anything," said Kirsten, heading for the door.

After she had left, Rupert picked up the coffee cup again and tipped the contents swiftly down the hand basin in the corner of the room. Laura lifted a quizzical eyebrow at him, but before he could explain his action, the door swung open again and Kirsten returned, carrying a clarinet.

"Panic over! It was taken by some chap who hangs around the place – apparently he is a familiar figure and virtually lives here. They said that he's a bit odd, but harmless. The floor manager saw him wandering about with the clarinet in his arms and retrieved it. I'd better check it over, but it looks fine. I need a drink first: did I see some coffee?"

"It went cold," said Rupert disingenuously. "I'll go and get you something."

"I've got some spring water in my bag," said Laura, reaching for it.

"Oh, that'll be fine. Thank you. Sorry this has been such a muddle. We'll be able to have a proper chat after the performance."

Just then Suzy returned carrying the spare clarinet in a case. The next few moments involved explanations and – after handing Kirsten the bottled water – Laura and Rupert made a discreet exit as Kirsten sat down to drink the water and calm down, the clarinet safely nestled in her lap.

"What was that all about?" asked Laura.

"What – the missing clarinet?"

"No: obviously the fellow in the aviator hat wandered off with that as a prank – I meant the coffee."

"Well, for starters, why did our friend from the audience come all the way backstage to provide the coffee?"

Laura shrugged.

"Did it smell odd to you?"

"No."

"Well it did to me. Did you notice Kirsten's initials?" pursued Rupert.

"K.C.N. – you read them out. What was the relevance of that?"

"Just that it is the chemical formula for potassium cyanide. The coffee smelled of bitter almonds to me."

"Rupert, your mind works in the most peculiar ways."

"Yes: that's why you love me!"

This statement was perfectly true, which was why Laura declined to respond – except to return the gentle squeeze that Rupert gave to her hand.

Rupert and Laura were only just back to their seats in time for the second half of the concert. The smart man was sitting with his wife and for a second Rupert caught his eyes in a glance. He had small, bright and very dark eyes; but gave no indication of recognising Rupert from when he brought the coffee to Kirsten's room. Likewise, the vagrant was quietly seated and seemingly indifferent to the fact that his little escapade behind the scenes had nearly scuppered the performance. Kirsten, confident and elegant, made her entrance with a swift smile at the audience and nod to the orchestra, the conductor following deferentially behind her. Taking her place, Kirsten shook her hair and struck her stance: there was nothing in her demeanour to suggest the minor drama that had just occurred. The orchestra set off with a grand melodic opening whilst Kirsten swayed gently in concentration, lifting her instrument to her lips once or twice as if to moisten it, and giving the merest hint of an adjustment to the mouthpiece. Almost from the moment Kirsten started to play it was clear that something was amiss. She made the first high note and the three octave drop, but even in the few notes after that Kirsten seemed to be struggling. For a moment she tried to continue, the conductor glancing at her as if to decide whether he needed to adjust the pace of the orchestra. The first impression was that of a soloist who had lost the plot; but when the clarinet finally dropped from Kirsten's hands and she clasped her throat, it was clear that the problem was more fundamental.

There was the moment's pause, followed by the slow chaos which can so often accompany an unexpected calamity. The conductor dropped his baton and turned to Kirsten, but the orchestra carried on playing for a few more phrases, and then petered out in an almost comical way down to the last peep from the last instrument. The audience, at first embarrassed and then confused, seemed to draw a collective breath before breaking out into excited mutterings. The conductor, stooped over his fallen soloist and seemingly trying to raise her head as she struggled for breath, frantically indicated that medical help was needed. One or two members of the audience rushed forwards to assist. After that, Laura lost sight of Kirsten, just catching glimpses of her shiny green dress through the cluster of bodies. She registered the sight of Mr and Mrs Posh quietly leaving, whilst the man in the aviator hat seemed to push forward in the hope of making out what was happening. And then she saw Rupert, pulling himself up onto the stage and picking up Kirsten's discarded clarinet. He was thoughtfully sniffing the mouthpiece.

Laura and Rupert were sitting in the champagne bar comforting a tearful Suzy. Chaos had come and gone and officialdom had taken over. Pronounced dead where she had fallen, Kirsten had nevertheless been taken away in an ambulance. The consensus seemed to be that she had suffered some kind of fit, but the police had appeared at the scene and were searching her dressing room. Rupert was looking thoughtful and saying very little. Laura was allowing Suzy to talk. The bar was doing a roaring trade.

"I wasn't even there," Suzy was saying between gulps. "I was about to come around to the front and listen; and then there was all the commotion. By the time I got anywhere near Kirsten, she was dead!"

Laura, never the most adept at comfort, patted her hand.

"Has she ever had fits before?" asked Rupert. "Is this the first time she has collapsed?"

Suzy shook her head. "Kirsten was perfectly healthy. She was allergic to nuts but we have an EpiPen for anaphylaxis: we've used it once or twice when she has eaten something with an unexpected trace of nuts in it, but she has never had a really bad reaction."

"Could she have eaten anything with nuts in it this evening?" asked Laura.

"Absolutely not," Suzy shook her head emphatically. "Kirsten would never eat before a concert – she tended to feel a bit queasy. She would have a good lunch and then nothing but coffee or water."

"She didn't have any enemies, I suppose?" pursued Rupert as Laura gave him her disapproving look.

"Enemies?" Suzy looked shocked. "No; she was the loveliest person."

"But she was successful, and success – especially in the entertainment business – can lead to jealousy. Well, what about rejected lovers?"

Again Suzy shook her head. "Her longest relationship was with Hamilton Gilbert; she met him at the Royal Academy – he was a cellist. They were an item for about five years, but he was a really intense, slightly unstable character. Very good-looking and a brilliant musician, but Kirsten found his moods and emotional dependence too much to handle, especially when her career started to take off."

"What happened to him?" asked Laura. "Did he become a professional musician?"

"No. He was very talented, but he didn't have the temperament to be a musician. I thought he might make a mark as a composer, but I haven't heard of him again and Kirsten never mentioned him. But why are you asking? Do the police think that she was murdered?"

"I don't know what the police think," admitted Rupert. "But the manner of her death, and the timing, were extraordinary."

Suzy looked aghast and Laura, disapproving again, said, "Why don't you go and get us all a drink, Rupert; the crowd at the bar has subsided a little."

Rupert nodded and left Laura listening to some more of Suzy's worries and regrets. However, rather than making his way straight to the bar, Rupert – catching sight of Mr and Mrs Posh sitting alone at a table – made his way over to join them.

"You were in the audience just near us," Rupert said, by way of introduction, as he sat at their table. "Are you both all right?" Up close he could see that the man, who was in his sixties with a tired, pale face which accentuated his dark eyes, looked on the verge of exhaustion. His wife, well groomed and with a bone-structure which bespoke good looks in past years, seemed almost dazed.

"Fine, thank you," replied the man. "Just a bit of a shock."

Rupert nodded slowly and then, with barely a moment's hesitation said, "It wasn't the cyanide that killed her."

At this statement the man gave a convulsive jump and his wife actually emitted a little scream. After a moment of horrified silence, the man replied,

"I don't know what you are talking about."

"I'm sorry, I should have introduced myself: I'm Rupert Latimer. You saw me when you brought the coffee in to

Miss Norman."

"I don't care who you are and I don't know what you are talking about. I'd rather you left us alone; you are upsetting my wife."

"You brought the coffee in," persisted Rupert, "and it looked like there was sugar in the saucer, but Miss Norman didn't take sugar. I'm rather a nosy person, and I took a sniff of the coffee. After that I swept the white grains into my handkerchief, where they still are. And then I threw the coffee away – so, like I say, the cyanide didn't kill her. What I want to know is: did you put poison in anything else?"

"But she must have drunk the coffee," said the man. "If she didn't, why...?"

"Why indeed!" said Rupert. "So I gather that you didn't poison her – at least, not successfully. The question is: who did?"

When Rupert eventually returned to his wife with three glasses of brandy, Suzy had disappeared.

"She went to make some phone calls," explained Laura, her pale, pretty oval face looking a little weary. "What's going on, Rupert? I know you have probably solved the case by now, but did you have to ask tactless questions of Suzy?"

"Yes and yes," replied Rupert, putting one of his long, angular arms protectively around his slender wife. "At least, I can deduce what happened, but whether it is susceptible of proof is another matter."

"Was she poisoned?" asked Laura, who had been following at least some of Rupert's thought processes.

"Well, that is an interesting question," said Rupert happily, sipping his brandy. "You know that I was suspicious of the coffee, but even when she collapsed I knew that poison in the coffee wasn't the cause. I don't know much about poison, of course, but the classics are strychnine or cyanide. Well strychnine takes the biscuit for drama – violent death throes and all that. Can be concealed in coffee, which masks the bitter taste, but death is not instantaneous. Anyway, Kirsten's death was sudden and without the spasms, so we can rule that out. So the stuff that looked like sugar wasn't strychnine, but it could have been cyanide. A teaspoon of cyanide in the coffee would have caused death within minutes – and Kirsten did seem to die struggling to breathe as if she had swollen airways. The only problem is that she was looking just fine when she came on stage, so cyanide wasn't the cause."

"And, in any case, she didn't drink the coffee; you saw to that," Laura pointed out reasonably.

"No, but it did have a good old dollop of cyanide in it!" said Rupert, almost triumphantly.

"Rupert! – how do you know that?" exclaimed Laura.

"Because I just wheedled a confession out of George Gilbert, father of the very Hamilton Gilbert whom Suzy told us about – the brilliant but insecure musician that Kirsten gave the push because his emotional demands were getting in the way of her career. The two, it turns out, were engaged and Kirsten had been welcomed into the bosom of his family. After she broke off with him he went to pieces, never played the cello again and drowned his sorrows in drink. He alienated himself from his loving family – father is a chemistry lecturer, mother a music teacher – and became little more than a tramp."

Understanding dawned in Laura's eyes. "So the father was after revenge and, as a chemist, a little bit of cyanide posed no problem. Are you going to tell the police?"

Rupert shook his head slowly. "Tell them what? That I thought that the coffee smelled funny? That a disturbed old man told me that when he heard that Kirsten Norman was coming to his home town it was more than he could stand?

And, after all, she didn't drink the coffee."

"Rupert, it is not up to you to make judgements as to what the police should and shouldn't know and whether or not a man deserves to get off with what was certainly attempted murder. And, anyway, I'd bet my last penny that you took a sample of that white powder."

"As a matter of fact I did," admitted Rupert, "But it might well get left in my pocket and come out in the wash! If I am asked I will tell the police; is that good enough?"

"I'm not sure that it is. After all, Kirsten did die and her death is consistent with poisoning, so you can't rule out the possibility that Mr Gilbert had a backup plan."

Again Rupert's expression seemed doubtful. "He was disbelieving when I told him that she hadn't drunk the coffee – and, I suspect, a trifle relieved. And, as I said, I'm not sure that her death was consistent with a great dollop of cyanide. Furthermore, the only thing we know she did actually drink was the water you gave her. If the police do start asking questions they will be focusing on that!"

"That did cross my mind," admitted Laura. "But I bought it in the garage shop earlier today and never opened it. Unless someone tampered with it, intending to poison me!"

"I really don't think so," said Rupert. "Kirsten seems a much more plausible target and no one could have known that she would be the one to drink the water. No, I don't think it was that at all."

"What do you think happened?" asked Laura.

"Well, there was the other half of the aggrieved family here on his home territory tonight: Hamilton Gilbert himself – the man whose promising career and entire grip on life were derailed by Kirsten's rejection. This was the first time she had played here; he too might have felt the moment had come for revenge."

"How do you know that he is here?" asked Laura,

flummoxed for the first time.

"Because his father told me. Hamilton is our very own vagrant in the aviator hat who loves music so much. After his relationship broke down he turned to drink and dropped out completely. In fact, I could see a resemblance between Mr Posh and his son – the same intense, dark eyes."

"And he took the clarinet! Didn't Kirsten or Suzy recognise him?"

Rupert shook his head. "No. I think Kirsten had a fleeting recognition of his parents. But I'm not sure that either she or Suzy actually came into contact with him."

"So he somehow poisoned the clarinet?"

"Not even that – and now I am only making deductions; I know nothing. At least, I do know that the mouthpiece of the clarinet smelled of almonds. I was thinking of cyanide at the time, but the clarinet didn't smell of bitter almonds, it had a sweet smell."

"And Kirsten was allergic to nuts! You think he soaked the reed in almond oil – or simply replaced the reed with one he had treated? But how could he be sure that would kill her?"

"I don't suppose he could. In fact, I rather doubt that he meant to kill her. As her long-term boyfriend he would have known that she had an allergy to nuts. Perhaps he was just trying to embarrass her: she would have a reaction, gasp a little, mess up the playing. I don't think such a violent reaction was predictable."

"But it is still murder."

This time Rupert's shrug was eloquent with indifference. "Like I say, all that is guesswork. The police will soon know that she died of anaphylactic shock if that really is the case. That will lead to her allergy and they will look at the clarinet and find out that Hamilton Gilbert fiddled with it. If they are worth their salt they will get that far, no problem. As to whether a murder change will stick: who knows? Definitely a case of diminished responsibility. Best case scenario, Hamilton ends up getting the sort of treatment he needs."

"So you will say nothing?"

"They would treat me like an interfering fool if I butt in with my harebrained scheme; and rightly so."

"What shall we do then?" Laura looked dispirited.

"Find Suzy and take her home if the police have asked her all the questions they want to and then return to Claresby Manor. You can check in and see if Florence has settled for the night."

At this final suggestion Laura's face brightened up and she took her husband's hand and went with him to find her cousin.

The Floods Murder

"Getting through the ford could actually be quite dangerous," said Rupert to Laura with a note of satisfaction in his voice.

"Yes, well you knew that the river was in flood and chose to come this route, so I can only assume you fancied the challenge," returned Laura.

Rupert gave her a wicked little smile and ploughed the four wheel drive vehicle through the water, creating a small tsunami in their wake. Ignoring her husband's smile of exhilaration Laura continued to address more practical matters.

"I imagine that Sunley Grange may be flooded too. It is a beautiful house, but being so near the river has always been a problem and this autumn has been as bad as I can remember for persistent rain."

"I'm sure that Damian and Flora were at our wedding, but I can't honestly recall them."

"They weren't at our wedding, as it happens," said Laura. "We spent some time together as children, but were never particularly close – I preferred Suzy."

"She's coped well since Kirsten's death," mused Rupert.

"Yes, I'm glad to see her in a more balanced relationship; she was too much in Kirsten's shadow, but Peter obviously adores her."

"She was your cousin on your father's side?"

"Yes. It was my father's sister, May who was her mother. George Reckless was mother's brother and his wife was Sylvia: Damian and Flora are their children. They are very slightly older than me. I do remember staying at Sunley Grange as a child, but I've not been there as an adult. To be honest, I was pretty surprised when Damian contacted me and asked that we come to stay; especially at such short notice. It's just lucky that Veronica was happy to babysit for us."

"I suppose that his father's illness has been a bit of a shock. Still, Reckless is a wonderful name: he should have been a solicitor!" Another smile brightened Rupert's large featured face.

"Actually he was an estate agent: Reckless and Knocker. They went out of business years ago; I don't think my Uncle George had much of a business brain. His real interest was antiques and books. He spent any money he did have on beautiful old furniture – or so my father said. He always used to think that Sunley Grange was the worst place for such things because of the pervading damp."

At this point in the conversation, Rupert and Laura Latimer arrived at their destination. Sunley Grange was a gracious Georgian house of balanced symmetry and old-fashioned elegance. Its best feature was that it had light, well-proportioned rooms; its worst that it was in a poor state of repair and tended to be chilly because of the expense of heating a large, five-bedroom residence. Neither Damian nor Flora actually lived with their father anymore, but since his illness Damian had moved in, ostensibly to look after the place. It was a well known fact that Damian had been left the house in his father's will. There had been some speculation amongst the wider family that this was rather unfair, as George Reckless had no money to speak of other than the capital that was represented by the house and therefore Flora would receive almost nothing on her father's death.

It was still raining with steely persistence as Laura made her way to the front door, improvising with a pashmina to keep her glossy hair dry whilst Rupert wrestled their two bags out of the back of the Range Rover. Fortunately Flora stood with the front door already open and the couple were able to enter quickly. Despite the fact that the cousins were not particularly close, Flora's rather mousy face was lit with a smile and an almost relieved expression as she welcomed Laura. Her brother, joining her in the hallway, seemed equally pleased to see them and shook Rupert – whose tall, angular frame towered over him – firmly by the hand. Flora herself, with her almost childlike height and figure, made Rupert feel as ungainly and oversized as he ever did, and he had to stoop almost double to give her a polite greeting peck on the cheek. They were led into a comfortable reception room where a log fire blazed in the fireplace. Despite the warmth this exuded Rupert was immediately aware of at least the smell and feel of damp in the room. Flora went out to fetch coffee and the other three sat down in some plum coloured eighteenth century mahogany armchairs.

As Laura exchanged preliminary courtesies with her cousin, Rupert allowed his curious eye to rove around the room. He was used to the recently reinstated opulence of Claresby Manor, but was nonetheless impressed by the quality and style of the furniture he saw about him. The showpiece was a Queen Anne walnut cabinet, splendid but rather ugly with its mottled veneer and urn-finials above the doors. An olivewood long case clock with floral marquetry also caught his attention and impressed him more with its quality than its intrinsic beauty. Damian noticed his interest.

"Beautiful furniture was my father's hobby," Damian explained to Rupert. "He bought and sold items over the years, usually at a loss. He did have good taste, but he was not a business man. The best stuff we keep in this room as we usually have a fire burning in here. We are quite lucky not to have been flooded this week. You will find we have sandbags at the side door, which is where we are most vulnerable." He spoke about the house in a proprietorial way although Rupert knew from Laura that he actually lived in a modest bachelor flat in the neighbouring town. He also spoke about his father in the past tense. Before they could discuss the furniture more, Flora returned with a tray laden with coffee cups and a plate of biscuits which she settled on a small table, passing the coffee around with milk and sugar as requested. When she too was settled in an armchair, it was Laura who recommenced the conversation.

"How is Uncle George? When I spoke to you yesterday, Damian, you sounded concerned."

"I'm afraid it really is only a matter of time," replied Damian, his pale eyes fixed on his coffee cup. "He had a massive stroke about a week ago and since then the doctors have told us of serious cardiac problems. I'm not sure he would be alive now without their intervention, but without hope of recovery I gather that they will let nature take its course."

"Was he treated promptly after his stroke? I know he lived here alone and wondered how quickly he was found?"

"Ah, well," said Damian in measured tones, as his sister looked uncomfortable, "you haven't heard the whole tale. He wasn't alone: his wife, Elsa, was with him."

"Wife!" exclaimed Laura. "I didn't know that he had remarried."

For the first time some colour came into Damian's rather insipid complexion. His was a dull rather than an ugly face, but when his expression kindled, as it did now, the effect was not a pleasant one. There was a hint of bitterness in the tight line of his mouth. However, he spoke in an easy enough tone,

"No, neither did I, Of course I knew that he was friendly with Elsa. She lives in one of the terraced cottages down by the church and I think my father had taken to going for walks with her. I bumped into her once when I came around to help my father with some gardening in the summer. She was just

134

leaving. We saw her at the hospital too, didn't we, Flora?"

"Yes." Flora had the same pallor as her brother, but on her the result was merely to make her look washed-out. "It was Elsa who was with him when he was taken ill."

Damian, not waiting to see if his sister had more to say, took up the story. "We were called by Mrs Talbot, father's housekeeper – it happened to be her day. She left text messages for both Flora and me, just to say that father had been taken ill and was in hospital. I phoned the hospital and, as soon as I knew it was serious, I picked Flora up from Brightfields and we went in together."

"The school was very understanding," said Flora with a weak smile. Laura knew that she was the secretary at a local preparatory school.

"Of course when we got there, we were confronted by Elsa – all tearful and wifely. She had been having lunch here and said that father had complained about feeling funny and, before she could do anything, had collapsed. It was only when the doctor came in and addressed her as Mrs Reckless, that I had any idea that they were married. It was a shock, I can tell you!"

Somehow Rupert was left with the impression that Damian had been more shocked by the discovery that his father had remarried than by the possibility of his imminent demise.

"Was she not living here, then?" asked Laura, picking up on Damian's mention of her coming for lunch almost as if she were a guest.

"No; that's the funny thing. Apparently they were married in a civil ceremony just over a month ago. Other than two friends of Elsa's, who live in the village and attended as witnesses, no one else knew about the marriage – not even Mrs Talbot. I can only assume that it was a romantic gesture." This final statement was said in such a tight-lipped way as to suggest absolute contempt for any such motive. "Beyond that, she was still living in her house and my father here at Sunley Grange. And, of course, he has still left the house to me in his will. You know how important it was to him to keep the house in the family – it was almost an obsession with him. It wasn't a case of him having any particular fondness for me." Another bitter twist moved the edges of his mouth. "Anyway, the will is over on the desk." Damian nodded his head towards the fine oak and ebony Victorian desk where a formal looking document was indeed placed on top in sole occupation.

"It's the will he wrote five years ago," added Flora, nervously. "He would never have changed it."

A slightly awkward silence followed these revelations as if something indecent had been said. It was Flora who changed the subject.

"I've got the lunch in cooking. I hope you like hotpot? The weather is so chilly that I've started to cook my winter menu. After lunch we can go for a walk along the river – I hope you have brought your welly-boots?"

"We've got some living in the back of the car," smiled Laura. "And we'll brave a walk however rainy or windy it is."

Whilst Flora was in the kitchen putting the finishing touches on the lunch, Rupert and Laura took their bags up into a pleasant bedroom with a pink floral theme on the rather faded wallpaper. The view was out of the side of the house where the willows that lined the river could be seen, although the course of the river itself was hidden behind a handsome stone wall. The lawn in the garden, however, was already under an inch or so of water which was edging its way relentlessly towards the house itself. The fact that they were welcome guests was attested by the fact that a fire was burning in a bedroom fireplace which looked like it hadn't been used since the time of King George III. The blustery wind outside was making the smoke filter into the room and Rupert's eyes were watering slightly. Laura emerged from their en-suite bathroom, her hair freshly brushed and glowing around her pretty face.

"Is what Damian said true?" asked Rupert abruptly.

"Which thing?" asked Laura.

"About his father being obsessed with keeping the house in the family?"

"Oh, yes." Laura herself, as the inheritor of Claresby Manor – a house which had been in her family since before 1066 – knew a thing or two about the lengths one would go to in order to retain the family home.

"So he might not, for example, have wanted to leave something to a young wife, even if he was besotted with her?"

Laura cocked her head on one side, thoughtfully. "You are wondering why Damian went to such lengths to tell us that his father had left the house to him? It was a bit inappropriate. You have to share my family's mentality to understand the importance we place on keeping the house in the family. No, Uncle George would have left Damian the house even if he loathed his son – which he may well have done. Six new wives would not have changed that fact. And I doubt that there is any money outside the house to give to either Flora or a wife."

"That's what I wanted to know," said Rupert more comfortably. "It seems that there may be troubles ahead."

"What do you mean?"

There was a tap at the door and a call of, "Lunch!" from Flora.

"Wait and see," said Rupert with an enigmatic wink.

They had polished off the hotpot and Damian and Rupert were helping themselves to apple crumble and custard whilst Laura finished off her wine and chatted amiably to her cousins.

"Have you been able to take time off work without any trouble?" she was asking Damian.

"Sadly, yes. Working in an estate agent's office in the current climate is pretty undemanding. It is a good thing my father's business collapsed years ago; it would never have made it through this recession. I'm honestly wondering about retraining as an English teacher. Perhaps I could get a job at Flora's school!"

"Oh, that would be lovely!" exclaimed his sister, apparently not picking up on the note of sarcasm in his voice.

"You could write crosswords," suggested Rupert. "It doesn't pay much, but it keeps the brain sharp."

"All right if you happen to have a rich wife!" said Damian bluntly.

The silence that followed this conversation-stopper was broken by a sudden, very loud jangling noise which made both Laura and Rupert jump.

"That's my message tone," apologised Damian, reaching in a pocket for his mobile phone. "I never hear it go off unless I have something dramatic."

"Mine just beeps gently," said Flora with a small smile as her brother glanced at the message which he had received and returned the phone to this pocket without comment.

Laura stood up to begin clearing the plates from the table and Flora hastened to help her. The plan for the afternoon was that Damian would visit the hospital whilst the others went out for a blustery walk. Damian departed promptly, leaving the ladies washing up together. Flora then spent some time showing Laura an album which included photographs of them both as bridesmaids at a family wedding when they were children and Laura reciprocated with some pictures of her little daughter, Florence. Eventually the three of them pulled on raincoats and ventured out in the direction of the village.

It was as well that they all wore boots, as the river had washed over the banks, across the road and was now encroaching on the row of cottages opposite. The first large batches of leaves had been whipped from the trees and were slippery on the wet ground. The church itself was on slightly higher ground and their route took them through the churchyard and up and across the fields beyond before they retraced their footsteps from the church again. As they walked past the row of cottages opposite the river one of the doors opened and a woman in coat, hat and boots stepped out. Flora looked at her with instant recognition and the lady walked over.

"Hallo, Flora: I was just about to walk along the riverbank to see how bad things are getting. I left my umbrella behind in case it took off!" She was pleasantly spoken and attractive, with large grey eyes and a sensible face.

"Oh, Elsa – nice to see you: this is my cousin, Laura, and her husband, Rupert. We've just been for a walk." Flora seemed flustered and did not meet Elsa's eyes as she spoke. "Damian's at the hospital," she added.

Elsa, in contrast, seemed quite composed and merely raised one eyebrow very slightly at the mention of Damian. She then greeted Laura and Rupert before saying, "I went in to see George this morning – not that he is able to recognise anybody. Still, I talk to him and tell him where I've been walking: maybe he can understand." There was a real but gentle sadness in her eyes. She fell in to step with them as they walked back down the road towards Sunley Grange.

"The water's not quite reached you?" commented Rupert.

"Like the rest of the houses in the row, I have sandbags. Still it wouldn't be the first time I've had the river in my front room. It is for that very reason I don't have carpets downstairs – just quarry tiles and rugs which I can take up if in doubt. Of course there is always something that gets spoiled if the flood is bad enough, but it comes with the territory."

"Although Sunley Grange is closer to the river, we are actually up a little rise, so the cottages are the first to get flooded," said Flora.

They had reached home and Flora and Laura moved towards the entrance.

"I'll walk a little further with Elsa," said Rupert. "I want to see what the floods are like downstream." He carried on around the path by the side of the house whilst the other two went in.

"Oh, it's right across the path here as well," said Elsa. "It must be across George's garden. Oh, well, that's something he won't have to worry about," she added a little wistfully.

"I gather that you haven't been married long?" ventured Rupert, cautiously.

"Just over a month. Of course we had no idea that George would become ill: he always seemed so robust. We walked together a lot," she explained.

"Were you going to move in to Sunley Grange at some point?"

Elsa shook her head. "No. George was funny about the house – this whole "inheritance" thing that I don't really understand. I wasn't after his money, if that is what Damian has told you. We had been friends for a couple of years and the wedding was George's idea. To be honest I was amazed. I think it was just his way of marking me off as an official possession; not really romantic at all. I do love him, though.

My first husband was abusive; George is a gentleman. It made a nice change. Do you know him well?"

Rupert shook his head. "I only met the family today. They are Laura's cousins, but even she hasn't seen them for years. Damian contacted her yesterday to say that her uncle was dying and asked if she would come to stay. I suppose he wanted some family support."

"Most likely he wanted you to witness the fact that the will was in his favour!" said Elsa with the first sign of bitterness.

Rupert thought that this was very likely the case, so did not comment.

"I'm sorry," said Elsa, after a pause, as they picked their way around the edge of the flood and back onto a path. "That was ungracious of me. The fact is that when we met at the hospital and Damian realised who I was, the first thing he did was to quiz me about his father's will. And that was *before* he had been in to see his father! He wanted to know if George had written a new will to include me. I told him the simple truth – that when we married we agreed to be completely financially independent; not even move in together. After that Damian was tolerably polite to me."

"It must have been very difficult for you." Rupert settled for a safe platitude.

Elsa shrugged. "Honestly, I'm still in shock over George; I can't bear the idea of losing him. George never spoke well of his son, so I wasn't expecting to like him. The funny thing is, when I saw Damian at the hospital the night before last, I caught him looking at me with pure hatred in his eyes – just for a moment. It was actually rather unnerving. He was still polite to me, but it seemed to be a struggle. I don't know what had happened to make him so hostile again."

"That's interesting," said Rupert, more to himself than to Elsa. Then, after a short pause, "Do you mind if I ask you rather a personal question?"

Elsa gave a little smile. "By all means ask: if I don't like it, I won't reply!"

"Well, if George legitimately left you money – to Damian's detriment – would you accept it?"

After the merest hesitation Elsa replied, "Yes: if it was legal. I have no liking for Damian. But you have to understand George – there is no way he would countenance breaking up the house, even to provide for all those closest to him. Ask Flora. I was also going to add that not one in a thousand would turn down a legitimate legacy, and that includes me: but then I remembered Flora. She may be that one in a thousand. George always said that her devotion to her brother was beyond reason."

For a while the two of them walked on together in silence. The rain was beginning to get heavier so in wordless understanding they turned back when they reached a stile. As they neared Sunley House Rupert spoke again.

"Are you going to the hospital tonight?"

"Not unless there is any change in George's condition and they call me. I'll go again in the morning. Tonight I'm just going to curl up on the settee and watch television."

"Laura and I are here for at least a couple of nights. If there is anything you need in that time, just ask."

"Thank you." Elsa gave him a warm smile and carried on down the road to her own home, Rupert pausing, despite the rain, to watch her go.

Sunley House was warm and welcoming after the rain. Damian had returned home just before Rupert and was still in the entrance hall removing his coat and sorting through some newspapers he had bought for them all to read. He looked grey and anxious, his thinning hair plastered damply on his scalp. Flora and Laura had started on tea and scones, but on hearing the men return Flora came out to get a fresh pot from the kitchen. As she passed Damian, he took her briefly by the elbow and said in a low voice,

"I really don't think he will live another day."

Flora gave a brief understanding nod and carried on into the kitchen. Damian and Rupert went to join Laura. Damian sat in a chair by the fire, placing the newspapers on a low table in front of him, and then seemed to make an effort to rally himself and talk to his guests.

"How was the walk?" he asked.

"Wet," said Laura. "The church is beautiful, though. If we have the chance tomorrow I thought that Rupert and I might take a look around it."

"Perhaps we can have lunch in the pub – all being equal," suggested Damian. "I do appreciate you both coming. I just thought it would be better for Flora and me to have family around at this difficult time."

They carried on chatting in a slightly stilted way until Flora returned with the tea. All of them accepted a fresh cup and Flora and Damian exchanged a few words about their father. After that they spent the remainder of the afternoon fairly companionably, reading papers and making the occasional comment about the articles they read. Eventually they all freshened up ready for dinner, which was only a light meal of seafood and pasta. When they had finished eating Damian said,

"At the risk of seeming rude, I'm going into the study to listen to some Beethoven and check my emails online for an hour or so. You two are welcome to watch some television. There are some videos in the drawing room at the back. I turned on an electric fire in there, so it should be warm. I'll join you for drinks later. What are you going to do, Flora?"

"Oh, I've got a birthday card to post to a friend – I forgot all about it earlier. I'll just walk to the post box and drop it in. I might even take a stroll through the village and clear my head. I should be back in under an hour." Her voice seemed a little high pitched and nervous.

"Well, take care out there now that it's dark," said Damian with a show of brotherly concern. "But I will be interested to hear where the floods have reached. He left the kitchen and they heard the study door gently shut and the strains of Beethoven's familiar Fifth Symphony strike up. Laura and Rupert sorted through a collection of films and Rupert picked out "Jaws" whilst Laura chose a book from the bookcase and snuggled down next to him. They heard Flora call out to say that she was leaving and the front door slammed behind her, probably caught a little by the wind. After about ten minutes, Laura heard the jangling sound of Damian's phone from his study. Then his music changed abruptly, as if his mood had changed, and he put on some George Melly. Laura glanced up at the film, wrinkled her nose in distaste at what she saw, and returned to "Ivanhoe". In the study, Damian took off the jazz after about twenty minutes and reverted to Sibelius. After an hour the front door banged again, there was a brief pause and then Flora entered – still in her coat but without her boots.

"The flooding is right up to the doorsteps of the cottages," she announced. "I texted Damian and told him."

"Is it still raining?" asked Rupert.

"Oh, yes, a bit. We'll have to see what has happened in the morning."

Just then Damian came in looking flush-faced. "Thanks for the text, Flora: I just hope the really heavy rain lightens up over night, or we could be in trouble. Right! – what can I get you all to drink?"

Soon they all had a drink in hand and they watched the end of the film. It still wasn't quite bedtime and Damian suddenly and uncharacteristically declared, "You know, I don't think I could sleep tonight: who fancies watching "The

Lord of the Rings" films back-to-back? I've only seen them once."

Laura and Flora both made varying sounds of dissent, but Rupert – who loved the films – looked like Christmas had arrived early.

"Well, I'm game," said Rupert. "As long as there are snacks and toilet breaks!"

"Excellent!" Damian looked genuinely pleased.

Flora made it half way through the first film and then went up to bed, quickly followed by Laura. The two men, who had moved on to beers, could be heard occasionally chatting down the stairs. At about one o'clock Damian went to make some cheese on toast and Rupert crept into his bedroom to see if his wife was sleeping. She wasn't; she was deep in her book, but put it down when Rupert came in.

"Having fun?" she asked.

"Oddly, yes – and I was ready to thoroughly dislike Damian," Rupert said in a low voice. He sat on the bed and kissed Laura fondly on the cheek.

"What did you mean earlier – about there being trouble ahead?" Laura had obviously been waiting for an opportunity to ask this question.

"Only that everyone seems to be painfully ignorant about the facts concerning George's will. Everybody seems to be going to great lengths to tell us that George has left everything to Damian and did not change this provision – and had no intention of doing so, despite his recent marriage. But no one seems to have grasped the obvious – that a will is automatically revoked on marriage – if George dies, he will be intestate!"

Laura sat up straight in surprise. "What does that mean; in practical terms?"

"Well, that his estate will be distributed according to the intestacy rules. I'm not a hundred percent sure of the details, but the gist is that, after tax, his wife will get the first two hundred and fifty thousand, his children half of the remainder divided between them. The other half of that amount – about three hundred and fifty thousand by my calculations, will be set aside and Elsa will have a life interest in it. Damian and Flora will only get it after her death – and she is hardly any older than them, so it may be a long wait. In other words, taking into account inheritance tax, Damian and Flora will be getting little more than a hundred thousand up front – and the house will go!"

"But that isn't what Uncle George wanted! Doesn't his will count for anything?"

"Frankly, no," said Rupert. "If he had lived and someone had pointed all this out, he could have re-written the will leaving everything to Damian – but that never happened. From what I gather, he didn't have the kind of mind to grasp the fact that he would have to rewrite his will."

"Could Elsa refuse her share?"

"She could; but somehow I don't think she will."

"Are you going to tell Damian?"

"Well, not tonight – we've got a whole lot of film to watch! Saying that, I'd better get back down there; we can talk tomorrow." He kissed his wife again and left her looking thoughtful and concerned.

The small hours wore away as Damian and Rupert followed Frodo and Sam on the tortuous journey to Mordor. Damian had pulled out the extended version of the final film with something of a flourish, so it was clear that they would not see their beds at all that night. Then, just when the two men were beginning to discuss the possibilities of breakfast, the telephone rang. Rupert paused the film as Damian leapt up to answer it. Even from the couple of words he could hear, Rupert gathered that George was dying. This impression was confirmed when Damian re-entered the room.

"Father is dying. I will take Flora straight to the hospital. They have called Elsa too."

The house was in a flurry for a while as Flora was roused and dressed herself, and the two siblings departed to attend their father in his last few moments of life. Laura got out of bed to offer any help required, but in default of that returned with an exhausted Rupert to catch an hour or so of sleep before they had to get up. In fact, they were woken by the telephone after less than an hour. Laura ran down the stairs to answer and then returned and started to dress quietly with the intention of leaving Rupert undisturbed. A weary voice, however, questioned her from the bed,

"What's the matter?"

"That was Damian from the hospital," said Laura as she pulled on a jumper. "They have left messages at Elsa's house and on her mobile, but no answer. Damian thought I might go and knock on her door. George is still alive."

Rupert sat up, suddenly awake. "No! Don't you go: I'll walk down there. I chatted to her yesterday, remember?"

"If you like," said Laura, only mildly taken aback by his vehemence. "I thought you needed to catch up on your sleep."

"I can do that later," said Rupert, who was already pulling back on the clothes he had only recently pulled off. "I'll go and see what's happened to Elsa."

When Rupert left Sunley Grange he was greeted by mist and damp. The rains had ceased and the flooding had stopped short of the houses, but everywhere was wet and cold. When he reached the house he had seen Elsa leave the previous day, he gave a long ring on the bell. The frontage was that of a small terraced cottage and the one downstairs window had the curtain pulled firmly across it on the inside. A second ring and a firm bang on the door with his fist elicited no response. He was just wondering whether there was some back entrance when the front door of the adjacent house opened abruptly. The lady at the door – a short, plump figure in a track-suit – placed a tabby cat on the doorstep and looked at him sharply.

"Bit early, aren't you?" she said. The cat yawned and stretched and turned back into the house.

"I was trying to wake Elsa," confessed Rupert. "Her husband, George Reckless, is seriously ill in hospital."

"Oh, I heard some such thing. Isn't she answering?"

"No. The curtains are closed so I imagine she is still asleep. You don't know if she was going anywhere, do you?"

"Well I know she was in last night at about eight o'clock – I heard her banging about whilst I made my cup of tea," said the woman slightly resentfully.

"I hope she isn't ill," said Rupert. "I wonder if anyone has a spare set of keys?"

"As a matter of fact," came the slightly complacent reply, "I do have some keys myself which Elsa leaves with me in case she loses her own or suchlike – but I don't usually lend them to strangers!"

"Quite right," said Rupert, approvingly. "But I don't suppose that Elsa would mind you taking a look inside."

The lady seemed to think for a moment and then said, "It wouldn't hurt to take a look, and it's not like Elsa to go away without telling me." There was a pause whilst she receded into the depths of her home and then emerged with a small bunch of keys and carefully closed her own front door behind her. She gave Rupert a look which clearly informed him that he was expected to wait outside, and then she let herself into Elsa's cottage. Rupert, standing obediently a step or two back from the front step, waited seconds before the half-expected shriek reached his ears.

After a chaotic morning Rupert drove his wife to a nearby village for a pub lunch followed by a muddy walk across the fields and up a hill. Damian and Flora were still at the hospital and the police were all over Elsa's house. The skies had become clearer and the mist was beginning to lift, although it still clung in pockets. As they reached the summit the view below opened out, showing clearly where whole fields were still partly submerged under flood water. Despite this, the view was one of beauty and tranquillity. Rupert sighed aloud.

"Come on," encouraged Laura, "tell me what you are thinking? It must have been a nasty shock finding Elsa like that."

"I think Mrs Parsons was more shocked than I was – that is, I was shocked, but not wholly surprised. What really shook me was the sheer brutality of the murder, her head beaten in, struck from behind again and again: it was beastly and vicious and cowardly." He shuddered.

"Why would anyone do such a thing?"

"Well, she mentioned to me in passing that her first husband was violent, and if there is any documented proof of that – previous assaults or hospitalisation – I imagine that the police will check up on his whereabouts."

"We know nothing of her life, of course; but the timing of her death does seem a bit, well, *convenient* – at least for Damian."

"Doesn't it just," agreed Rupert.

"But if he thought that he was going to inherit everything from his father, what motive did he have?"

"And if he did know the will was invalid? Elsa told me that his attitude changed towards her a few nights ago – about the same time he invited us to come and visit."

"What's the connection there?"

Rupert's usually benign face showed a twist of anger, "Just that we may have been asked along to serve a purpose. So that we could be witness to the fact that he was certain of inheriting the money and could have no reason to kill Elsa. So that we could be witness to the fact that he was in the house all evening from the time he returned to the hospital until the time he was called back to the hospital."

"But we don't know what time Elsa died, so we don't know if we can provide an alibi." Laura's own delicate features were questioning rather than angry.

"We do know where Damian was for pretty much every moment of the night. I watched Elsa return to her own house yesterday after our walk, and Damian was already back at Sunley Grange. We had tea, read the papers and had some dinner. Then, at about half past seven, he disappeared into his study to listen to music whilst Flora was out for about an hour. After that I was with him watching our film-fest all night."

"So he was in the house all the time. But when was Elsa killed?"

"Well," Rupert mused, "When I found her body it was cold and stiff – she had been dead maybe ten or twelve hours. That means that she was probably killed at about the same time that Flora went out for her walk."

"You are not suggesting that Flora killed her!" exclaimed Laura. "I know she would do almost anything for her brother, but that would be a step too far. Anyway, she's tiny. The way you describe the attack on Elsa it was brutal: I can't believe for a moment that Flora was capable of such an attack either physically or temperamentally."

"Can you believe Damian capable of such an attack?"

"Frankly, yes," said Laura unhesitatingly. "But doesn't it

seem like a bit too much of a coincidence, her being killed on virtually the same day as his father? – it inevitably throws suspicion on him. Why not wait a bit and be more subtle?"

"Because if she died after George, even by one day, she would still inherit according to the rules of intestacy. That money would not revert to his estate if she died, it would go to her next of kin or in accordance with her will. Admittedly Damian and Flora would get more, because the sum which would have been used for her interest would pass to them; but it wouldn't be enough to preserve Sunley Grange unless Damian has his own money to put into the pot."

"Which he doesn't," said Laura, thoughtfully. "As always, Rupert, I really hope you are wrong. Apart from anything else, the thought that Damian asked us here to provide an alibi for him makes my blood boil. But the fact remains that he does have an alibi. We know he was in the house. We heard his phone go off. We heard him change his music. In any case, it really wasn't very long between us seeing him; an hour at most."

"An hour would have been plenty," said Rupert, thoughtfully. "After all, his going in to the study and changing music only creates an illusion of his presence. The text message only implies that he was there."

"But these days, can't you trace where messages were sent from and if they were received?"

"You could probably prove that the message about the floods was sent from Flora's phone at a certain time and that it was received on Damian's. But, that doesn't prove who put the message in!"

"Are you suggesting that it was Damian who went out with Flora's phone and Flora who covered for him in the house?"

Rupert's eyes suddenly lit up. "Yes, of course! How clever. Of course nobody would believe that Flora could commit such a murder even if she had a theoretical opportunity. But if it was Damian who called on Elsa with the pretext of talking to her about his father..."

"But if the murder was as vicious as you suggest, wouldn't there have been blood on Damian's hands and clothes?"

"It was a cold night; he could have worn a coat and gloves. If he did, we need to find those garments. Of course he could have burned them on the fire in his bedroom, but he didn't give himself much time because he insisted on us being together all night watching the film. But, you know what else comes into my mind: the fact that Flora didn't seem wet after her walk, and yet Damian was so flushed after relaxing and listening to music!"

"But we don't have any evidence and we have just gone out and left Damian with the perfect opportunity to come back from the hospital and dispose of any bloody clothes!"

"So we have, damn it! And I have a strong urge to do two things: run back and see if there are any suspicious remains in Damian's fireplace – and find out if any of his friends mentioned that his father's will was invalid."

When Rupert and Laura reached Sunley Grange there were two cars already outside: Damian's and a police car. Rupert had already been thoroughly questioned by the police following the discovery of Elsa's body, and it seemed that the connection between Elsa and her stepchildren had led the police to at least ask some preliminary questions. As they came into the entrance hall it was clear that Damian had only just returned, released from the hospital by his father's death and leaving Flora behind to sort out final details in a rush to be home. His arrival had coincided with that of the policeman and he looked like a man attached to his reason by one last thread. He seemed almost pathetically grateful to see Laura.

"This is my cousin," he explained to the policeman. "She will tell you that I have only just left the side of my father who died less than an hour ago. Whatever you need to ask, surely it can wait until I have had a few moments to compose myself? I am still in shock!"

"We are dealing with a particularly vicious murder," insisted the policeman. "I have a few very important questions to ask, but anything more detailed can be left until later."

"Uncle George is dead?" said Laura. "Come and sit down, Damian. I will make some tea and this officer can wait just a few minutes, I'm sure." She ushered them firmly into the first reception room. Rupert, meanwhile, disappeared.

By the time tea had arrived Damian was looking desperate. "I must just go to my room for a few moments," he said. "Then I will answer all your questions." He got up, but met the considerable bulk of Rupert Latimer in the doorway.

"It's no good," said Rupert, restraining him gently. "I've seen the bag with your clothes in. I know what happened! And I'm sure we can track the friend who explained to you how you were going to lose Sunley Grange."

For a second it seemed that Damian was going to make a wild dash, but suddenly he just collapsed making horrible gulping sounds of dry sobbing. A call on his radio from the policeman and a few words from Rupert and it wasn't too long before Damian had been taken away in a police car for questioning. Flora was to be apprehended at the hospital.

It was with relief that Laura found herself in the Range Rover with Rupert at the wheel on the pretty rural drive back to Claresby Manor.

"I'm so glad to be out of the whole poisonous affair!" she exclaimed. "I suppose we will probably have to go to court, but other than that, I hope I never see Sunley Grange again."

"Um," began Rupert tentatively. "That might not be so easy."

"What do you mean?"

"Well, outside Damian and Flora you were your Uncle George's closest relation. Damian and Flora won't be allowed to profit from their crime. Certainly they won't be allowed to inherit the money which would have gone to Elsa if Damian had not killed her. There is another little technicality too. Because Elsa died before George he, as her next of kin, may inherit her house too – unless she has drawn up a recent will, which somehow I doubt. There is no way that your cousins will be allowed to inherit that element of wealth from their father. One way or another, you will probably end up with Sunley Grange!"

Laura looked aghast. "Oh, I do hope not! If I do I really will give it away to become a refuge for homeless cats."

Rupert Investigates

A late June day in picturesque Cambridge is always a pleasure, but doubly so when attending a traditional graduation ceremony in the elegant setting of the Senate-House. For Laura Latimer the occasion might have been a poignant reminder of the fact that, by dropping out after her first term of studying the History of Art, she had robbed herself of the opportunity of ever participating as a nervous graduand about to kneel before the Vice-Chancellor's deputy. However, she was not predisposed to such introspection and was ready to enjoy the day as a spectator for whatever entertainment it might provide. She and her husband, Rupert, were currently accompanying the procession which was making its way from Pelham College, past King's College and on to the Senate-House. The object of their attention was a rather beautiful raven-haired young woman in a black gown and a hood edged with white fur. Considering that the majority of other women in the procession were similarly dressed in the academic costume of a Bachelor of Arts, she seemed to be attracting a disproportionate amount of interest both from casual passers-by and strategically placed press photographers. Bumping accidently into one of the latter, Rupert grumbled loudly,

"You'd think that they could leave her in peace for one day!"

"No chance of that," replied Laura. "At least they won't be allowed in the Senate-House without an invitation."

"I wouldn't be surprised if at least one photographer tries to wangle his way in by posing as a proud parent. Poor Tizz, she's quite right – she will never be able to blend into the background." Rupert cast his eyes around as if to detect every possible nook and cranny which might conceal a zealous member of the paparazzi, but seemed to suddenly catch sight of something else that galvanized him into instant action. With surprising agility for a man with a long, rangy, rather badly-put-together look about him, he leapt forward and caught hold of the raven-haired woman just as some projectile shot past them at tremendous velocity, slightly grazing Rupert's arm.

The day had commenced more peaceably with Laura and Rupert meeting up with Tizz – as she was affectionately known by family and close friends – and her Uncle Fred in the beautiful gardens of the exclusively female Pelham College. The sun was shining and there was a bustle of activity as the students arranged their gowns and hoods and deployed a derangement of pins and brooches to try and sensibly keep the garments in place. Laura and Rupert were the invited guests of Tizz – better known by her real name of Emerald George. Emerald George had been in the public eye from the moment of her birth as the daughter of Hollywood actor Victor George and his aristocratic English wife, Lady Rose Thorley. Emerald's father was part of a famous acting dynasty, her mother the daughter of Earl Thorley of Hampton and a renowned beauty. Having inherited her mother's looks and her father's talent, Emerald George's celebrity was compounded by her appearance in the box office hit *Barnstable* when she was only eleven years old. After the phenomenal success of this film, Victor George's career had sunk gradually into the doldrums until he finally decided to agree to the inevitable *Barnstable: A Crime Revisited*. By this time Emerald was sixteen and quite certain what she wanted out of life – and it didn't include an acting career. It just so happened that, along with her already abundant gifts, Emerald had inherited the Thorley brains – which had bypassed her mother – and was much more interested in scholarship and mathematics than anything Hollywood had to offer. Unfortunately, the plot of her father's film required a reprise of her role in the sequel. Somehow she had managed to cut a deal with her father that allowed her – on completion of filming – to finish her education at an English boarding school and go on to study at a university of her choice.

The sequel to *Barnstable* was a huge success and Victor George won his Oscar and Emerald George travelled to England to reside with her beloved uncle, Fred Thorley, who was currently Viscount Hampton. Fred was her mother's much younger half-brother and only thirty years old. He was also heir not just to his father's title, but also the Thorley tendency to reclusiveness and scholarship. His greatest pleasure was concocting excruciatingly difficult number puzzles and crosswords – and it was through their shared interest in crosswords that he had become acquainted with Rupert. As Rupert frequently went to stay with Fred, he soon got to know Tizz and encouraged both her and her uncle to contribute crosswords to his books. It was as a consequence of this friendship that Rupert and Laura had been invited to join Fred and Emerald for her graduation, her parents being otherwise occupied in the United States. Like Laura, Rupert was familiar with Cambridge, having been a student there himself. Unlike Laura, he had completed his studies and emerged with a creditable first. As the two of them watched Fred's inept attempts at securing Emerald's hood with a hairclip, the question of the classification of degrees had surfaced.

"Did you say that Tizz got a double first?" asked Laura, arranging her fascinator, which kept sliding down her silky hair.

"Yes, pretty effortless stuff for her," Rupert allowed himself a warm glance at Emerald. Her luminous beauty, which was much praised for lighting up the cinema screen, was un-dampened by the sombre black of her academicals. Aware of her husband's admiration for the younger woman, but confidently untroubled, Laura pursued her questions.

"I've never quite sorted out the Cambridge system of marking degrees – being a dropout myself."

"Well, strictly speaking the degree does not have a class at Cambridge and is awarded to any student who scrupulously attends every term. In reality everyone attaches the mark from the final examination to their degree. That is why I can claim a first having made such a poor showing in my earlier exams. Tizz gets a double first by virtue of achieving a first in two sets of exams."

"So what is a starred first?"

"If you get a first in every paper you sit – which, come to mention it, I thought Tizz did."

"And she even found time to produce some crosswords for your new book." There was a grudging respect in Laura's voice.

"A pity her parents couldn't come," mused Rupert.

"I guess their presence would have caused too much of a fuss and taken the attention away from the students, which wouldn't be fair." Laura looked at the girls, just starting to form a vaguely orderly queue under the instructions of a college official with scarlet edging to her gown. The parents fell back to the periphery, waving and smiling at their offspring as they began the short walk into the centre of Cambridge. It was all very relaxed and informal as they followed the road, stopping the traffic. It was as the students finally approached the Senate-House that the photographers, straining to catch a picture of the modest and reluctant Emerald George, were rewarded by the spectacle of what looked to them liked a crazed fan leaping onto her and knocking her to the ground. A moment of confusion

158

followed in which some well-meaning onlookers sought to restrain Rupert and to help Emerald to her feet. Emerald soon made it clear that, not only was she unharmed, but that her concern was for Rupert, who was bleeding profusely from the small cut to his arm.

"What happened?" she asked him, pushing her thick dark hair off her face and trying to staunch the bleeding from his arm with a silk scarf.

"I saw a person – it looked like they had a weapon." Rupert was pulling away from Emerald and scanning the shop fronts for a sign of the assailant.

"What is going on? Are you all right?" It was the Praelector, Dr Alice Bean, who had been organising the young ladies at the College and was leading the procession. Her concern was obviously to get things moving again and she did not seem to notice Rupert at all. Fred too, who had been a little ahead of Rupert and Laura, came to check up on Emerald, a worried look on his fair and kindly face.

"I'm fine," Emerald assured them both, as Rupert slipped off through the crowd. "Really; there isn't a problem." The Praelector gave her a cursory glance, which seemed to suggest that as her head was still clearly attached to her shoulders there was no possible reason not to continue with the ceremony, and hurried off to set things in motion again. Fred seemed more genuinely concerned and turned to Laura;

"What was all that about?"

"I don't know," admitted Laura. "Rupert saw someone. I'm not sure if they threw something or a shot was fired."

"I didn't hear a shot," said Fred. "Was someone targeting Tizz or was it just a random object being chucked about?"

"I don't think anyone would deliberately attack the students," Laura reassured him. "Whatever it was, I expect that Rupert will get to the bottom of it. I think we might as well carry on with the others and wait until he catches up."

159

Fred nodded, obviously wanting to follow Tizz and somewhat mollified. Laura, however, looked with a frown of concern after the now distant figure of her husband, but decided to carry on with Fred and the other parents and friends who were all talking animatedly amongst themselves. Sure enough, the young ladies of Pelham College continued on their way as the visitors filed into the Senate-House to take their seats. Laura followed the stocky figure of Fred up the stairs to sit in the gallery, firmly placing her handbag on the seat next to her for Rupert's benefit. However, it was not until the ceremony was nearly finished that he arrived. He had missed the entrance of the Esquire Bedell bearing his mace, and the Vice-Chancellor's deputy in her scarlet cope. He had also missed the moment when Emerald knelt down to have her degree conferred upon her and left the building clasping her certificate. There was quite a lot of Latin which he missed too – which was a pity because, unlike most of the audience, he might actually have understood it.

"Has she been up yet?" he asked in a whisper after clambering apologetically over people's knees to reach Laura.

"Yes; just a minute ago. But we are nearly half way through and no clapping, so we should be out soon too."

Rupert sat down and showed all signs of concentrating on the graduation ceremony. Laura, however, looked him over carefully and noticed that, as well as having a blood stained scarf around his left arm, he had acquired a carrier-bag with some item concealed within it. Although curious, she decided to wait until they were outside again to question him. Fortunately the event was mercifully brief and one of the Esquire Bedells called them to order and everyone stood whilst the officials left in another procession. As soon as they could make their way down the stairs, the three of them went to find Emerald in Senate-House Yard.

The sun shone warmly and Fred quickly spotted Emerald amongst the throng of new graduates. He gave her a little wave and she came to join them. All around them families were posing proudly for photographs. Rupert indicated that he would use his camera and Emerald stood smiling next to her uncle. Although not especially tall herself, in heels she was on a level with Fred, whose diminutive stature and rather washed-out complexion was pure Thorley. A series of portraits of past Earls at Hampton Hall displayed the same pleasant, insipid face. It was a face that was only redeemed by the intelligent dark eyes which shone out. In comparison, Emerald's beauty was vivid, with red lips, dark hair and deep blue eyes, and family portraits demonstrated that these looks came from her grandmother, Earl Thorley's first countess, who had been a model. His second wife and Fred's mother had been a distant cousin and childhood friend whom he married after ten lonely years as a widower. A few more photographs of the beaming Fred and the surprisingly shy Emerald were taken by Rupert and a couple of lurking press photographers took advantage of the moment too. Then Emerald indicated to her uncle that she wanted to move away before she attracted any more attention – not least because the state of Rupert's arm was arousing curiosity - and the four of them started to make their way back to Pelham College where a reception was to be held.

"What have you got in that bag?" Laura asked Rupert at the first opportunity.

"A crossbow bolt," said Rupert in a matter of fact voice, pulling out something that looked more like an arrow to Laura.

"Wow!" exclaimed Emerald, turning pale and looking suddenly confused, "is that the thing that hit your arm?"

"Luckily it only grazed me – this is a no-nonsense

missile."

"It could have killed her!" exclaimed Fred, as if only just realising the gravity of what had occurred. "Rupert, I think you saved Tizz's life."

"Yes; I don't think that anyone else saw what happened properly or they might have called a halt to proceedings and brought in the police."

"Just as well that didn't happen – Dr Bean would have gone spare!" commented Emerald, whose pale face had now taken on a flush.

"But why would anyone try to hurt Tizz?" pursued Fred.

"She's famous," said Laura simply. "Unfortunately that may be all it takes to attract the attention of some crazy person."

"Dad's had problems," admitted Emerald. "Hate-mail and threats and suchlike. Most of his fan mail is positive, although even some of the "I love you!" stuff can be pretty disturbing. I've never actually received anything threatening – at least, not that I know about – but I guess it does go with the territory. I'm hoping to be able to drop out of the limelight as time passes, but with the *Barnstable* sequel being so recent and such a success, I guess I'm stuck with a public profile for a while longer. There are action figure doll-things of me available at the moment; one of the girls in my corridor bought one to show me – it's not possible for me to be unrecognisable with that level of publicity, which is why I never wanted to be part of the film. But dad wanted it, so..." Emerald shrugged helplessly.

"Perhaps we should tell the police: you may need protection," said Fred looking anxiously at his niece.

"Give Rupert a chance," said Laura gently. "I've never known him not to get to the bottom of any mystery – and it may be best if we can solve this one without it becoming newsworthy."

"There were photographers present at the time," said Rupert, "but no one spotted the crossbow bolt."

"The use of a crossbow must be pretty unusual," commented Laura. "Does that tell us anything about the person?"

"Not really," Rupert replied with a shake of his head. "But make no mistake; this was a top of the range businesslike weapon. It amazes me that it is still possible for anyone over eighteen to buy such a weapon without the need for a licence or any form of registration. There's all this fuss made about possessing knives at the moment, but a good crossbow is easily as dangerous as a gun and anyone can purchase one after a couple of minutes' search on the internet."

"But a hunting crossbow is a pretty big contraption," said Fred. "Somebody must have seen who was holding it in a busy King's Parade."

"I saw it from a distance," said Rupert. "But the person was standing in the shadows of a doorway and everyone was looking at the procession. I expect they put it quickly back into some kind of bag or hold-all. I didn't know it was a crossbow straight away, I just caught sight of something odd and instinct told me that Emerald was the target."

For a moment Laura thought from the expression on Emerald's face that she was steeling herself to say something important, but in the end she just said, "Well, I'm very grateful – and we must do something about your arm when we get back to college."

"It should be fine," said Rupert dismissively. "But I will pop back to the car and put a jumper on so that I don't look quite so much like the walking wounded."

After Rupert had tidied himself up and they had all availed themselves of the Pelham bathroom, they made their way into Hadleigh Dining Hall where a buffet was set out. Having been purpose built as a women's college in the nineteenth century, Pelham was not amongst the medieval colleges which are often considered typical of Cambridge University and certainly had nothing to offer to equal the architectural splendour of King's College Chapel. However, it was a pretty and elegant example of Victorian architecture and what it lacked in history it made up for by being charming and welcoming. Long tables were laden with food and fresh fruit and the celebratory champagne flowed freely. Rupert, Laura and Fred took their glasses of champagne and settled in a quiet corner whilst Emerald was waylaid by various friends. When she eventually joined them she asked,

"Can I get you some food, Uncle Fred?"

"No, it's all right; I'll take a tour around the tables. The strawberries look good." He got up and the others followed him, helping themselves to smoked salmon, salads, cold meat and a selection of vol au vents. When they were all seated again, Laura asked Emerald to point out notable members of the academic staff.

"We are possibly not the most distinguished college for mathematicians," said Emerald "although as a Pelhamite it is sacrilege for me to say so, and you will notice that I am keeping my voice low. The colleges do vary in the quality of supervisions they offer and my school tried to persuade me to go to Kings, which boasts a couple of professors. Kings was a bit too prominent for me, however, and I have nothing to complain about here. Rose Tallford was my DoS – that's her in the grubby looking dress with short dark hair. She was all right, but I preferred Eustace – Dr Neill – who was my acting DoS for a term when Rose had a sabbatical. To be honest, I tended to go to him for advice. That's him over there helping himself to a mountain of food – the short man with the glasses. He really is a sweetie."

Laura, who understood a DoS to be a Director of Studies, nodded with interest as she watched the two academics fill their plates. Further chat was prevented by the arrival of a couple of other graduates.

"Georgie says someone tried to shoot you – what's that all about?" asked a rather dumpy blonde girl with cheerful unconcern.

Emerald shrugged. "Don't know. Anyway, they missed."

"Probably someone from the Assassins Guild or a LARPer," commented her taller companion.

"This is my Uncle Fred," Emerald said as her uncle came forward to hear what the two girls were saying. "Lucy is natsci and Georgie is another mathmo."

Fred smiled at the girls and rightly translated Emerald's introduction to mean that one had studied science and the other mathematics. Another term, however, required explanation.

"What is a LARPer?" he asked.

"Oh, LARP is live action role-play – recreation of battles or fantasy battles, that sort of thing. Those are the guys who are likely to have a replica Cromwellian sword amongst their most prized possessions."

"Or a crossbow?" asked Rupert, suddenly interested.

"Probably – I was never much into that sort of thing," Lucy replied. "I know Gavin, who is into the Assassins Guild, but they are really strict about weapons and just use things like rubber band guns and pea-shooters. It's all about the stealth, and even replica guns are a big taboo."

"Yes, but some of them are plumb crazy," added Georgie.

"Probably," agreed Lucy. "But they are mostly nice guys. If they wanted to target you as a challenge they'd ask first and offer to buy you a pint for your troubles – and even then they would only use water balloons or flour."

"Which brings us back to who tried to shoot you? It's funny it should have been a crossbow – didn't you have that one in your room for a while, Emerald?" inquired Georgie

165

chattily.

Emerald blushed a becoming shade of magenta and said, "Yes, but that was just a project thing – I was working out draw weight and power stroke and things like that." Then, changing the subject abruptly she informed her uncle, "Georgie is going to be studying for a masters, like me."

"Only because I want to wear a different gown. Don't imagine that I'm in Emerald's league, however; she is the outstanding mathematician of our year, everyone is in awe of her – even the lecturers."

"Yes, there was some grumbling at first about how it was against the laws of nature for anyone to be so clever and so beautiful, but then we got to know how sweet she was and forgave her," added Lucy. "We also know all her secret addictions – like the chocolate biscuit dunking and the marmalade – so we know she's human like us really."

"Well I have the inside story of your early morning hot-chocolate drinking," returned Emerald.

"Yes, but I shall take care never to be famous, just so you can't sell the story to a hungry press."

"We'll just sell them the secret chocolate recipe," said Georgie, and the girls all laughed at their private jokes.

Just then the woman whom Emerald had identified as her Director of Studies passed close by, her back to them, and Emerald hailed her,

"Dr Tallford, come and meet my uncle." The academic turned somewhat reluctantly and allowed Emerald to introduce her. "This is my DoS, Dr Tallford. My uncle, Lord Hampton."

Fred held out his hand: "Fred," he said – never one to feel comfortable with a more formal title. "Good to meet you. We are all very pleased with Emerald's achievements."

"Yes, she is a very talented young lady," conceded Dr Tallford in a soft voice. Rupert, watching from a few paces

166

away, couldn't help noticing what a singularly unattractive figure she cut. Whilst not actually ugly, her face was plain and she had what his mother had always termed "a pudding face" – pallid and slightly pudgy, although she was not overall a bulky figure. She seemed to have no single redeeming feature; even her eyes were pale and watery, her hair lank and dull. The overall effect was not helped by the shapeless black dress she wore or the flat brown sandals, nor by the slightly sour expression on her face. "It was, of course, no surprise that she has chosen to continue her studies."

"I know that she is very much looking forward to next year," said Fred, obviously deciding to stick to small talk. "It is a beautiful college you have here and a lovely place for peaceful study."

"We are particularly proud of our library." Dr Tallford continued with the platitudes. "We may not be the oldest college in Cambridge, but we have more space than some."

"I'll be here next year too," chipped in Georgie, with a slight twinkle in her eye.

"I'm aware of that," said Dr Tallford, turning her pale eyes onto the student. "I was interested to see that you achieved the grades."

The conversation continued coolly for a few more minutes before the academic moved off.

"Old cow!" said Georgie in a hushed tone. "I knew she didn't want me to stay on. I honestly worried that she would try and scupper my chances somehow."

"Oh, I don't think she'd do that," responded Emerald. "Anyway, everyone knows what a good mathematician you are, so I don't think that an unexpectedly low grade would pass without raising a few eyebrows."

"Just as well," said Georgie darkly. "She never seemed to like you much either, although you are too polite to

167

comment on the fact."

"I'm not sure she shows much liking for anybody," replied Emerald evenly, "so I never took it personally. She did her job well, so I've no complaints."

They continued to chat and enjoy the strawberries and cream, wandering out into the garden to eat them. After a while Rupert positioned himself confidentially beside Emerald and asked in a low tone, "What was all that about a crossbow in your room?"

"I thought you'd get round to quizzing me about that," said Emerald with an embarrassed smile. "It was something I bought off the internet – pretty impressive object – but it really was because I was curious about the mechanics of how it worked and I experimented with it a bit. The odd thing was that when I packed up to go back to Fred's after May Week and our post-exam wind-down, I noticed it was missing. I guess I should have reported it or asked at the Porters Lodge, but I wasn't sure that it would go down well that I'd had the thing in the first place – and, before you ask: yes, the bolt you picked up matched the ones that came with the crossbow."

"Who knew you had it?"

"Well, Georgie, because I discussed some of the mechanics with her and a couple of other mathmos. I did actually take it down to the copse at the edge of the Pelham sports field and fire a few shots at a tree – just to take measurements of distances the bolt travelled and stuff. James came with me then. And there were people in and out of my room who might have seen it; but only friends, because I don't like having a lot of people in my room – my space and that sort of thing."

"And, just out of interest – any other funny stuff happened to you?"

"Funny in what way?"

"Anything else which could be interpreted as someone trying to get at you, or anything else taken from your room?"

Emerald mused for a moment and then said, "Well, there was an incident with my bike just before finals. I was riding along Silver Street on my way to see James when I had to brake suddenly and was nearly thrown right over the handle bars – I tore my dress and scratched my arm, but no harm done. When James looked over my bicycle later he found that the nut on the back brake was loose – he just tightened it up. It didn't occur to me that anyone would tamper with it, but I guess they could have done. They'd have to know it was mine, though, because it's usually chained up along with dozens of others."

"Who's James – boyfriend?" asked Rupert with a touch of curiosity.

Emerald smiled. "Just friend and fellow mathmo. He tended to hang about with me and Georgie – and Tom too, before he degraded. We punted together a few times, and sat around in the Botanic Garden, that kind of thing. James and Tom are both from Sackville College, which does really cool formals, so I've been over there."

"So Tom didn't graduate this year – is he coming back to finish?"

"Yes, he's pretty clever but just didn't get himself together the last couple of terms, so he's going to retake the year."

"What about other things being taken from your room or any signs of any break-in?" asked Rupert.

"There never was any sign of anyone breaking in," admitted Emerald. "I tended to leave my lock on the latch if I just popped down to the buttery or the library, so anyone could walk in." When she saw Rupert raise an eyebrow at this lack of security she added, "That's nothing – Georgie leaves hers on the latch all the time because she lost her keys in the first week. Anyway, we are both on the second floor and it's pretty safe, although there isn't really anything to stop anyone from wandering up there. As for the crossbow, I'm ashamed to say I didn't miss it until I came to pack when I was going home to Fred's, so I don't know when it disappeared."

"Is James around today?"

Emerald shook her head. "No. Even though he did the same course as Georgie and me he has already graduated – because we do it by college not by subject group. He's gone home. Georgie is the only one who is staying in her room a bit longer; mainly because she can't stand her stepfather and keeps her holidays short. I'm hoping to get a new room when I come back next year, but they don't guarantee accommodation to post-grads and I may share a house with Georgie and a couple of others."

At this point in the conversation, Laura came up with some coffee for her husband and Emerald wandered off to say a few goodbyes.

"Fancy a walk over to the Fitzwilliam to look at the paintings?" Laura asked Rupert.

"Yes – how about you, Fred?"

"Absolutely; when Emerald can tear herself away."

A little while later the four of them made the short walk to the museum with its imposing Neoclassical Corinthian portico which seemed almost too grand for the otherwise modest small city street. There they spent a peaceful hour before wending their separate ways, Fred and Emerald back to his lodge in the grounds of Hampton Hall and Rupert and Laura back to her ancestral home of Claresby Manor where their small daughter, Florence, had been left in the care of a close friend. The couple enjoyed a peaceful summer, which included the recently revived Claresby Fair, which was held in their extensive grounds. Fred came up for the day, but there were no mishaps to report from Emerald, who was

170

camping with friends, and it seemed to have been decided that the incident with the crossbow was to be forgotten.

The summer passed with a fitful mix of sunshine and showers, and autumn arrived with a more promising period of settled weather. Students returning to Cambridge for the Michaelmas Term early in October included Emerald to her new ground floor room in Pelham College, her friends James and Georgie to a house shared with a couple of others, and Tom to have a second go at his final year in Sackville College. The first few weeks were quiet enough, but then a couple of things happened which had Fred Thorley picking up the phone to speak to his friend, Rupert Latimer.

"Some funny things have happened, and I am worried about Tizz," Fred said once they had exchanged greetings.

"What things?" asked Rupert.

"Well firstly, the crossbow reappeared. Tizz is certain that it is hers and the bolts were returned too – minus the one you picked up at her graduation. Georgie found it in her bedroom one day. There are four people in her house – two postgraduates, including herself, and two Cambridge graduates who are working in casual jobs. James is doing a bit of bar work and I think the other chap does the same sort of thing – I think he is a classicist and does a bit of writing too. Anyway, there are plenty of people in and out of the place and there are no locks on the bedroom doors. Still, it would limit who could reasonably wander about the place."

"Is the front door kept locked?"

"Mostly: or so I gather from Tizz, who is a frequent visitor. All four residents have keys – and I guess the landlord does; but apparently the front door is sometimes left on the latch when someone is expecting guests and is too lazy to answer the door."

Rupert sighed. "I hope Emerald is keeping her door locked

this year?"

"Yes she is," replied Fred. "Unfortunately she has a ground floor room and with the weather so warm, she left one of her windows open a few times."

"And?"

"And, when she came back after lunch today, she made a rather unpleasant discovery in her room: a dead rabbit. It was left on her pillow. She is terribly upset – far more upset than with the crossbow incident. In fact, I'm about to drive up there to see her. I wondered if you could meet me there?"

"Of course, I can be in Cambridge in under two hours, traffic permitting. I imagine it will take you a bit longer?"

"No; actually I'm at the London flat, so we could meet at the Porters Lodge at about five, if that's all right for you?"

"That's fine. Laura is in London with Florence anyway, so I won't be missed and I can join her there when I've finished in Cambridge or vice versa."

The two men were greeted by a visibly upset Emerald when they reached Pelham College. She insisted on making them coffee first in the buttery, and then she took them to her room. It was a typical student room with bed, desk and cupboard and a few posters on the wall. This particular room had large sash windows which looked out across some parking spaces onto the road at the front of the college.

"I didn't move the rabbit, but I had to cover it up, poor little thing, because I couldn't stand looking at it," said Emerald.

Rupert removed the tea towel as Emerald averted her eyes. The rabbit was a small white Netherland Dwarf – the type sold as a pet, rather than a wild rabbit. The sight of the limp body was enough to upset the robustly matter-of-fact Rupert and he quickly covered the body again. Fred glanced once and turned away.

"We'll take it away and get you a fresh pillow," Fred

reassured Emerald, "but I really think that you should ask about having a second floor room, or at least keep the room secure." By this time Emerald was in tears and her uncle put an arm around her.

"It's just such a horrible thing to do – who would do such a thing?"

"I expect the rabbit died naturally," Rupert said comfortingly.

"No it didn't!" responded Emerald. "Some monster cut its throat!"

Rupert was silenced, because this was quite true, although he had hoped that Emerald might have overlooked this fact as the rabbit had been dead for a while before being placed in her room and there was very little sign of blood. Nonetheless it was clearly intentionally gruesome and intended to frighten her. Emerald, however, was made of stern stuff, as she demonstrated by her next comment.

"I don't know why someone is doing this, but I won't let it get to me – and I refuse to move rooms!" Then, seeing her uncle's face she added, "but I will be more careful about locking things up when I go out."

"What about your food in the kitchen?"

"You think someone might tamper with that? Well, since I have a fridge in here, I'm quite self-contained, so that shouldn't be a problem. But it is a bit depressing to have to worry about things like that. I've left a couple of packets out there, but I can get them now." Emerald left the room and Fred turned to Rupert,

"I really do think we should tell the police some of what has happened."

"Of course. Best to ask Emerald if that is what she wants when she comes back."

"Have you any idea what could be going on?"

"Well," replied Rupert slowly, "I know *what* the

perpetrator is, I just don't know *who* they are yet – it's just a case of working it out."

"Explain," said Fred.

"Well, the perpetrator of the three incidents – and I include the time that someone tampered with Emerald's bicycle brake – is obviously a Cambridge insider, not a crazed fan. They know their way around and can go in and out of students' rooms without arousing suspicion. They have a sense of occasion – the graduation ceremony – and they obviously want to get Emerald off the scene; hopefully just by scaring her, although they are obviously malicious and callous as well as jealous, so I wouldn't like to guarantee her safety."

Fred was looking alarmed. "Tizz never told me about her bicycle – what happened?"

"I expect she didn't want to worry you," said Rupert. "Anyway, she didn't attach any significance to the incident until I asked about it. Put simply, she nearly had an accident last term when the nut on her back brake became – or was made – loose."

At that moment Emerald returned to the room with a few packets of food and followed by three other people. "I met Georgie, James and Tom outside," she explained. "They were coming to see if I fancied a walk down to the river and I told them what had happened." The three students came in, Georgie acknowledging Fred and Rupert and glancing at the tea towel on the pillow as Emerald introduced everybody.

"White rabbit, eh – that's a classic!" exclaimed James with heartless indifference. He was a nice looking young man of middle height. His friend, Tom, was slighter with a narrow face and long nose. He stepped forward and tweaked the towel so as to expose what was underneath.

"Oh, we'll have to get rid of that," Tom said more practically. "Are their some bin bags in your kitchen?"

Emerald nodded and she and Tom went off to find one.

"How horrible!" exclaimed Georgie. "What is going on?"

"It seems that Emerald has an enemy," said Rupert. "All we need to do is to establish who and why."

"Well, my money is on Rose Tallford," said Georgie without demur. "She's been positively toxic to Emerald recently."

"Can you see her wandering in here with a dead rabbit in her handbag?" asked James, doubtfully.

"Easily!" replied Georgie. Just then the others returned and the James and Tom lifted the pillow with its grisly burden into the sack and then departed with Emerald, like a small funeral cortège, to find the outside bins. Taking advantage of their momentary absence Rupert turned to Georgie and asked,

"Can you quickly fill me in on Emerald's relationship with the two boys – any feeling in any direction there?"

"Well, not from Emerald," replied Georgie. "She just sees them as friends. But James is very interested – she just doesn't seem to notice."

Rupert nodded knowingly – this had been the state of affairs between him and Laura; although he had finally persuaded her into marriage, probably more by slow attrition than outright conquest. "What about Tom?"

"Well, he is a close sort of person – inscrutable; so it's hard to tell. I tend to assume as a default that all men will fall for Emerald. Tom's a physicist, but a great reader – I think he gets distracted, which is why he went off-course last year. But I didn't put his distraction down to romantic troubles; at least, not with Emerald as the object."

Further disclosures were precluded by the return of the others. A little discussion between them and Fred and Rupert were persuaded to book into a hotel and stay for the weekend at least. No one ever needed much excuse to spend

175

time in Cambridge whilst the weather was fine and river and parks inviting, but the real reason was Fred's anxiety and desire to stay until he was sure that Emerald was safe. Emerald refused to involve the police – on the basis that the story would be sure to end up in the press and attract even more adverse attention. Rupert phoned Laura to explain, and then he and Fred took Emerald out for a fish supper. The following day dawned cloudless and a brief exchange of texts secured an arrangement for the two older men to meet up with Emerald and her friends for the obligatory punt down the Cam. Scorning the chauffeured punts, the group secured two boats with Rupert, Fred and Emerald in one, Georgie, James and Tom in the other. Both Rupert and James had previous experience and manoeuvred the boats out with graceful skill, making the handling of the pole and the standing position balanced on the back of the punt look easy and natural. A number of newcomers belied this impression, losing their poles in the mud, wedging their boats horizontally across the river, and committing every error in the catalogue short of falling into the water.

Their trip on the river took them past St John's College and under the Bridge of Sighs, the ladies relaxed and graceful in their summer frocks which were out for their last showing with just the help of a cardigan in deference to the hint of autumn in the air. The excursion did the trick and, after stopping off for a pub lunch, Emerald returned to her room with the group for a cup of coffee feeling relaxed and calm. There was a little coming and going as various members of the company popped to the bathroom and Fred went out to buy a pint of milk. Eventually they were all settled, making themselves comfortable on the bed and an odd assortment of chairs such as is usually found in student accommodation. Only Emerald was missing – and nobody could remember if she had slipped out to the toilet, to fetch

176

some more mugs or to borrow some milk.

"She's probably gone to the kitchen – I'll go and check," said James.

"I'd better go to the girl's bathroom," said Georgie.

"Why not just phone her?" suggested Rupert. "She always keeps her mobile in her pocket." And he and Fred went down the corridor and outside in search of a signal. Tom followed them for a moment and then wandered off in the opposite direction on a search of his own. Amidst all this fuss and movement, the door to Emerald's room was left on the latch until they all reassembled after their various failures. In the meantime, Emerald, who had set off for an upstairs kitchen in the search for borrowed milk, returned to find her door ajar and the room deserted. A quick glance around told her that Georgie's handbag was still there as was her uncle's jacket, so she deduced that they hadn't gone far, although she couldn't understand why everyone had disappeared. She was just about to look out into the corridor when something caught her eye. On her bed was a doll, its head broken from the body. A closer examination confirmed that this doll was one of the replicas made of her character from *Barnstable* – a truly grotesque Emerald lookalike. Beside the doll was a piece of paper with a single word scrawled on it: "Tonight." Coming on top of the rabbit incident it was too much for Emerald who felt a sudden rush of nausea and dashed to the nearest toilet. It was only then, of course, that the others returned.

"No sign of Emerald?"

"No. You?"

"Nothing."

The five of them looked one to another until Rupert caught sight of the doll and the note. He picked up the note and passed it to Fred.

"What does this mean?" asked Fred.

"Other than a threat, I don't know. Anyone could have walked into the room and left it whilst we were out looking for Emerald," responded Rupert.

"The *someone* who has abducted her! We really must call the police now," exclaimed Fred. "This is virtually a death threat." Just then there was a knock on the door and they all jumped. Tentatively Rupert opened it to reveal an alarmed-looking female student.

"There's something going on in the bathroom. Someone is shouting and screaming, but the door's locked."

Rupert shoved almost rudely past her, closely followed by Fred and the others. The bathroom contained a couple of sinks, a shower cubicle and two toilets with doors locked by old-fashioned key and keyhole. One of these was being rattled vigorously from within and what was unmistakeably Emerald's voice was calling, "Get me out! Who locked me in! Get me out!" almost hysterically.

"But I searched for her in here!" exclaimed Georgie. "It was the first place I looked and all the toilets were empty."

Rupert, meanwhile, put his shoulder to the door and broke it down and Emerald emerged, sobbing. The key was later found neatly dropped into the second toilet.

Once Emerald had washed and composed herself, the sequence of events was unravelled and it was clear that she was locked in only after they had all gone to look for her, and after she had seen the doll.

"I felt sick, and had just pulled the door closed behind me. I didn't see the key in the lock my side where it usually is, but I wasn't bothered. Someone must have put it the other side and I suddenly heard it turn and realised I was trapped and just panicked."

"And whilst we were running all over the place, someone was able to place the doll and take the opportunity to lock you in the toilet," said Rupert bitterly. "And, of course, no one saw anything!"

"But the note says something will happen tonight," mused Tom. "So why don't we just take it in turns to watch? There are four of us to be on guard, even if we just sit in the room – so Emerald need never be alone."

"But Emerald doesn't have to stay here at all," exclaimed Fred. "She can stay at the hotel tonight or, better still, I can take her back to Hampton."

"But then we won't catch whoever it is," said Emerald in a low and now composed voice, her eyes flashing and her pale, beautiful face resolute.

Fred took her by the shoulders. "I just want you safe!" he said.

"She would be safe," said Rupert, picking up on Tom's suggestion, "if we watch over her – one man in the room with her, one on the lookout outside for whoever comes."

"And what if they have a gun!" said Fred desperately.

"If they had a gun, they wouldn't have used a crossbow. This is England! – guns are rare, and this has descended more into scare tactics than a genuine threat. If someone wanted to kill Emerald and had the wherewithal to do it, they would have done it by now. This is all about intimidation, and it's time it stopped."

Against Fred's objections and with Emerald's insistence to carry the decision, it was agreed that Fred and James would watch for the first half of the night, Rupert and Tom for the second.

Although the day had been warm, the mid-October night came on cold but dry, and the watchers all bundled up in thick jumpers and scarves. James had taken the first stint, quietly moving from the long corridor and through the outside door to the car park. Although the College was locked down at night and access was only through the main entrance where the Porters Lodge was manned, the door nearest to Emerald's room had card access and James had her card so that he could let himself back in after taking a look outside her windows for any signs of a would-be intruder. It was both a possibility that her stalker was already concealed somewhere in the building or that they were prepared in such a way that locked doors posed only a slight challenge. Fred had stayed with Emerald in her room and when Rupert came to begin a second shift, he found his friend ashen-faced and anxious.

"I tried to get Tizz to sleep," Fred confided to Rupert in a low voice. "I made her some cocoa and I think that she dozed for a bit. She seems calmer than I am."

"Well, it's not long until morning now," said Rupert. "In a way I'm more worried about nothing happening than something. At least we are here and prepared tonight. It is going to be very difficult for Tizz to carry on with a vague threat hanging over her at all times."

Fred nodded in reluctant agreement. They were standing just outside Emerald's door and Tom joined them.

"You stay with Emerald in her room," Rupert instructed him. "I'll keep an eye on things out here – and you, Fred, get back to the hotel and try to sleep. I'll text you and let you know if everything is all right."

The three men parted and Tom gently closed Emerald's door behind him and smiled at her. She was dressed in a soft, grey tracksuit which served reasonably well as night clothes. Her dark hair was loose and her blue eyes bright in her pale face.

"All peaceful?" asked Tom.

"Yes. Would you like me to make you some coffee?"

"Thanks."

Emerald made a cup for them both and they chatted a little in low voices about the book she had been reading and then half-dozed in their chairs. There was no sound from Rupert outside and as dawn crept in through the windows a feeling of anti-climax stole over Emerald. She had wanted matters resolved so that she could get on with her life. Tom had gone to the widows a couple of times to look outside. Doing this for a third time he gave a sudden gasp and, with great speed, threw up the window and climbed out. Emerald, who had been all but asleep, jumped up too and went to stare out after him. There was the short space of the car park and then a gate to the pavement beyond, and it was there that Tom was grappling with a figure in a blue cagoule with the hood up. There was a light drizzle in the air and a feeling of early morning chill. The person in the coat seemed to be a stronger build than the slender Tom and soon managed to thrust him to the ground. Just then Rupert – who must have heard the kerfuffle – emerged from inside the building and called to Tom: "Stay with Emerald!" Tom had picked himself up and seemed to be examining himself for bruises before returning through the now open door and back into Emerald's room. Rupert was seen running down the road in a long-limbed dash that was more effective than elegant. Emerald stood anxiously by her door ready to usher Tom back in and closed it behind him.

"Who was the person – anyone you recognised?"

Tom shrugged indifferently. "No idea: just the first innocent early morning passerby who caught my eye. I just hope they can run fast and fight well and keep the annoying Rupert out of the way for long enough."

Emerald's stomach performed a nasty twist inside her. "What do you mean?"

"Just what I say." Tom was rubbing one wrist with his hand as if to test if it had been damaged. His narrow face was pale and set, his cold eyes flicking up to observe Emerald with only the smallest sign of interest. "I'm just amazed that you hadn't realised that the person trying to make you leave was me – you ruined my life! But I guess you are so wrapped up in yourself you didn't notice."

"I ruined your life! How?" Emerald was too flabbergasted by this sudden and unexpected announcement to feel fear for the moment.

"My first year at Cambridge was the first time I had ever been happy – the first time I'd had a true friend. James and I meant everything to each other from the first day we met – and then you came along."

Emerald looked confused. "But James and I are just friends – and I thought you and James were just friends."

Tom shrugged. "Who knows what James and I might have been – you ruined all that. Of course you knew what you were doing to him with your film star looks and oh-so-glamorous life. I did hope that you might go back to America and then James and I could be like we used to be – but you just couldn't take a hint. I don't care anymore. I'll make sure that you are out of James's life for good!"

There was something about the cold voice and frozen expression of the young man that told Emerald more than his words. She knew that he had decided to kill her and she knew that he wasn't rational. Extraordinarily she felt more annoyed by the nonsense of his attitude than frightened by the danger it put her in. Somehow it wasn't personal – he had just focused on her and blamed her for his failures rather than taking responsibility for his own problems.

"Killing me won't give you James. And even with Rupert out of the way, it will be pretty obvious that you are to blame for my death. Honestly, this isn't going to get you anywhere."

"You are missing the point – I said that I don't care anymore. My life's over anyway – I just don't see why you should get to enjoy yours." Tom had stopped rubbing his

182

wrist and looked at Emerald with cool calculation. He was only slightly taller than her and of a wiry rather than a strong build. However, when he put his hands about her throat he had an iron grip and an equally resolute determination to continue despite her kicks and blows as she struggled. Emerald's anger still hadn't given way to fear when her eyes flicked shut.

They were sitting in the lounge of the hotel. "When did you realise that it was Tom?" Fred asked Rupert as he poured a second cup of tea for himself and his niece.

"Well, I'd had niggling doubts about him ever since he suggested the night watch – and I was pretty sure someone quite close to Emerald was responsible; but I just couldn't fix him with a motive. Then I caught up with the man that Tom had sent me after, tumbled him to the ground, and realised when I was sitting on top of him that it was Felix Hammond – a fellow archaeologist lately of Pembroke: just the sort of man to take an early morning walk and not at all the sort of man to obsessively target a beautiful young film star. And I suddenly thought of Emerald alone in her room with Tom."

"Well I'm glad your mental processes were so quick or Tom might well have throttled me for good and all," said Emerald, cautiously fingering a light silk scarf which concealed the bruises around her neck. The colour had come back to her face as they munched on a plate of teatime scones, lunch having been more or less missed in the chaos of the day. She wore a plain skirt and blouse and still managed to draw the eyes of all in the room by her classic but vibrant beauty.

"Funny; I never suspected Tom," said Georgie. "I noticed that he was obsessed with James and I knew that James was besotted with you, but Tom was always such a cold fish I

183

never thought that murderous resentments burned within. I always fancied Dr Tallford in the role of malefactor."

"And apparently I don't notice anything much about anyone," said Emerald ruefully. "I just thought of James and Tom as friends that it was pleasant to pass the time with."

"That's me and Lucy," said Georgie, cheerfully helping herself to strawberry jam. "I don't love her, she doesn't love me and neither of us fancies you one little bit! – you are quite safe with us."

"That's good to know," replied Emerald uncertainly.

"What have they done with Tom, anyway?" asked Georgie.

"He has been arrested," replied Rupert. "However, it seems that Tom has had some sort of breakdown and Emerald made his attack sound more like a pitiful cry for help that a real attempt at murder."

"And some people say I'm not a good actress..."

"But you will stay at Cambridge, Tom or no Tom?" asked Georgie.

"Yes. But Uncle Fred says he is going to buy a house here, so I think I'll move in with him and get a bit more privacy and security."

"Laura and I are going to help him house hunt," added Rupert. "She's due here with Florence in about an hour and we can stay the whole week."

"So all's well," added Emerald.

"Except," continued Rupert, "that once the story of unrequited passion and attempted murder hits the press, your chances of remaining low profile will be even less than before..."

The Coach House Mystery

It was one of the hottest days of a dismal summer, coming a bit late as September ousted August. At midday it was too hot for the fair-skinned Rupert to enjoy the heat of the sun, and he had found refuge in one of the dilapidated outhouses of Claresby Manor. There were stables, a coach house and an old granary; none of which had been renovated since his wife, Laura – the Lady of the Manor – had discovered treasure on the land of her impoverished family and rescued Claresby Manor's fortunes. When Laura came out to find her husband, she was holding the hand of a tottering Florence – now nearly two years old and a vision of prettiness in a flower-sprigged dress and a straw hat on elastic, which kept slipping from her head. Rupert had opened wide the rickety doors to the coach house and saw them coming. As befitted a young father, he immediately stopped what he was doing and exclaimed,

"What a pretty dress, Florence! And I love your hat."

Florence beamed happily at her father and said, "My hat!" whilst attempting to rescue it again with her free hand as it slipped rakishly over one ear.

Laura, who was also wearing a light summer dress and neat straw hat, looked curiously into the dark interior of the coach house.

"Have you unearthed anything interesting in there?"

"I've disturbed a few mice and about a century's worth of dust," admitted Rupert. "I was looking at the Rolls Royce – but it doesn't seem to have an engine; which is a pity."

Laura let go of Florence's hand – leaving her to assiduously pick the dandelion leaves which grew through the cracks in the flagstones – and went to join her husband by the remains of the car.

"It must have been a real beauty," commented Rupert,

brushing debris from it with a loving caress. "It's a Silver Ghost – probably about 1924. I think the fittings are actually silver-plated underneath the tarnish. It's all leather and mahogany inside; although the mice seem to have been eating the seats. It does seem to be an awful waste – I wonder if I could restore it to its old grandeur?"

Before she could reply, Laura was distracted by the sight of Florence, who had taken her hat off and turned it upside down to use it as a basket, with the elastic serving as a handle.

"What are you doing, Flo?" she reprimanded. "You'll get your hat dirty!"

Florence's lower lip jutted dangerously. "For Bluebell," she explained.

Laura peered into the hat and saw the leaves and understood that Florence was collecting them for her pet rabbit. "Oh, all right," she conceded. "We'll take them over to him, and when he's had his lunch, we'll make yours." Then, to Rupert – "With any luck, she'll have a nap after lunch. When you've finished out here I'll make yours – say about half-past-one."

Rupert nodded his acknowledgement and turned his interest back to the Rolls Royce, whilst Laura and Florence went to where Bluebell's hutch stood in the corner of a walled garden close to the house.

Rupert came in dusty, hot and dirty, and washed himself at a large porcelain sink. The lofty medieval kitchen of Claresby was always as cool as a cave, which made it a pleasant refuge on a hot day. Laura was preparing a salad, and some fresh rolls and a platter of cheese and ham were set out on the long oak table, as was a jug of homemade iced lemonade. Rupert sat down and poured himself a large glass of the lemonade and drank it down in one go.

"Florence settled down to sleep easily enough," commented Laura.

"Well, she'd been up since six," replied Rupert.

Laura placed the bowl of fresh salad on the table and joined her husband. "Any hope with the car?" she asked amiably.

"Well, it wouldn't be a cheap enterprise because of the need to repair the engine. As a matter of fact, I found most of it abandoned in a far corner, but it will need a lot of work and expensive new parts. I do quite fancy the idea, though."

Laura nodded as she uncorked a bottle of chilled Chardonnay.

"But I found something else of interest in the car," continued Rupert.

"What, other than mice nests?" asked Laura.

"Yes: it was in the trunk, actually. The trunk was probably fitted later – onto what looks like a custom made aluminium rear luggage rack. Anyway, inside it was a wedding dress."

"A wedding dress? Was it in good condition or had it decayed?"

"Oh, it wasn't old," continued Rupert. "In fact it was brand new and in pristine condition, all rolled up in a plastic bag. A good one too, if I'm any judge – designer made."

Laura frowned. "By brand new, do you mean never worn or put in there recently? – I was imagining it had been dumped there out of the house; although I can't see why."

"I mean that is was put there recently – in the last year or so. The bag was modern enough and it was all still clean; no damp at all."

"Why would someone bother to break into Claresby coach house to dump a brand new, expensive wedding dress?" mused Laura.

"That's what I wondered. Perhaps you can have a look after lunch before Flo wakes up. I also found a tool box in

187

the car – all original tools from 1920; but that is more useful than intriguing."

Lunch was finished, Florence still slumbered, and the dress was spread out, a gleaming white against the dark polished oak of the table in the Great Hall. It was quite a voluminous dress and would have swamped the svelte Laura had she chosen to try it on. It was also of an elaborate style with flounces and bows, and the neckline was cut daringly low. Laura wrinkled her nose in mild distaste,

"It wouldn't be my choice of style – far too fussy – but there's no doubt it was expensive. This isn't a readymade dress and the fabric, as least, is fine quality: satin with handmade lace. The beadwork is done by hand too; beautifully done, but way over-the-top given the lace and flounces. This was made to the customer's request – I can imagine the designer and dressmakers wincing as they carried out instructions. Someone wanted all the bells and whistles on their wedding day."

"Do you think it was ever worn?" asked Rupert eyeing the garment.

Laura examined the dress carefully, paying special attention to the hem and small train. "My guess is that it wasn't. If you marry in church you will be walking outside at some point and the train at least will gather a bit of dirt and dust. Even if the whole wedding was conducted inside on a single site, say in a hotel, you'd expect a bit of a grubby mark on the pure white of the hem – and this is pristine."

"Which begs the question: why would anyone dump a lovely dress, unworn, in the back of a derelict car?"

"Perhaps the engagement was broken off," suggested Laura. "The bride couldn't bear to look at the dress that she would never get to wear and dumped it."

"Possibly: but why come all the way out to Claresby

Manor?" replied Rupert. "She could have stuffed it into a black plastic bag and left it out to for the bin men."

"What a waste!"

"Well; she could have taken it to a charity shop."

"Maybe – but perhaps whoever it was didn't want to be rid of it. Perhaps she hoped that the marriage might go ahead after all and she could retrieve it."

"Or she planned to find another man to marry," suggested Rupert, cheerfully.

Laura frowned at this suggestion and then said, "Well, if the bride-to-be was local to Claresby, the person to ask would be our very own vicar, Veronica Dahl: she would know about any cancelled wedding. I was going to walk down to the vicarage with Florence for tea – why don't you come along and we can see what she has to say?"

An hour later Rupert, Laura and Veronica sat in the cool of an arbour drinking tea whilst Florence ran around with a pink balloon which was doomed to pop on one of the rose bushes. Veronica, whose dark beauty and voluptuous figure always held Rupert's gaze – despite his devotion to his pretty, auburn-haired wife – was looking particularly striking in a red dress with a tight black belt.

"We don't get many weddings in Claresby Church," she admitted in answer to Laura's preliminary question, "mainly because I'm not very accommodating to people from outside the village who want to get married here just because it will look picturesque in their photos. They don't come to church and have no intention of ever setting foot in the village again. I'll always marry villagers, of course, regardless of whether or not they are regular churchgoers. My two most recent weddings were both for villagers. Well, both brides and one of the grooms were local. Just this Saturday I married Lisa Jones and Bill Smith – he was divorced, but his wife had left him for her boss. She actually came to see me

189

to say that he was blameless in the divorce – and as a committed Christian it was important for him to have a church ceremony. He wasn't local, but Lisa is and they are settling here, so I hope to see more of them both after the honeymoon. The wedding before that was over a month ago. That was Amy Price, and what I most remember about her was the fact that, at our pre-wedding chats, all she could talk about was how she wanted to festoon the church with flowers and satin bows and how they were going on a romantic honeymoon to Bermuda. I do find it depressing how some of these girls seem to think the wedding day is the point of the exercise and that the marriage itself is a regrettable by-product. Admittedly Dean Phipps impressed me as a particularly uninspiring young man, but I almost felt sorry for him – it was as if she was just marrying him so that she could have her dream wedding. She was talking about having a chocolate fountain at the reception, vintage champagne; all that sort of thing. I guess all girls have their dreams – anyway, the reality was somewhat more modest, with a reception at The Claresby Arms and a few pints for Dean's mates, followed by a week in Eastbourne. I do remember that she wore a particularly beautiful lace veil – it didn't match the dress, which was a cream off-the-peg number, rather frilly. When I commented on how lovely the veil was, she said that it had been her grandmother's and she wore it for sentimental reasons. I counted this as a point in her favour."

"No weddings cancelled or broken engagements?" asked Rupert.

Veronica shook her head. "Not that I'm aware of. I had one cancelled wedding in my last parish which caused all sorts of upset; but nothing like that here. By the way, if Keith and I marry, it will be very private, with just two witnesses and a slice of cake afterwards."

"Yes – but you must promise that Rupert and I can be the witnesses," smiled Laura, who knew Keith Lowe, the local doctor, very well. She also knew that, many years ago, his fiancée had left him only weeks before his wedding; but this fact was not alluded to.

"Maybe," replied Veronica inscrutably.

Further discussion on this sensitive subject was precluded by a sudden bang and a howl of grief from Florence as the inevitable happened to her balloon. Rupert, the doting father, had come prepared, and immediately fished a new balloon (also pink) out of one of the pockets in his trousers and started inflating it. Florence, her attention caught by the apparent magic of a new balloon appearing from her father's mouth, ran over and clambered up beside him, poking the expanding balloon with an investigatory digit, the fresh tears still beading the peachy skin of her cheeks. Laura smiled indulgently at this scene, and gazed fondly on Rupert, whose face – which was ugly at the best of times – was distorted by the process of blowing air into the balloon. Naturally he could not resist letting a few squirts of air out of it, so that Florence giggled at the "rude" noise produced. Eventually the new balloon was tied off and the little girl happily resumed her game.

"I hope you have a whole pocketful of those things," commented Laura. Rupert obligingly put his hand into his pocket and displayed a hand full of multicoloured balloons. "You spoil that girl!" Laura retorted – but with a smile that said she both understood and approved.

"Why the question about cancelled weddings?" asked Veronica, returning to their original topic of conversation.

"Simply because I discovered a very beautiful, apparently expensive and unworn wedding dress in the old Rolls Royce in one of our outbuildings."

"Oh: I didn't know that you had a Rolls Royce."

"It's left over from the 1920s and has most of the engine missing," replied Laura. "Rupert's thinking of restoring it."

"And the dress was in the car? What makes you think it was put there recently?"

"Style, condition, and the fact that it was in a supermarket carrier bag," said Rupert. "It certainly wasn't from the same period as the car."

"Not ominously bloodstained?" asked Veronica.

"No: immaculately clean."

"So just a mystery about why it is there – no hint of a crime?"

"Anything like a mystery intrigues Rupert," said Laura. "It wouldn't surprise me if he did unravel a crime linked to the dress in due course."

It was a blustery October evening and Rupert was sitting in his favourite corner seat at The Claresby Arms, a virtually untouched pint in front of him as he waited for his friend, Keith Lowe, and amused himself by eavesdropping on his fellow drinkers – most of whom were familiar to him. The topic of conversation was the troubles of Pam Holmes, a local woman of about forty-five whom Rupert had occasionally encountered at the village church.

"Well, of course suspicion fell on her," a plump little woman was saying. "It's been nothing but spend, spend, spend since Christmas. They've had that conservatory put on the back of their place and now she's talking about booking a winter cruise in the Caribbean."

"Yeah, but she said that aunt of hers from Australia left her all the money," commented a skinny man who was leaning against the bar.

"So she *says*," replied the little woman, scepticism in her every syllable. "She'd never even mentioned the aunt before – and I've known her these forty years. And she's got some silly name like "Eunuch"!"

"Eunice," corrected a voice from further down the bar, helpfully.

"Whatever! She never visited Pam and I know Pam never went to Australia: so why would she want to leave her pots of money?"

"I've seen these programmes on telly about people who die without writing a will and they've got no close relations at all – and then they trace someone who is a distant cousin and they get all the money: maybe that's what happened with Pam." The man down the bar seemed to be full of helpful explanations and the little woman gave him rather a sour look.

"I've seen that programme too," confirmed the skinny man. "Maybe this was a long-lost aunt and Pam didn't even know about her until she was told about the money."

"Hope I've got a long-lost aunt with pots of money," commented another man, and everyone laughed.

"Still, I can understand Pam being annoyed," said the skinny man. "I'd heard rumours that they thought that someone had been pinching money from Baines and Hayes, but there's no proof it was Pam."

"Yes, but she does work in accounts, so it looks a bit suspicious," chipped in the little woman, who seemed determined to think the worst.

"Not if they don't have any evidence: innocent until proven guilty," said the man down the bar.

"Yes, and Pam could sue if they suggest it was her – that's defamation!" added the skinny man, as if he too wanted to look like he had inside knowledge of the law.

"No smoke without fire," muttered the woman.

Rupert was distracted by Keith's arrival and, by the time the two men had exchanged greetings and Keith had gone to fetch a pint for himself, the conversation had moved on.

Keith soon returned and launched into the subject of the Rolls Royce which Rupert was repairing, more than usually eager to offer his assistance as he shared Rupert's love of classic cars. By the time Rupert had bought them both a second pint, his mind returned to what he had heard about Baines and Hayes, which he knew to be a small engineering company based in the nearby town and which employed a number of people from Claresby village.

"As a GP, you must get to hear a bit of local gossip: have you heard anything about someone helping themselves to money at Baines and Hayes?"

"As it happens," replied Keith, after taking a long swig of beer, "I was chatting with Bill Baines just the other day – we play golf sometimes on a Saturday. They have picked up on the fact that there seems to be an unexplained black hole in their finances. He's checked through the accounts himself, but can't find any anomalies. They haven't called in the police yet, because they are not sure whether this is actually a case of fraud, poor accounting, or just that their expectations were unrealistic."

"You mean they don't know for sure that someone is taking money?"

"Not for sure. The problem started when one of the people who worked in accounts was seen to be splashing cash around in such a way as to start tongues wagging. This made Bill take a look at things and he did wonder if there might be something in the rumours. Having said that, they don't have any hard evidence that anyone has been siphoning money off and, now that they are keeping a sharp eye on things, everything seems above-board."

"I suppose it would – if someone thought they had been rumbled, they might be a bit more careful,"

"Perhaps. You know me; I hate rumours. It brings back memories of when Veronica was first appointed vicar here

194

and there were all those malicious stories about her just because her first husband was so much younger than her and died suddenly. I hear all sorts of things said, but I never pay much attention unless there is incontrovertible evidence."

Rupert nodded his agreement and decided to file the matter away for future consideration.

On a Tuesday morning, the Reverend Veronica Dahl ran a playgroup in the James Mortimer Rooms – a small extension at the back of the church which included a kitchen and toilets as well as a meeting room. Since the room was named after Laura's father, she thought it appropriate to take his granddaughter along once in a while. There were never more than a dozen mothers and grandmothers in attendance, with a selection or under-fours, who could play with a couple of boxes of toys whilst their carers drank coffee and chatted. The relative popularity of the group was put down to the fact that Veronica always provided generous supplies of chocolate biscuits and homemade cakes. As soon as Laura arrived, Florence made a beeline for a farm set, which was a particular favourite, and started setting up the somewhat chewed plastic animals. With half an eye on her daughter through the hatchway, Laura began to make tea and coffee whilst Veronica chatted to some of the mothers. Just as she was slicing the Victoria sponge, her attention was caught by the arrival of a rather flustered looking middle-aged woman who entered, exchanged a few words with Veronica, and left a small child of about two holding hands with the vicar. Laura recognised the little girl, who sometimes played with Florence, and her grandmother, Pam Holmes. Veronica gently led the little girl over to Florence, and the two of them seemed to settle to playing with the farm animals in an agreeable manner. Veronica came over to help herself to a coffee, and she and Laura went to sit in a quiet corner whilst one of the other mothers passed some biscuits around. It was generally a scene of content and friendly chatter.

"What was the problem with Pam?" inquired Laura.

"Well, she always babysits her granddaughter on a Tuesday – her day off work – and usually brings little Chloe along here. However, there has been some unpleasant gossip about her recently, and she pretty much said that she didn't want to deprive Chloe of playing with her friends as usual, but wasn't prepared to make friendly conversation with some of the other women, who had been so spiteful about her."

"Ah, I see. Rupert mentioned about the gossip surrounding Baines and Hayes."

"It makes me mad!" said Veronica, her green eyes flashing. "She actually came to see me after church on Sunday and showed me all the documentary proof that she had inherited money from an aunt. I assured her that I did not require to see anything of the kind, but she insisted. I think she thought that if I put it around that it was all legal and proper, people would stop attacking her. Of course, I will mention the facts when appropriate, but I also pointed out to her how hard it is to stop malicious gossip. Remember when Arthur first came up to my house to take a shower and to have dinner with me? I could tell people he was my brother and needed a bit of help until I was blue in the face, but it didn't stop some of them drawing their own conclusions and calling me "harlot" and other nice things."

Laura nodded understandingly.

"I did suggest that she showed the documents to Bill Baines, so as to remove any suspicion that she had taken money from his company, but I think she was just too angry with him. I can't say I blame her. She's still doing her job – mostly out of bravado, I think – but she said that all the pleasure has gone out of it. The girls from the office used to be really friendly – they even had weekly pub lunches out together – but I think all that has changed. She's had the same job for twenty years and carried on there more for the comradeship than the money in any case. She even showed me an album she kept of some of their lunches at The King's Head just down the road from where they work: I think it's all been a bit traumatic for her."

Laura nodded again and stored away all these snippets of information to pass on to Rupert – knowing that where there was mystery or misunderstanding, he would want to dip his fingers in. Sure enough, when she relayed these facts to him over their supper that night he said,

"I wonder if I could persuade Pam to show me those pictures of the pub lunches."

"Well, you'd have to be sensitive if approaching her, as she's feeling pretty sore at the moment. What do you expect the photos to show anyway?" asked Laura.

Rupert shrugged his wide, angular shoulders, "I don't know. I never know what will provide helpful information and what won't; but I am curious about the goings-on at Baines and Hayes, and if Veronica has seen evidence that Pam was not in any way responsible for a possible cash-shortfall, it makes me wonder who else might be."

"As it happens, I've arranged to take Florence to have lunch with Chloe at Pam's on Saturday, so I'll see if I can borrow the album."

True to her word, Laura managed to tactfully request a viewing of the photograph album of the girls from Baines and Hayes, and passed it into the hands of a curious Rupert, who flicked through the pages with intense interest.

"So; does it tell you anything?" asked Laura, as she watched her husband stoop his long frame over the coffee table on which the photograph album was placed.

"Well, yes – it tells me who was taking money from the

company; why, what happened to that money – and why no suspicion fell on them!" declared Rupert. "What it doesn't provide is one scintilla of proof of these assumptions!"

Laura looked at her husband with a doubtful expression, her pretty oval faced creased in concern.

"Really, Rupert, sometimes I can't tell if you are serious or not. How can you possibly glean all that information from a few photos of a group of women having a pub lunch?"

"Quite simply – because I started off with a bit of background information and put two and two together. Let me show you..." He shifted companionably along the chintz settee until he was sitting close to his wife and placed the album between them. "You will recognise some of the women from Claresby village. There's Pam, obviously – and that is Susan Hamble and Ellen Finch."

Laura nodded. Claresby was a small village and everyone met up from time to time either at the church, outside the village school, at the post-office, or in the pub: so these were all familiar faces.

"I don't know who those two are," continued Rupert, pointing to some figures in a smiling group, "but that is Amy Phipps, née Price, just after her honeymoon."

"Yes – she does look well in that picture," acknowledged Laura.

"Doesn't she just," agreed Rupert. "Something to do with the glowing suntan, perhaps: which is interesting, because Veronica told us that she spent her honeymoon in Eastbourne."

"Maybe it is just the glow of a happy newlywed."

"More like a Caribbean tan!" rejoined the unromantic Rupert. "If you remember, Veronica told us that Amy seemed to have grandiose plans for her wedding – to include a honeymoon in Bermuda – but in fact settled for a modest wedding and a week in rainy Eastbourne."

"Well, she certainly didn't get that suntan is Eastbourne this July – but she might have used a sun bed to get a pre-wedding tan."

"Maybe – except that Pam happens to have been a guest at Amy's wedding: and here is the picture of Amy with a classic English pallor. She is also wearing the lovely white lace veil which doesn't match her cream dress."

"Didn't Veronica say that it had belonged to her grandmother?" said Laura.

"Yes; and that may explain the difference in style and quality." Rupert's voice expressed scepticism.

"You have a different explanation?" said Laura.

"I do. I think the veil was meant to go with another dress altogether – in fact, the very dress we found in the Rolls Royce."

"It would seem to have been designed to match that dress," agreed Laura, studying the veil in the photograph with care.

"So, let us assume that Amy had started off with the lavish wedding plans and the extravagant dress – what would make her change her plans?"

"The fact that her friends from work would wonder where she had found the money to pay for such an event," said Laura, following Rupert's train of thought.

"Exactly. Suspicion had been raised by Pam's spending, and the boss at Baines and Hayes thought that money had been siphoned off."

"But there was no evidence of Pam doing anything amiss."

"But Amy might have been taking the money to fund her dream wedding and exotic honeymoon."

"Then she panicked and decided to play things safe and settle for a modest wedding," continued Laura.

"She dumped the dress, but couldn't resist wearing the lovely veil."

"And hung on to the honeymoon in Barbados – but lied to

everyone about where she was going."

"Precisely," said Rupert.

"In that case, Dean must have known what was going on – or he would have wondered where the money came from. But, Rupert, this is all the merest speculation; and I wouldn't want to spread unfounded rumours about Amy and Dean."

"No more would I," agreed Rupert. "But I have an idea how we might prove the connection between Amy and the dress. I'm guessing that she wants it back – it is her design and her dream. As it happens, on the walk between Baines and Hayes and the pub where the ladies from the office lunch, is a charity shop. I'm going to arrange for the wedding dress I found to be displayed in the window at a very modest price. The lady in the shop will inform anyone interested that the dress is reserved, but to leave their name and telephone number in case the buyer changes her mind. I want to see if Amy Phipps tries to retrieve her dress."

"It wouldn't prove anything."

"No, but it would make me sufficiently suspicious of her to feel justified in letting Bill Baines know that he should be checking out Amy, not Pam," concluded Rupert.

October was mellow and lovely, delivering more sunshine than the summer months, and Laura and Rupert were able to enjoy walks in the grounds of Claresby Manor, looking back at the medieval house nestled serenely amidst its shrubberies and walled gardens. The blackberries were over, but Florence always managed to pick up a few more conkers for her vast collection. Despite the warmth of the weather, the draughty and dark interior of the manor required log fires to make it welcoming, and Rupert even picked up a few fallen branches from their woods to add to the fire in the Great Hall, where they crackled and spat wetly. Shortly after they had returned, and Laura had taken Florence to the kitchen to make hot chocolate, the phone rang. Laura could hear Rupert's voice for a few moments, and then he came to join them, declining the chocolate and making himself coffee.

"That was the lady in the charity shop," he informed Laura. "Not only did Amy Phipps come in to buy the dress, but she became pretty agitated when it was explained to her that someone had already tried it on and reserved it and was going to come back with a friend before making a final decision. Apparently Amy insisted that no one had any right to reserve something when she was ready to buy it upfront with cash – twice as much as the asking price if necessary. The lady held her ground, however, and promised to phone her up if the dress was not sold."

"Did Amy give any explanation as to why she would want to buy a wedding dress a few months *after* her wedding?"

"She said she was getting married at Christmas – which my lady found pretty unconvincing as she could clearly see her wedding ring!"

"What a pity," said Laura, adding cold milk to Florence's drink. "It does suggest that the dress was hers – and I can't think of any reason why she would have hidden it other than that we surmised."

"Well, I'll suggest to Bill that he takes an unobtrusive look at what she's been up to at work. As it happens, he's going to be at the vicarage for dinner on Sunday night, so perhaps we'll find out what transpires."

"I hope it turns out to be a case of another rich Australian aunt," said Laura.

Florence had been left with a babysitter and Rupert and Laura had taken the short walk to the vicarage so that they could enjoy the excellent red wine that Keith always brought along to Veronica's dinners in liberal quantities. The group around the table enjoying roast beef and Yorkshire puddings included the bluff and somewhat rotund Bill Baines and his plump, friendly wife, Louise. Initial conversation turned on Rupert's progress with the Rolls Royce.

"I'm going to have the entire chassis rebuilt," Rupert was saying happily. "And Laura wants it painted in navy blue with silver accessories."

"It has precisely two thirds of its engine, at present," added Laura, "so it will be quite a mission to find authentic working parts to complete it. Rupert's been scouring the internet, but some things will have to be custom made."

"You don't expect to be driving around in it anytime soon," said Bill Baines, with a wink.

"I think we are talking more fun than function," said Laura. "And I will be keeping the Range Rover for everyday purposes."

The plates were dexterously cleared by Veronica who soon returned with a large apple crumble and jug of custard.

"Claresby Manor apples," she announced. "Laura let me scrump in her orchard."

"It was a particularly good year for apples," explained Laura. "I have boxes of them in the cellar, so just drop round, Louise, if you want any."

"I like apple crumble," said Bill, his mouth full.

"Oh, well, I'd better take up the offer," smiled Louise.

"So," said Keith, addressing Bill, "did you tell Rupert and Laura the outcome of your office investigations?"

Bill's pleasant, round face creased into a frown at the memory. "No; but I will give you an update – in confidence. Unfortunately Rupert was quite right to tip me off about Amy Phipps. It seems she's been siphoning money off for several years by the simple expedient of double and triple ordering various items of office equipment. It was her job, you see, to keep the place up to date with coffee makers, photocopiers, fridges and even hanging baskets and tubs for out the front. Apparently her husband, Dean, was selling things on over the internet. Amy was signing off all the orders and we didn't have an adequate system of double checks."

"Bill's paying the price of being too trusting by half," said his wife.

"Well, there may be a bit more to it than that," said Bill cryptically, "but you get the gist. Of course I've apologised to Pam for ever suspecting her."

"How sad," said Veronica, earnestly, her beautiful face cast down. "All for a bit of extra frippery at a wedding. I think I'll ban flowers from the church and insist that all brides wear a standard issue dress – with coffee and biscuits at the back of the church afterwards."

"I don't think that will catch on," said Laura with a smile.

"Perhaps not," admitted Veronica. "But maybe Keith and I will model a new-austerity style wedding and hope that we set a trend."

Postscript: Rupert's renovated Rolls Royce made its first outing shortly after Florence turned five.

The Curious Legacy

Rupert Latimer's benign face creased into a frown as he sat in the kitchen of Claresby Manor eating his eggs and bacon. He held his fork in one hand and a recently opened letter in his other, and it was the latter that caused him to frown.

"How odd!" he exclaimed.

"What's odd?" asked his wife, Laura, with her attention still mostly on her own, rather larger, pile of morning post.

"Do you remember old Mr Hodge who lived at the big house near the other end of the village?"

"Little chap, very elderly, something of a recluse – didn't he die recently? I know that Veronica and Keith visited him a lot earlier this year because he needed a bit of help."

"Yes – that's the chap: Gordon Hodge. Well, this is a solicitor's letter informing me that he left everything to me in his will."

Laura put down the document she was reading and frowned back at Rupert. "Why did he do that? I didn't think you knew him."

"I didn't," said Rupert. "I recall wishing him a good morning once about two years ago when I happened to pass him in the lane, but I think that was the highlight of our acquaintance."

"Well, he must have been without any family and was just searching for someone trustworthy to look after his estate," said Laura, to whom this seemed quite reasonable. Having inherited her family's ancestral home – subsequently discovering a small fortune in treasure hidden in the grounds – not to mention acquiring further property which had come her way from an uncle, the sudden bequest of a house didn't strike her as anything out of the common way. "Perhaps Veronica can find some use for it in the parish," was all she contributed.

Rupert sat thoughtfully whilst Laura returned to perusing her letters. For some reason a verse he had stumbled on whilst flicking through his bible in one of Veronica's less interesting sermons the previous week popped into his mind: *Matthew 25:29 For everyone who has will be given more, and he will have an abundance. Whoever does not have, even what he has will be taken from him.* He hadn't been able to make sense of this at the time as he had taken it to imply that those who were already well off would be given more, whilst the poor would lose out. He thought that this was probably reflected in the world he saw around him, but it didn't seem very fair. He'd have to ask Veronica to explain the meaning of the verse to him – he was probably taking it out of context. Anyway, the fact remained that he and Laura were already very comfortably situated in life and hardly in need of a sudden windfall of this kind. Having said that, the fact of the matter was that everything they owned really belonged to Laura. Admittedly he lived in the lovely, historic house and had access to a well stocked joint bank account; but the reality was that these were his by marriage and he had never personally owned more than the clothes he stood up in and a few personal possessions. His only earnings were generated by the writing of crosswords, and a generous description of the income produced would be "pocket money". For this reason, the notion of inheriting a house – albeit from a virtual stranger – had more of a charm to him than it would to Laura.

Rupert folded the letter carefully and tucked it into the inside pocket of his jacket as he helped his wife clear the table. It was a chilly but dry November morning and, leaving Laura to occupy their daughter with some building bricks in the cosy morning room, he went into the village, ostensibly to pick up some fresh eggs from the corner shop, but actually

206

with an interest in walking past the house to which the solicitor's letter had referred. Claresby wasn't a large village and from the manor house – which stood on the eastern corner, close to the church – it was only a brisk walk into the centre, which incorporated a few shops and a pub next to the village green, and out the other side to where The Red House stood in a rather isolated position. It was a handsome rather than a beautiful house, taking its name from the red bricks with which it was constructed. It had a Victorian appearance, large windows and an imposing front door with a stained glass panel in a tiled porch. As would-be proprietor, Rupert took the liberty of opening the little gate and walking up the path, taking in the over-grown garden and dilapidated appearance of the main building. The former occupant had given the impression of being rather eccentric, and the whole place exuded an air altogether unwelcoming. The only thing that struck Rupert favourably was the pleasant view which the house commanded across the lane and over the fields to the low hills beyond.

As it happened, on the way back from his visit to The Red House, Rupert encountered Veronica Dahl. She gave him a friendly smile.

"Good morning, Rupert. It's a nice day for a stroll. I've been doing my parish rounds. Carrie Floyd has a new baby: a little girl called Tiffany."

Rupert fell into step with his friend whose beauty and feminine appeal were undimmed by the fact that she wore a clergy shirt and dog collar with plain black trousers. After a brief exchange about the weather he asked,

"What do you know about Gordon Hodge, former resident of The Red House? I've just been taking a look at the place."

"Very little: he was private to the point of being reclusive. When I held his funeral the only people present, apart from myself, were Keith, Bernie Smith – his solicitor – and old

Annie Hart, who has attended almost every Claresby funeral for the last thirty years. Oh, and Vince, who had done the digging."

"Laura mentioned that you and Keith visited him in his last months."

"Well, Keith was his GP, so his visits were mainly professional, although I know he did do a few jobs about the house – Gordon got very upset if things weren't just-so. My visits were professional too, but I tried to keep an eye on him and took a bit of shopping in from time to time. He was a very courteous gentleman and seemed grateful for the help. I even got the odd cup of tea out of him, but he never opened up to me as some people do, particularly in a final illness."

"He never mentioned any family, then?"

"No. There were a couple of photographs in the house, but I think they were of the previous owner; or so he said."

"Is there anyone in the village who might know anything about his past? – he must have been living here for decades."

"Well, as it happens, I'm just calling in to see Annie. She's lived in Claresby all her life and never misses a thing. She'd be absolutely thrilled if you asked her to delve into her memories. Why the interest, by the way? – there wasn't the slightest hint of his death being anything other than nature taking its course."

"Just that I've learned that he left me his house: I rather wonder why."

Veronica raised a quizzical eyebrow. "I didn't know that you were acquainted with him."

"I wasn't," admitted Rupert, "other than bumping into him on the occasional walk. That's why I am curious about what made him tick."

"Well, let's see what Annie has to say. She'll be delighted to have you drop in on her."

Annie's little cottage looked out onto the village green and

208

was as near to the centre of Claresby as it was possible to be. For someone of Rupert's stature the low beamed cottage presented all sorts of hazards and, other than when he was sitting down in one of the sagging settees in the crowded little room, he was virtually stooped double. There was a merry fire blazing in the grate, and a couple of tabby cats came to wind round their legs and present their ears to be tickled. A quick glance around revealed a collection of ornaments and a number of magazines; but although the old lady had a radio, there was no sign of a television – Claresby village provided her with all the entertainment she needed. It was as well that Rupert had the insatiable appetite of a young man with a large frame and very little flesh to fill it, so that the two slices of Dundee cake and a scone lavished with jam which accompanied the cups of tea he was given proved no problem, despite his having eaten a full English breakfast little more than an hour before. Talk revolved around the more good-natured end of village gossip as Annie insisted that Tiffany Floyd, whom she'd seen the previous day, was the image of her great grandmother, who had been at school with Annie. At some point Veronica skilfully entered the name of Gordon Hodge into the conversation. This was all the encouragement Annie needed to divulge everything she knew.

"I remember Gordon from the bank over in town – he was cashier there for many a year, always polite, but never friendly. Kept himself to himself. You could see him every week for years and he'd still keep you at arm's length. And he was a neighbour of mine to begin with – had the cottage two down from me for twenty years or more, but I hardly saw him, except when he would come and go to work. Took the bus every day, he did. Not a Claresby man, he moved here – oh, it must have been mid-sixties. I think he was in his thirties, but looked older. He always had a pale, washed-out look to him. Little, insignificant man he was, who never made his way up in the bank, although I don't doubt that he was clever enough. He was the kind of person who would always be overlooked and was too mild-mannered to make a fuss about the fact. He never married. Of course, the really interesting thing about him was that he was bequeathed The Red House. It belonged to Janice Lacey – real beauty, she was – but no one knew much about where she came from either. She must have moved to Claresby in about 1980. Didn't know that the two of them were friends, although there were rumours that he would slip up to visit her from time to time. Couldn't see it, myself: why would a woman like her take a fancy to a man like him? Still, there must have been something in it, because when she died, the house was his."

"Did he get many visitors to The Red House?" asked Rupert.

The old lady shook her head. "No: only those in Claresby who felt a duty. Your lovely wife's father would pay a visit once in a while – old Mr Mortimer was a real gentleman. Used to bring produce from the manor gardens to all sorts, although we all knew he didn't have much money himself back then. The only time Gordon seemed to come out of his shell was when we started an art club once a month in the old village hall. A group of us used to get someone in to demonstrate how to do a watercolour – that sort of thing. Sometimes we'd bring our own bit of work along and have a practical evening. I used to do watercolours; until my hands became too unsteady."

There was a brief interlude as Annie selected a few little framed pictures of beautifully executed botanical studies and Veronica and Rupert showed that they were suitably impressed. Then the old lady picked up a miniature to show them. It was an oval of no more than at inch long at its widest and showed a delicate profile like a cameo brooch.

"This is exquisite!" exclaimed Veronica. "And I do believe that this is you, Annie."

Annie smiled happily, "So it is," she said. "And that was drawn in pen on paper by Gordon one evening at our art group. An amazing talent he had for working in tiny detail. He could have carved into a pinhead. Just worked on that quietly one evening, and handed it to me before I went home. The group folded not long after – not enough interest in the village – and I don't think he ever spoke one word to me again. I went to his funeral, though. Of course Bill Smith recently revived the club, but I no longer attend."

Annie soon went to unearth some more of her paintings and tried to ply them with yet more cake and tea, but eventually Veronica and Rupert had to offer their thanks and leave the slightly stuffy cottage for the brisk air without.

"What did you make of all that?" asked Veronica.

"Nothing to tell me why he should choose to leave me his house, other than the fact that he appears not to have had any particular friends – and also, I suppose, that he had come across it somewhat fortuitously himself. I wouldn't mind knowing a little more about the original owner – Laura might even remember something from her childhood. Also, when I have the keys to the place, the contents might tell their own story."

"Looks like you'll have something to occupy your winter evenings," smiled Veronica. "Well, I'd better be off; I'm meeting Keith for lunch."

The two parted and Rupert continued his walk back to Claresby Manor deep in thought.

Rupert was unable to make any further progress in discovering why the elusive Gordon Hodge should have bequeathed his property to him until he was given the keys to The Red House. The only snippet of information which had been added to what Annie had said was that Laura vaguely recalled Janice Lacey as a very pretty lady who had died quite young. So it was with a considerable sense of anticipation that Rupert opened the front door to the empty house. The first thing that struck him was the chill. This, of course, was inevitable given the time of year and the fact that the place was uninhabited. Someone had been in since the former occupant's death – perhaps at the behest of the solicitors who were the executors – so that everything was in order, the fridge empty of food, dirty laundry removed, and all signs of a final illness swept away. There was a small heap of post on the doormat, but most had already been set on a neat little side table in the entrance hall.

The house was grand but rather formidable, with heavy staircase and gallery with oak banisters. In contrast all the furnishings, pictures and ornaments that met Rupert's eyes as he entered the downstairs rooms one by one had a rather feminine feel to them. Ornaments were dainty, the upholstery pink and floral and the paintings obviously chosen to match the decor rather than for any intrinsic artistic value. The main upstairs bedroom was similarly feminine in feel with lots of lace and ruched pink curtains. Clearly this was the room inhabited by Gordon Hodge, the other bedrooms showing signs of having being locked up and discarded for a long period of time, but he had left no mark upon it. Even the towels still hanging in the bathroom were pink. Other than a wardrobe of men's clothes, there was no suggestion of male habitation. Indeed, the little collection of trousers and jumpers clearly belonging to Gordon Hodge paled into insignificance against the larger wardrobe which contained a fine array of designer dresses and the long racks of high-heeled shoes. Not only had Gordon inherited the house from Janice Lacey, but he had moved into it virtually as a camper, leaving her personal effects in place for over twenty years. The house had more to say about the long-gone Janice than the recently deceased Gordon.

It was perhaps indicative of Rupert's personality that he did not stop at taking a look around the reception rooms and bedrooms on this, his first visit to The Red House, but took the trouble to pull down the loft ladder that gave access to the wide, draughty, boarded space above. Fortunately, for the purposes of his investigations, there was a light switch and a single light bulb rigged up, which produced a dim, shadowy light. As well as a functioning water tank, and an old one which had been too bulky to remove, there were three suitcases and a couple of items of broken furniture. There was also a very old perambulator which must have belonged to previous occupants unknown.

The three suitcases proved to contain a selection of paper bags and carrier bags, all carefully folded and saved as if by a thrifty person who thought they might prove useful. Rupert was reminded of his maternal grandmother who, at Christmas, had always removed the wrapping paper from her gifts with extreme care, smoothed it out, folded it up and preserved it for reuse the following year. Rupert had put this down to a frugal wartime mentality which she had developed and never shaken off when more profligate and comfortable times had come. He rather thought that the meticulous and prudent Gordon might have shared this attitude. Having assured himself that there was nothing more than paper bags in the cases, he took a quick look in the pram, vaguely expecting more of the same. Sure enough, there were a number of carrier bags containing what looked like more paper. Rupert opened one up to examine it further and was presented with bundles of crisp new banknotes. A rapid search through the other bags in the pram revealed the same – bundles of unused notes, mostly for ten, but some for twenty pounds. In the last bag of all he also found an envelope. It was addressed quite clearly to "Rupert Latimer" in a very small but clear hand. Rupert opened it with eager interest and read the note inside.

Unusually, Laura has set out their dinner that night on the big oak table of the Great Hall. Even with a fire blazing in the broad stone fireplace, the place could never be cosy. It didn't help that the carved gargoyles of the musicians' gallery above looked faintly sinister in the shadows created by the fire and the candles that Laura had lit. There was an unwritten understanding between them that this was the anniversary of when they had become friends, exchanging their troubles during a difficult first term at university over a formal dinner at Rupert's Cambridge College. In fact, in contrast to the medieval grandeur of the setting and the fine old goblets into which Laura poured the champagne, the rest of the table was strewn with the boxes containing a takeaway Chinese meal – Rupert's favourite. They sat in the tall backed, carved oak chairs and tucked in to the food whilst discussing Rupert's visit to The Red House that day.

"Were there any documents or photographs that told you anything about the background of Gordon Hodge or Janice Lacey?" Laura was asking as he ladled steaming rice onto her plate.

"No," replied Rupert. "Nothing so obvious. In fact I think that Gordon had gone to pains to destroy any useful documents. The only two items which he seems to have been uncharacteristically sentimental about were two photographs – one of a young Janice standing outside a pub, and one of an old lady, perhaps his mother, standing outside a rather run down Victorian terraced house. There were some more recent pictures of Janice too; but always on her own, never with Gordon. She was a very pretty woman with fair hair and blue eyes. There was also Janice's death certificate carefully folded in an envelope. She died in 1990 of lung cancer. It gave her place of birth as Rotherhithe. She was only forty-five."

"But you said that he had left a letter for you explaining why he gave you the house: aren't you going to read that to me now? I don't know why you were being so mysterious about it earlier." There was a slight scowl on her face which did nothing to mar her delicate features and natural prettiness.

"Simply because of where I found the note," explained Rupert, his chin jutting out as he shovelled large forkfuls of food into his mouth. "Considering that he could have left an explanation in his will or even a confidential letter to me with the solicitor, it indicates quite a tricky turn of mind that he hid it in an old pram up in the attic! Also, I didn't tell you everything when I got in – partly because I was still processing the facts myself. The pram in which I found the letter also contained a small fortune in brand new bank notes."

Laura stopped with her fork midway to her mouth. "Bank notes? – stolen from the bank?" she asked in surprise.

"Well, he was a cashier," admitted Rupert, "but he spent most of his working life in our own local branch, and if there had been a big scandal or theft there, it would have been talked about in Claresby for years to come. Of course, I can't rule out that possibility and I will make some inquiries."

"You still haven't told me what the letter said," continued Laura.

"Oh," Rupert reached into his pocket and unfolded some paper whilst finishing his mouthful of food, "it says – *With your reputation for investigatory skills, you should be able to unravel my story. I would like the satisfaction of the*

215

details being made public. After that you may dispose of my wealth as you see fit. It's signed by Gordon Hodge."

"Interesting. And yet you say he seems to have destroyed most of his personal papers? Why would he do that if he wants you to find the truth?"

Rupert shrugged, "Either he destroyed them at a point in time when he didn't want anyone to find the truth or he just liked the idea of me having to do some leg-work. In a perverse way I prefer the challenge. If he had just written an explanation or confession, I would not have become invested in unravelling the story – perhaps he wanted someone to take a real interest in his history. We'll have to wait and see what I turn up – that may explain his motives."

"And in the meantime, he's done you more of a favour by providing you with a mystery to solve than he did by leaving you his possibly-dodgy fortune."

"Precisely!" said Rupert cheerfully.

The following morning Rupert commenced his search into the history of Gordon Hodge and Janice Lacey courtesy of the evidence provided by the two photographs. He was helped in this search by that fact that picture of Janice showed a young woman in her early twenties standing outside what he took to be a London pub with its name prominently displayed. She was holding an empty tray in one hand and had an embarrassed, slightly furtive smile on her face as if not expecting to have her picture taken and unsure whether it was a good idea to allow it. Rupert was starting off by using the internet as his search tool. The pub bore a very common name and he searched this name along with Janice's place of birth and soon found an up-to-date picture of the same pub. He knew little about this particular area of London, except that it was historically a port but the docks had been closed and it was now a residential area. He thought the picture of the old woman outside a house quite likely to be taken in the same sort of area of inner London. It showed a common type of meagre Victorian terraced house with just a front door and a lower and upper window. The simple process of searching a street-view map of the area immediately around the pub quickly revealed the very house. If, as he thought, this was Gordon's mother and he had grown up in the house, it was a fair guess that Gordon had met Janice when she was a barmaid at the pub around the corner where he went for a pint, either when he still lived there or when he visited his mother. Rupert gave a grunt of satisfaction. A visit to the area might confirm his guess.

The second thing that Rupert did was to put on his coat and take the bus from Claresby into the nearby town to visit the bank where Gordon had started working about forty-seven years before – if Annie Hart's memory was to be trusted. His inquiries at the bank were rewarded by the name Gilbert Howe – a man now in his eighties who was manager at the time that Gordon would have been there. He still lived in South Marlesby, a neighbouring village which Rupert knew very well. The retired manager was apparently held in some esteem at his old branch and visited weekly to conduct his banking business. Rupert left his name and telephone number, asking that these be passed on with a request that he could meet the old gentleman at a time to suit him. The time and place that suited Gilbert Howe turned out to be lunchtime at The King's Head in Marlesby the following day.

The unspoken understanding was that Rupert would provide lunch and Gilbert would provide memories. The pub was homely and warm and Gilbert seemed to be well acquainted with both the barman and the menu. He had soon ordered the liver and bacon and Rupert followed suit. On Rupert's inquiry he expressed a preference for white wine;

so Rupert bought a bottle, hoping that it would prove sufficient to loosen the man's tongue whilst not fuddling his mind. Over the first glass of wine Gilbert brought up the name of Gordon Hodge,

"When I originally got your message, I struggled to remember much about the fellow," confessed Gilbert, who had a round, boyish face which belied his years, and astute, twinkling eyes sunk a little in the folds of age. "I do recall your wife's late father, James Mortimer, very well. I've dined at Claresby Hall with him more than once. Affable fellow. And I recall Laura as a bright little girl. Anyway, Gordon was one of those men you could work alongside for years without ever getting past the surface impression – and that impression was not very edifying. He was a Londoner; not well educated but probably no fool. I imagine that he had been expected to leave school at the first opportunity to help out with the family bills. He never rose above cashier and never seemed to make much effort to recommend himself, although he was reliable enough. I think he retired in his late fifties with ill health – although I've just heard that he died only recently, so his health must have been reasonably good. Mind you, I took early retirement too and am still enjoying a pub lunch with a new acquaintance; so I can't complain! Why the interest? He always struck me as a rather dull character?"

"I inherited his house and found a good deal of cash in the attic," replied Rupert frankly. "He had inherited the house himself from a friend, and the money could have come from anywhere; I don't mean to imply the money was dishonestly obtained."

"Good-grief! Well, I can assure you that he was always considered scrupulously honest; whatever his other foibles might have been. I can't pretend to have liked the man, but there was never any hint of impropriety in my time or since."

"No, I've never heard any such suggestion," Rupert replied carefully. "It just seemed odd for the man to keep so much cash about the place. Wouldn't it be better to keep gold if you want to store your money under the mattress, so-to-speak?"

"Oh, we'd all like some gold under out mattress," smiled Gilbert, whilst acknowledging with gratitude the arrival of the liver and bacon. "But if there's one thing you learn as a bank manager it is that people can be very funny about money. Some want to hide how much they have from a spouse or children. Then there was one person – whose name I will not mention - who lived the most frugal of lives in a very modest house, whilst keeping a fortune of money in the bank untouched. It all went to charity in the end. Then there were those with deposit boxes full of gold jewellery which was never worn – a form of insurance policy, I suppose. But you say that it was notes you found? Were they recent? By the way, even if they are old and have been withdrawn from circulation they can be redeemed at the Bank of England – in my experience most high street banks will accept them."

"Some of the ten pound notes show Florence Nightingale – I checked it out and think that particular note was introduced in 1975. Some are the older, brown note which was withdrawn in 1979. Then there are the twenty pound notes with a Shakespeare theme which I believe were available from 1970 until 1991. So it seems is that the notes all date from the time that Gordon was working in the bank in the 1970s. I haven't tried to spend any of it yet. How easy is it to spot a forgery?"

"Oh, I used to pride myself on being able to tell a forgery just by feeling the texture of a note," beamed Gilbert, helping himself to a third glass of wine. "And of course now when they make bank notes they use sophisticated devices

219

such as holograms and embedded strips. There was always a small incidence of forged notes, but they were quickly removed from the system and destroyed. Probably you've heard of the best known case – Operation Bernhard?"

Rupert shook his head and Gilbert, looking gratified, mopped some of his gravy up with his mashed potato and took a mouthful before continuing,

"Well, during the war, the Nazis thought that they might be able to destabilise the British economy by dropping loads of forged banknotes into our country. The plan never quite came off, but some of the forged notes did enter into circulation. One practical upshot of this was the fact that we did away with many of the larger denominations whilst forgeries of five pound notes were gradually removed from the system. We no longer have a one hundred pound note and, after the war, it wasn't until 1981 that the fifty pound note was reinstated. I'm not saying that forgeries no longer occur, but it's not an easy game. If Gordon was stockpiling money in his attic it was because he was an odd fellow – I don't for a moment think they would be forgeries."

The two men finished up their lunch with spotted dick and custard and Rupert returned to Claresby Manor with the question of why there was so much money concealed in a pram in Gordon Hodge's old home unanswered. He found Laura in the kitchen making apple pies. She kissed him briskly, leaving flour marks on his jumper sleeve, and carried on with her rolling and cutting whilst he sat at the large, well scrubbed table.

"How was your lunch?" Laura asked.

"Nice lunch, pleasant man; no progress on finding out where the money came from. Gordon's old manager just hinted that some folks are a bit odd about money. He was a little dismissive of Gordon – uneducated Londoner, that sort of thing. There might be the hint of the snob in Gilbert

Howe, and it may explain why Gordon was never promoted, despite the fact that Gilbert acknowledged that he was intelligent, hardworking and reliable."

"But you don't know that it was Gordon's money in the first place, "said Laura sensibly. "He inherited the house from Janice and we don't know anything about her. She must have been pretty well off to buy The Red House in the first place. Where did her money come from?"

"I guess the house is worth over half a million now – so, yes, she must have had some money; but the picture I have of her shows a barmaid."

"Perhaps she robbed a bank?" suggested Laura helpfully.

"Maybe she did," acknowledged Rupert. "I'm going to see the pub where she worked tomorrow. A lot of time has passed, but I might find out something about her there."

As it turned out, Rupert's luck was in when he made his way to the Rotherhithe pub pictured in the photograph of Janice. It was a free house which had been in the Bullock family for three generations and still had a fine selection of real ales on tap. The family lived on the premises and there were a couple of rooms available for guests. It was a smart, square fronted brick building, very well maintained and comfortable within. But the first thing that struck Rupert as he entered was that the landlady, who was pulling a pint and chatting to the customer at the bar, bore a striking resemblance to Janice Lacey. Rupert waited his turn before ordering a pint himself and asking if sandwiches were available, it being still before midday.

"Yes, no problem," smiled the woman, who was a shapely blonde in her late thirties or early forties. "Beef and mustard, ham, cheese?"

"The beef would be nice," said Rupert with a smile. "By the way, if you have a moment, could you tell me if you

221

recognise the lady in this picture?"

The woman put Rupert's pint down in front of him and glanced over at the picture,

"Well, it's this pub, isn't it?" she said with mild interest. "She looks kind of familiar. When was it taken?"

"I don't know for sure," admitted Rupert. "Maybe forty years ago."

"Oh, my dad would be the one to ask, then. He's over in the corner keeping an eye on me – aren't you dad?" She gave a wink in the direction of an elderly man who sat on his own with a half finished pint in front of him. The man glowered back at her. He was a big, bullish man who didn't do anything to encourage Rupert to come and join him. Rupert, however, smiled and sat on the opposite side of the little round table,

"I'll sit here and wait for my sandwich," he said in a friendly way. "Nice pub this."

"Been in the family three generations," said the man. "Always managed to keep our independence: that's why people come here – best beer for miles."

"This is a nice drop," agreed Rupert, taking a good swig of his own drink. "I take it that you ran the pub before your daughter?"

"I still do my share," said the man, "but Trudy and her husband have taken over now. I'm John Bullock and my father, James, was landlord before me."

"So you'll probably recognise the lady in this picture?" Rupert passed the photograph across the table. The man only looked at it for a moment, but it was a long enough glance for Rupert to detect signs of recognition in it. No comment was returned, so he prompted, "One of your barmaids, was she?"

"Where did you get this?" was the response.

"It was in a house which I recently inherited – she was one

of the previous owners."

"Dead, is she?"

"As far as I know she died about two decades ago."

"She'd have only have been in her forties, then – not much older than Trudy here. They look alike."

"Yes, I thought there was a resemblance," said Rupert.

"The woman's my sister: Janice."

"That would be Janice Bullock?"

"That's right."

"And she moved away?" pursued Rupert.

"Disappeared more like. Didn't know what happened to her. My dad was furious. Don't know where she would have gone to. She didn't have any money and left with nothing more than what she stood up in. We tried to find her, but we never heard another word. What did she get up to, then?"

"I don't know much myself. She came to live in Claresby village, where I live now. She was well liked locally; that's all I know."

"Why are you bringing that picture in here then?"

"I was trying to make a connection with a man called Gordon Hodge: he's the man who left me the house."

"Never heard of him," replied John Bullock shortly.

"He was rather a slight man, fair hair, pale face. I think he grew up just around the corner from here. I wondered if you remember him coming into the pub to chat to Janice?"

"A couple of blokes used to hang around after Janice, but she never paid them much attention – my dad wouldn't have liked it."

Rupert's plate of sandwiches arrived in the hands of Janice's niece.

"Here – that's your Aunty Janice!" said the thickset old man, suddenly seeming to take an interest.

"Looks like me, doesn't she?" said Janice. "Except that I lighten my hair. It was a bit of a family mystery, where she

223

got to, wasn't it, dad?"

"This man says she died years ago."

"Oh, I'm sorry," said Trudy, automatically clearing away her father's now empty glass. "Where did she get to?"

"She lived in Claresby village until her death," repeated Rupert.

"Don't think I've heard of that place," said Trudy. "I hope she was happy. What my dad isn't saying was that my granddad could be a bit of a bully."

"Thought he owned my sister," admitted John Bullock. "I didn't always get on with him myself; but he was a good landlord."

"And you don't have any pictures of her or any idea if she had any gentleman friend?"

"My dad threw all her stuff out after six months," said John. "That was it, really. We never much spoke about her again, although I did think about her quite a bit. She was younger than me and I suppose I felt I should have done more to look after her. Still, that's water under the bridge. What about another pint for your dad?" he asked Trudy.

After that Rupert made small talk about football to his reluctant companion until he had finished eating his sandwiches. Then, thanking both father and daughter, he left the pub and made his way around the corner to where the terraced house he thought to have been Gordon's home was. There was really nothing much to be gleaned from looking at it. Two neighbours chatting in the street were young and unlikely to know anything about the inhabitants of forty or fifty years before. He decided that he had achieved as much as he could and set off home again, still having failed to unravel the story which Gordon had wanted him to make public.

Rupert had left the central heating on a low setting at The

224

Red House and returned there more than once to browse the items in the rooms and to make more careful searches in drawers and even between the pages of the few romantic novels which must have belonged to Janice; but without uncovering anything that explain the relationship between Gordon and Janice or where the money in the attic had come from. The only piece of information which moved him on in his quest was that imparted by the Land Registry entry for the house. It told him that it was Gordon, not Janice, who was named as the owner on the records. He was also now aware that Janice had changed her name from Bullock to Lacey – probably to stop her father from tracing her. For some reason, Rupert always felt uncomfortable in the house as if a hostile not a friendly spirit inhabited it. Therefore he was pleased when Laura accompanied him there one day for her first visit, having dropped Florence off to play with a friend.

"I can see why you don't love the house," said Laura after taking a tour of the rooms. "There is something empty and unsatisfactory about the place, despite the pretty furnishings. It's almost as if nobody ever lived here – although we know first Janice, then Gordon did. And you say it was Gordon's house all along?"

"Oh, yes. He must have bought if for her and everyone just assumed that it was hers because she moved in and he remained living in his own little cottage until she died."

"But why not live with her? Do we assume that she was his mistress?"

"Probably. I imagine that Gordon saw her at his local pub – the sort of beauty he never really stood a chance with. But she was trapped and unhappy and he had the money to offer her an escape. He bought the house and maintained her in reasonable style here until her untimely death."

"Yes, but how? You gained the impression he came from a

very modest background and he was not successful in his career – certainly not successful enough to buy and run a place like this as well as having his own home."

"Well, that's the mystery, isn't it? I suppose we can assume that he created the impression that the place was hers in case anyone inquired how he came by the money. No one knew anything about her, so they just accepted her as another independent lady come to live in Claresby."

"But if he bought the property, someone must have known: the estate agent, the solicitor? And his name was on the deeds clear as day."

"True, but nobody cared and nobody looked, it was all just taken at face value, right up to the point where everyone thought she had bequeathed him the place, although there was probably no will at all as everything she had was his anyway."

"So the only remaining question is how, in 1979 when the house was bought by Gordon, did he have the eighty or ninety thousand pounds it would have cost him then?"

"Exactly. And why did he want me to use my "investigatory skills" to find the truth, after he had so successfully covered it up?"

"Well, I'll take a look about the place, but I don't know what I'm looking for," said Laura, pushing her long auburn hair behind her ears as if to prepare herself for the search.

"We'll know when we find it, I guess," replied Rupert.

Again the search only went to prove the paucity of evidence available. Other than the handful of popular novels, it seemed that the only other form of entertainment available would have been provided by the television. There was also a box, rather like a toolbox, full of painting articles which backed up Annie Hart's reference to Gordon having been fond of art. Rupert looked through the collection for a second time. There were a number of sable brushes suitable for watercolour, a little case containing half pans of watercolours and a few tubes in addition. There were also some tubes of acrylic paints and some bristle brushes and an artist's knife and another tool for scratching out details. Then there were some bottles of ink and a collection of pens with fine nibs such as Gordon might have used to draw the little cameo which Rupert had seen at Annie's house. There were a couple of cameos of similar design which appeared to depict Janice displayed on the wall above a bookshelf, although most of the pictures in the house seemed to be shop-bought prints rather than originals. Rupert had also come across a couple of sketch books containing meticulous drawings of commonplace objects carefully initialled by Gordon and one book of watercolour sketches.

Laura returned from her own tour of the house as Rupert packed the art materials back into their box.

"I've discovered where Janice's interest lay, anyway," she said. "She obviously loved shoes and clothes and has some quite lovely things. Lots of makeup still in the dressing-table too – it's a wonder Gordon kept all that stuff. What did you find?"

"Nothing: just looked through Gordon's paint box again."

"There were a couple of lovely engravings in the bedroom," said Laura. "Nudes; very elegantly done."

"Show me!" demanded Rupert, suddenly interested. He followed Laura upstairs and into the main bedroom. The largest pictures in the room were matching prints of pink floral displays. To one side of the bed, however, were two beautiful black and white engravings which Rupert had previously overlooked. Examination proved Laura to be correct: they were exquisite pieces of work.

"Do you think Gordon did those?" asked Laura. "They are lovely – modelled by Janice, perhaps?"

"They have his initials on them so, yes, Gordon's work.

And haven't I just been an idiot and missed the obvious!" exclaimed Rupert

"What's obvious?" asked Laura.

"Gordon's talent for meticulous detail and painstaking work. These are engravings – you do know how they are made, don't you?"

"Of course. The engraver uses a sharp tool to work into a copper plate and then that is used to print the picture – at least, that's how I've seen it done."

"And that's not so dissimilar to how banknotes are made. Which reminds me..." Rupert galloped down the stairs, ungainly limbs flailing in all directions. Laura, following at a more moderate pace, caught up with him as he tipped the contents of the art box unceremoniously on the floor and started to scrabble though the resulting heap. "Look!" he exclaimed triumphantly.

Laura looked. He was holding a sharp tool with a wooden knob for a handle.

"This is a burin or a graver – a tool for engraving. Of course he must have had more, but he obviously disposed of them along with his finished plates. He must have been extraordinarily good, because no one ever spotted his forgeries. And he must have been putting something like fifty pounds worth a day into the system over a ten year period to buy the house for Janice."

"He was a cashier – so you think he was switching the notes with genuine ones?"

"Maybe, but he didn't really need to. He could simply have had an account with another bank which didn't know him and deposited the money on a weekly basis."

"Wouldn't they have thought it odd that all the notes were obviously crisp and new?"

"Perhaps. You may be right; he'd switch a few at his own branch to get a variety of ages and serial numbers."

"He was still taking quite a chance. Suppose someone had spotted that they were forgeries or seen him making the swap?"

"Some men like the thrill of a risk. Presumably he got a kick out of the fact that quiet, dull, over-looked Gordon was getting one up over all of them!"

"Is that why you think he did it? Or did he just want a way to provide a love nest for the girl of his dreams?"

"We'll never know," admitted Rupert. "He certainly doesn't seem to have wanted the money for himself, because he left a heap of it unspent. He also lived quite modestly, even after he moved here. And then there is the fact that he wanted me to find out what he had been doing and tell the world."

"Yes, that is odd," admitted Laura, sitting down on one of the settees. "Having so brilliantly covered up his tracks, why ask you to work out what he had done?"

Rupert sat next to his wife his broad, ugly face expressing puzzlement for a moment whilst he thought,

"I can only assume that what he really wanted was to prove how much cleverer he was than all the people at the bank. At first it must have been sufficient for him just to know that his forged notes were so perfect that no one ever noticed. Then he fulfilled his dream of winning the woman he wanted. Once she died, it must have been a more hollow victory as he lived a lonely life with a lot of money that meant nothing to him. I think in the end he just wanted to give the likes of Gilbert Howe the surprise of their life – he had been pulling off a fraud under his nose for all those years!"

"What will you do?" asked Laura.

"Well, I must admit I'm curious to see if the bank will accept some of the notes as genuine – and I suspect they will. Having said that, now that I believe the money to be forged, I can't in all conscience spend it. I'll tell the story to Veronica; perhaps all the proceeds can go to charity."

"What, give up the house?" asked Laura in mild surprise. "I got the impression you quite liked having a place of your own."

A very faint blush touched Rupert's cheeks, as his wife was very close to the truth. "In some ways I did," he admitted, "but at the same time I never felt comfortable with the whole deal and the house gives me the creeps."

Laura nodded understandingly.

"Also, Gordon's request was for me to make his story public, and I don't know that I will. The idea of his almost bragging about the deception from the grave is a little distasteful. And, as ever, I am only making deductions: it would be a whole different business to go back and prove that Gordon had pulled off a prolonged fraud, dumping tens of thousands of pounds worth of forged notes into the system."

"So Gilbert Howe will never know?"

"There is a possibility that I will buy him another pub lunch and run the theory past him," said Rupert, the hint of a wicked gleam in his eye."

The two of them tidied up the collection of paints and brushes that Rupert had spilled and carefully locked up the house, ready to pick up their daughter and return to the homely tranquillity of their own Claresby Manor.

The Twelve Days of Christmas Mystery

It was Laura Latimer, Lady of the Manor, who made her way down the draughty corridor to open the ancient double doors to her guests. She was greeted by the smiling face of Keith Lowe, the village doctor, and his wife of a few months, Veronica.

"Merry Christmas!" exclaimed Veronica. "We've even brought you a seasonal flurry of snow."

Laura squinted out into the darkness and saw that where the warm light from the mullioned windows of Claresby Manor fell on the ground outside it twinkled on a thin frosting of white. "You'd better come in. I see you came bearing gifts too. What is that you have, Keith? It looks like a small tree."

"A pear tree, if I am not mistaken," said Keith. "Complete with partridge. And I didn't bring it; I found it on the doorstep. At first I thought it was a decoration, but there is a gift label on it."

Laura raised an eyebrow at the thing, but ushered the couple briskly to the warmth of the Great Hall which boasted a blazing fire of apple wood and festive decorations of holly and mistletoe. Rupert, Laura's husband, rose from his chair, a flush on his benign but ugly face.

"I've been basting the turkey," he said. "Everything is just about ready. How was your day, Veronica?" He bent almost double to place a kiss on her face, not failing to notice how striking she looked in a scarlet velvet dress which complemented her dark hair and green eyes.

"Just about holding up," she replied. "Late service last night, early service today – and I noticed you weren't in the Family Service this morning to hear my Christmas address!"

"I always enjoy the carols on Christmas Eve," replied Laura smoothly. "And Florence enjoyed the crib."

"Where is my little goddaughter?" inquired Veronica.

"Taking a much needed nap," said Laura. "She's had enough food, presents and excitement for one day; although I don't doubt that she will wake up in time to eat Christmas dinner with us."

"I'm not used to waiting until the evening," complained Keith mildly. "I didn't realise the perils of being married to a vicar. I've sat through three services in the last twenty-four hours and the sides of my stomach are slapping together, I'm so hungry!"

"We had some smoked salmon for lunch," added Veronica, "but I must say there is a good smell wafting in from your kitchen. Anyway, Keith is on call, and there are a couple of nasty cases of flu in the village, whereas I am very much off-duty now."

"In that case, let me pour you a sherry," said Laura. "And I'm sure Keith can have a small one."

They were soon all seated in the big oak chairs which were set about the fireplace. Keith lifted his eyes to appreciate the view in the lofty Great Hall with its oak panelling, ornate plasterwork ceiling and shadowy musicians' gallery. He was just contemplating the grand scale of everything, when he fixed upon a very small, artificial Christmas tree placed in a far corner. It somehow seemed anticlimactic given the context.

"I thought you were going to have a noble Norwegian spruce?" Keith said to Rupert. "Did you change your mind?"

Laura and Rupert exchanged slightly humorous glances.

"Well, thereby hangs a tale," said Laura. "Rupert did indeed specially order a tree – the sort of thing the Norwegians donate for use in Trafalgar Square every year – about sixty-foot tall!"

"Laura is exaggerating," said Rupert. "It wasn't more than about twenty-foot tall – perfectly reasonable for the Great

Hall."

"Where is it then?" asked Veronica.

"I decided to put it up in the front drive instead."

"But only after a struggle to manoeuvre it around in here and the deposit of about a billion pine needles!"

"I didn't see it out the front. Are there lights on it?" asked Keith.

"Well, it's not actually up yet: I'm thinking it should be ready by New Year," admitted Rupert; and they all laughed.

"But what were you saying about a pear tree?" continued Laura, looking about to where Keith had placed a bag of Christmas gifts and what looked like a large potted plant with a brightly coloured soft toy wedged in it.

"The gifts are from us, but the tree was on the doorstep," Keith reminded her.

Laura stood up and went over to examine the object. "It looks a bit sickly," she commented.

"Pear trees are deciduous," responded Keith.

Laura removed the stuffed bird from the branches absent-mindedly and said, "Oh, well I'll put it in the orangery and see if it thrives. I'll take it there now whilst I go to see if Florence is awake."

When Laura returned, a still sleepy Florence snuggled into her arms, the others were discussing the gift and its possible origins.

"The label just says *Merry Christmas,*" observed Rupert. "I suppose the fact that it was left by our door indicates that it is meant for us – but there's no way of knowing who left it. I do hope it is not someone with a sense of the dramatic who is going to leave something on each of the twelve days of Christmas in accordance with the carol."

"The five gold rings would be acceptable," commented Veronica.

"Yes, but the eleven pipers piping could be annoying,"

replied Rupert. "Not to mention all the doves, geese, swans and calling birds!"

"Expensive too," added Keith. "I don't suppose eight maids to do the milking would come cheap!"

"Arguably it would be more than eight," said Laura, who had a quick head for mathematics. "In the traditional version of the carol the gifts are repeated every day up until the twelfth, so we can expect twelve partridges and…" she paused to calculate. "…forty maids-a-milking!"

"And forty gold rings," added Rupert, not to be outdone by his wife. By this time Florence had found the toy partridge and adopted it. With the perversity of a two year old child who was used to her own way, she then refused to be parted from it despite the enticement of all the other gifts she received.

Soon the dinner was served on the old oak table set with goblets of silver, which flashed in the candle light as they drank, and ivory handled cutlery. This was followed by a homemade plum pudding, and Rupert doused it in brandy so that it flamed with a blue light and they all clapped. By the time they finished and presents had been opened and examined, Florence was saucer-eyed with tiredness and dozed on her father's lap as he sat by the fire with Keith and Veronica whilst Laura played some carols on the piano. It was well after midnight before the two guests departed for a crisp, cold walk back to the vicarage, and Rupert and Laura retired to the four-poster bed in the fire-lit scarlet bedroom.

On Boxing Day morning, Laura was making porridge when Rupert came into the kitchen.

"Another inch of snow fell in the night," Rupert commented, "but the roads are still passable – not that we are planning to go anywhere today. Oh, and another gift on the doorstep."

"Gift? What gift?" asked Laura vaguely as she stood on tiptoe trying ineffectively to reach a pot of honey on one of the high shelves which lined the wall of the medieval stone-built room.

"A second day of Christmas gift, unless I am very much mistaken," responded Rupert as he made use of his lanky six-foot frame to reach the honey.

A slight frown creased the delicate brow of Laura's pretty, oval face: "Two turtle doves?"

"Actually two dead doves," admitted Rupert. "But I think that the symbolism is there."

"That's rather unpleasant," said Laura. "What did you do with them?"

"Disposed of them in a sanitary manner," replied Rupert. "And, for the record, there were two sets of footprints in the snow – one coming and one going. No snow had fallen on top of the prints. I think it stopped snowing at about five this morning and it's only seven now – so our Father Christmas made an early start."

"Well, late really – since Christmas Eve has come and gone," corrected Laura. "But why would anyone bother? You would think that on the day after Christmas everyone would be happily ensconced in a warm house with their family."

"I don't know," admitted Rupert. "The only other light I can shed on the matter is that the gift-giver had large boots on – probably a size ten broad-fitting."

"So what should we expect next? – Three French hens? Four calling birds?"

"I'm unconcerned right up until the ten lords a-leaping!" responded Rupert. "Still, I do wonder what message the sender is trying to convey."

The two following days produced three oven-ready chickens – possibly French – left on the bonnet of Rupert's car, and four small, artificial blackbirds, this time on the doorstep again. It was with some trepidation that Laura greeted her husband at the breakfast table on the fifth day. In response to her quizzical look he answered,

"Not five golden rings, if that is what you are wondering. More like five pork sausages – nice ones, actually, like the butcher usually makes with course cut meat and herbs."

The issue was discussed with Veronica and Keith that evening whilst the four of them sat in the cosy red drawing room with its fat leather settees and rich Turkish carpet. The room was free of any Christmas decoration other than a few sprigs of holly, being already elaborate enough in its decor. A large jug of mulled wine was keeping warm by the fire, and they helped themselves to the mince pies piled on a plate next to it.

"Does it feel sinister?" Veronica was asking Rupert. She had experienced the malicious actions of some parishioners when she first arrived in Claresby followed by rumours about the death of her first husband and a number of unexplained disappearances.

"Perhaps the dead doves suggested malicious intent," replied Rupert, "but the chickens and sausages were almost comical. The only thing that makes it all worrying is that anyone should be obsessed enough to carry on delivering these things day after day."

"And to manage without us being able to catch them at it," added Laura.

"Well, they've got another seven days to go if they are really obsessed," said Keith. "Personally I'm curious as to how they are going to produce the twelve drummers. Also, I calculated that the full cost of the twelve days of gifts as specified in the carol would be about twenty thousand pounds! But, seriously, is there anyone who could have a grudge against you?"

"Rupert did help put my cousins in prison for murdering their father," mused Laura. "But that's another story altogether – and doesn't explain the delivery of five sausages."

"There is a bit of a meat theme," observed Rupert. "Honestly, the chickens on day three looked so nice I regretted disposing of them! But I spoke to Phil Young this morning about our hog roast on Twelfth Night and he was as friendly as he could be."

"Yes, but he has had a few problems lately," interposed Veronica. "When I ordered my Christmas turkey from him he complained about how many people had used the new butcher in town this year – his orders were down twenty-five percent on last year."

"But you had Christmas dinner with us?" said Laura.

"Oh, it was only a small turkey," said Keith. "Just so we could have our own little dinner together last night – nothing like the splendid bird you had at Claresby. Was that from Phil?"

"Well, it was actually from the new butcher's in town," admitted Laura. "It's the first time I've been there and they had an offer on the organic birds if you ordered well in advance."

"So our own butcher, Phil, may be a little disgruntled," smiled Veronica, "especially with you being such a prominent person in Claresby."

"It is true that the Mortimer family have always bought their meat from the village butcher," acknowledged Laura, "but I can't imagine that Phil would set such store by this fact. Anyway, he will be here for our Twelfth Night party. He will have full range of the kitchen and will be roasting a whole pig on the spit in the fireplace. I'll have a gentle word with him then."

It was recorded in the Domesday Book that the Lord of the Manor of Claresby had the exclusive right to hold both a fair and a market on his land. As a descendant of the Mortimer family, who were named in the 1086 entry, Laura had reintroduced the tradition of the fair. Since discovering treasure in the grounds and restoring the family's fortunes, she had also revived the medieval tradition of a celebration on the fifth of January to mark the end of the winter festival considered to begin at Halloween. This was only the second year that this particular event had been held at Claresby Manor since its reintroduction, but the pattern had been set for the provision of a hot winter punch and a hog roast, as well as cakes and fruit juice for any children who attended. Entertainment included musicians playing medieval and renaissance music from the gallery in the Great Hall, as well as a raffle to support the village church.

The evening of Twelfth Night proved to be cold but dry and everything was merry within the Hall as villagers chatted and danced. Laura surveyed the scene with satisfaction, before returning to the kitchen to see that everything was under control. Phil Young, ably assisted by his teenage son, was carving the pork which was piled into rolls and carried away by the tray-full to the hungry revellers. He was a big, ruddy faced man in his fifties with an impressive beer belly and bright blue eyes. He smiled at Laura as she entered,

"Everything going well? It sounds like fun out there."

"Oh, yes – you must come and join us soon; you look as if you are almost done out here. The food has been splendid."

"Always good to be appreciated," replied Phil with a hearty wink. "By the way, there may be a bit of a surprise for you in a while."

"Oh?" said Laura uncertainly. "What sort of a surprise?"

"You'll just have to wait and see," replied Phil

enigmatically.

Laura went back to join Rupert and conveyed to him what the butcher had just said.

"I do wonder if he was put out by your not buying a turkey from him," mused Rupert. "It is interesting that the delivery of gifts stopped after the five sausages at the point when I confirmed that I wanted Phil to provide the hog roast – perhaps I should have sorted it all earlier. Anyway, all's well that ends well."

"But how do we know that it has ended well until we know what Phil means by a surprise!"

"I suppose we will just have to wait and see, like the man said."

Events continued to be a success and Laura ate some hog roast, drank some punch and danced an excitable sort of reel with her husband until the exhausted musicians went to take some refreshments. The celebration was set to end at midnight, but at fifteen minutes before the hour the partiers were distracted by the sudden striking up of music outside. Looking out onto the lawn, which was flooded with light from the house, they saw a Scottish Pipe Band of about a dozen players with bagpipes and drums. Everyone gathered by the windows to watch and clapped appreciatively at the end of the first tune. A second struck up and as Laura enjoyed the spectacle she found Phil at her elbow.

"Had I mentioned that my brother played in a pipe band?" said Phil with a grin.

"No – how wonderful – and it looks like we've got our drummers and pipers all rolled into one!" exclaimed Laura happily. "But I think we had better ask them in for some hot punch. It looks like our party is going to go on into the early morning after all."

19618739R00141

Printed in Great Britain
by Amazon